# Summary Justice

# Summary Justice

## John Fairfax

Little, Brown

LITTLE, BROWN

First published in Great Britain in 2017 by Little, Brown

1 3 5 7 9 10 8 6 4 2

Hardback ISBN 978-1-4087-0872-9
Trade paperback ISBN 978-1-4087-0873-6

Typeset in Sabon by Palimpsest Book Production Limited, Falkirk, Stirlingshire
Printed and bound in Great Britain by Clays Ltd, St Ives plc

Papers used by Little, Brown are from well-managed
forests and other responsible sources.

MIX
Paper from
responsible sources
FSC
www.fsc.org    FSC® C104740

Little, Brown
An imprint of
Little, Brown Book Group
Carmelite House
50 Victoria Embankment
London EC4Y 0DZ

An Hachette UK Company
www.hachette.co.uk

www.littlebrown.co.uk

For Ursula Mackenzie

All trials are trials for one's life,
just as all sentences are sentences of death
De Profundis, Oscar Wilde

# PROLOGUE

Friday, 23 July 1999. Court 1, the Old Bailey, London.

'William Benson, stand up.'

His Honour Judge Rigby stared across the court as if no one else was present, as if the prosecutor hadn't turned to smile at the girl from the CPS; as if Helen Camberley QC, Benson's defence counsel, hadn't momentarily covered her face; as if Benson's mother wasn't crying; as if Paul Harbeton's father hadn't been removed from the court after another outburst of swearing. Judge Rigby had seen it all before. Justice, played out, was always a dreadful business. But even he was saddened by this latest episode. It was his task to put fresh words on another banal tragedy.

'You have been found guilty of murder. You took a man's life. In so doing you have shattered the lives of those who were close to him. You have devastated your own, and of those who are close to you.'

He seemed to appraise the dead body of Paul Harbeton as if it were laid out on the exhibits table between the bench and the dock. During the trial, unsmiling and remote, he'd leafed through the pathologist's photographs, squinting occasionally at the close-ups while the expert serenely described every contusion and scratch. The butchery that had followed showed how seriously the courts took killing: every other possible cause of death had been excluded. Every internal

1

anomaly had been explained. Every organ had been examined and weighed. The cause of death had been nailed down. And then Paul Harbeton had been stitched back together. Benson could almost see him now, lying on that gleaming aluminium table, horribly clean.

'It should have been an ordinary Saturday evening in November. You went to the Bricklayers Arms in central London with your then girlfriend, Jessica Buchanan. She described you as a thoughtful, considerate young man, though she'd been drawn to a certain melancholy. Like you, she was a second-year student of philosophy; like you, she had a particular interest in ethics; like this court, and like everyone who knows you, she thought you incapable of shocking violence. The irony of your circumstances – a young man, aged twenty-one, fascinated by the structure of moral principles – is painful to observe.'

Judge Rigby paused, as if to turn a page. But his hand did not move. His eyes didn't shift from the ghost of a body between them.

'On that same evening, Paul Harbeton went to the same public house. He was a hospital porter at Charing Cross Hospital in Hammersmith. He was also an unpaid volunteer at Leadgate House, a day centre for people with Alzheimer's disease. By all accounts he'd had a hard day. He'd done a night shift at the hospital, slept a couple of hours, and then gone to the day centre. I imagine he was tired when he went to the Bricklayers Arms. He might have been short-tempered. That would explain why he shoved you brusquely when he came to the bar, where you were standing. It would explain why he spoke to you abruptly. Provocatively. You had a right to protest – and you did, verbally. And it should have ended there. I am sure the same kind of brief encounter occurred in every public house in London that night. But none of them led to a senseless killing.'

Benson glanced at the public gallery. Paul Harbeton's family were bunched along the front row, angry brothers flanking a broken mother. The spectators were lapping it all up – the same few who'd turned up every day of the trial, along with some tourists, chalking up a visit to the Old Bailey. Benson's parents were on the back row. But Eddie, his brother, wasn't with them. He couldn't be. There was no wheelchair access. But even if there had been, he wouldn't have come, and it was an act of wild imagination that made Benson look for him, wanting last-minute forgiveness. A wave. A sign. Anything.

'Shortly after this encounter you left the premises with your girlfriend,' said Judge Rigby. 'It was 10.15 p.m. Jessica went one way, and you went the other. You then made your first great mistake. You went back to confront Paul Harbeton. You waited for him outside the Bricklayers Arms. And when he emerged at ten forty-five, you followed him down the street. I accept what you say, because it is confirmed by two independent witnesses. You called out to him. Words were exchanged. Mr Harbeton gave you a headbutt that cracked your cheekbone. You retaliated. Ineffectively it would appear, since the fight concluded shortly afterwards, with you lying on the pavement. When you came to your feet, Mr Benson, you should have gone to the police. You lost your chance for proportionate justice. Instead – and this was your second grave mistake – rather than call the police, rather than go to hospital, rather than stand back and see things in proportion, rather than think *morally*, you followed Paul Harbeton into Soho. You have denied what subsequently happened, but this jury, who listened carefully to all the evidence, did not believe you. You killed him. You struck him from behind and walked away with his blood on your hands.'

'Bastard,' yelled one of the brothers. 'Rot in hell. You're

dead when you get out. You're finished. You're buried. You're— Get your hands off me, get off, leave me—'

Judge Rigby merely looked at the public gallery. He said nothing, waiting patiently for the ushers to restore order. Paul Harbeton's mother was staring into space, her eyes wide, her cheeks blackened by smudged make-up, seemingly unaware that her son was being carried away, arms flailing, spit flying from his mouth. The door closed. Benson thought he might be sick. He could no longer listen to the judge. A low sigh escaped from his mouth: he was with his mother by the blue wooden hut in Brancaster Staithe on the Norfolk coast. The front flaps were down and she was smiling, selling whelks and a crab to Mrs Pennington. The old woman came every week, same day, same time, with the same complaints about her husband, the weather, the state of her knees . . . He could smell the sea. He could taste salt on his lips. There were shouts from a fishing boat. The whisper of the surf filled a sudden silence and Judge Rigby's voice returned like the slap of a wave.

'. . . and they are heartbroken. The sentence of the court is fixed by statute, and I pass it now: life imprisonment.' He closed his red trial book, hesitated, and then continued. 'May I give you a word of advice, Mr Benson? Think long and hard about what you have done. Think carefully about what you might do . . . how you might salvage the ruin of your life. Take him down.'

A strong hand gripped Benson's elbow. Suddenly he was no longer in court. There were bright lights and long, airless corridors. Somehow he was walking, though he had no control over his limbs. They reached a chipped counter. He handed over his watch, some money and his belt. Keys rattled. A holding cell door swung open. For a second, he caught the gaze of his jailor and he received the distant look reserved for those who've crossed a frontier and can never,

ever come back. Benson belonged among them. He was a murderer.

An hour and a half later Benson stumbled into the late July sunshine. Two guards bundled him into a white van that looked like a rubbish truck. He was locked into a cubicle the size of an aeroplane toilet. The heat was stifling. Sweat ran into his eyes. He blinked at some scratched graffiti: YOU CAN BE A HERO . . . GEEZA . . . WELKUM TOO HELL. When the vehicle lurched out of the court block, cameras flashed at the darkened window. He turned aside, back to the conversation that had taken place in the holding room before the guards banged on the door.

'There is no chance of appeal,' said Camberley. She paused, knitting her fingers. One nail had been bitten. The torn quick was cherry red. 'I've just seen the judge in chambers. His recommendation is that you serve eleven years. That's lenient.'

She was searching Benson's face. So was George Braithwaite, his solicitor. So was the Oxford undergraduate on work experience, Tess de Vere. Benson wouldn't be free until he was thirty-two. For a twenty-one-year-old, that was getting on. Braithwaite spoke:

'You see, Will, you never accepted that you followed him; that the fight hadn't ended outside the Bricklayers Arms. But you did go to Soho. And that means it was always up to the jury to make the link. They—'

'Got it wrong,' said Benson. 'Because the fight didn't continue in Soho. Because I didn't hit him from behind. I am still innocent, regardless of what the jury think.'

'I know,' said Camberley.

'I know,' said Braithwaite.

Tess didn't speak because it wasn't her place. She was standing by the scuffed wall, arms behind her back. They were roughly the same age. They'd shared a coffee and memories of the sea, because Tess, too, had grown up to the sound of waves and the shifting colours of wet sand. She was from Galway on the west coast of Ireland. They'd joined voices with the Proclaimers. *But I would walk five hundred miles* . . . It was a rebel's song. Passionate. Adamant. Their eyes had locked in defiance.

'I am sorry,' said Camberley, aligning a stray, silver hair. 'I wish there was something I could do.'

She'd fought as if defending her own son. The prosecution were relying heavily on circumstantial evidence. She'd deemed it weak.

'There is,' said Benson. He was one step ahead of Judge Rigby. He'd already decided what he wanted to do.

'Well?'

'I want to come to the Bar. Just tell me whether I have a chance.'

Camberley was quite still. Her sharp, almost black eyes lost their intimidating shine. The finger with the bitten nail found the same, offending hair.

'You have to be serious, Will.'

'I am deadly serious.'

He glanced at Tess and she smiled her rebel smile. What was a thousand miles if you knew what you wanted?

The prison van lurched to a halt and then lurched again. For ten boiling minutes, Benson sweated and sucked in the hot, fetid air, then the door opened and he was taken into a yard surrounded by brick walls, coiled wire and high fencing. This was HMP Kensal Green. A pink cloud hung in the sky like a used swab. Benson's heart was racing. He was in a processing area now, surrounded by other men . . . only he felt like a boy who'd been kicked out of school, shifting dimension to a strange place on a distant planet.

'Try not to look green, son,' his dad had said, choked, as if he knew anything about prison. His mum took over. 'Don't let 'em know you're scared, Will.' She'd got that from a film. They'd looked at each other as if a grave had opened between them.

'Hey, yoo. Gottaburn?'

The speaker was about Benson's age. His limbs were shaking. He gnawed his lower lip. There were shouts and cries from somewhere behind, but he didn't react. His twitching eyes were on Benson's pockets.

'Gottaburn or what?'

'Pardon?'

'Whatyainfor?'

'Sorry?'

'You deaf? WHAT-ARE-YA-IN-FOR?'

Benson hesitated. 'Murder.'

The young man pulled at someone else. 'Gottaburn?'

Benson thought of Tess de Vere's smile. She'd believed him, even if the jury hadn't. He was going to walk a thousand miles.

'Inconceivable,' said Camberley, finally.

'Why?'

'The cost is too high.'

'Not for me.'

'In order to be rehabilitated, you'd have to admit that you killed Paul Harbeton; and you didn't.'

'I'll admit that I killed him.'

'You'd have to live a lie.'

'I can do it.'

'Not for the rest of your life.'

'But it's already the rest of my life. I was convicted. There's no appeal.'

Camberley shifted in her seat. 'Even if you managed to get qualified, there would be no point, because no Inn of Court would accept you as a member. The Bar Council would never let you join the profession.'

'Can't I fight them?'

'There's no guarantee you'd win. And even if you won, no chambers would grant you a pupillage, and even if they did, no chambers would give you a tenancy. You're talking madness, Will. This is the stuff of dreams.'

Braithwaite tried to lower the tone. 'You have to be realistic. Even if you could beat back the opposition, they'd join forces and banish you. The Bar would never acknowledge you. No solicitor would instruct you. The Bench would never trust you. You'd be an exile.'

'I didn't ask if I was being realistic. I just want to know if it's possible.' Benson turned back to Camberley. 'I chose to study philosophy because I was always asking "Why?" As a kid I drove my parents crazy. I got into trouble with my teachers. I annoyed my friends. But I've never known what I wanted *to do* with my life, not until this trial. Until I saw you asking "Why?" Until I entered a room where "Why?" is the most important question in the world, where no one can tell you to shut up, where God himself would have to give an answer if he dared to enter that witness box.'

'No, Will, you can't—'

'This is what I want to do, Miss Camberley.'

'It's too late.'

'Question people. Expose assumptions. Challenge—'

'I'm sorry.'

Benson looked her in the eye. 'You're sure about that?'

'I am.'

'Then why did you say there's no such thing as a hopeless case when we first met?'

'I was talking about a trial.'

'We were talking about persuading people to believe in me. Would you mind explaining the difference?'

Camberley glanced at Braithwaite as if he might know the answer but Benson wasn't going to wait. 'I want to come to the Bar,' he said. 'Is there a chance? I don't care how small it is.'

'A chance?' Camberley rose to go, a thumb nursing the edge of that ragged nail. 'Yes. A sliver of a wafer. So forget it. You may as well ask if you can visit the moon.'

'Gottaburn?'

This time it was someone else, but Benson was called to be processed. His details were taken down. He signed various forms. He was photographed. He was strip-searched. He was given some clothes and bedding. He became prison number AC1963. A doctor asked if he was suicidal. And then, strangely changed, he was taken up some stairs.

'You're going straight on to D Wing,' said the guard. 'The First Night Centre's full. So's the induction wing.'

They came to an iron lattice grille with a gate inset that opened on to a long, iron landing. New guards took over. Above and below, suicide netting stretched across the yawning well of the block, connecting three levels of endless blue doors. The lead guard stopped when he reached the middle of the landing. He pulled keys on a chain from his pocket. Moments later the blue door to a cell swung open and Benson froze in horror.

An old man was sitting on a toilet. He had greasy hair, pulled back in a pony tail. He was unshaven. Faded blue tattoos, more like graffiti, covered a scrawny neck. The lobe of an ear was missing. The man didn't even stop what he was doing to look at the open door. He just reached for a roll of paper.

'Remember what I said, Needles,' warned the guard. 'Break him in nice and I'll see you get some touches.'

The cell door slammed. The lock turned. Needles rose, not bothering to press the flush.

'Gottaburn?'

Benson wanted to scream. 'I don't understand.'

'A cigarette. Have you got any baccy?'

'I don't smoke.'

'Then start. There's nothing else to do in here.' Needles lowered himself slowly on to a chair, reached for some needles and yellow wool and started knitting. 'Except flush my throne.' He nodded towards the toilet.

'Good lad,' he said, after Benson obeyed. 'We're going to get on. What's your name?'

'Benson. William . . . Will.'

'Well, you can forget Benson, William, Will. I'm going to call you Rizla. And if anyone asks your name, you say "Rizla". That includes the screws. Got it?'

'Yes.'

'Good lad. What are you in for, Rizla?'

'Murder.'

Needles undid a stitch. 'Silly boy.'

That night Benson lay curled in foetal anguish listening to Needles snore and scratch himself. But his right hand was clenched tight – the same hand that had struck Paul Harbeton – and in it was the one thing that mattered: a sliver of a wafer of hope.

# PART ONE

## Two days before trial

# 1

'Another murderer?'

'Yep.'

'Who?'

'Have a guess.'

'I've no idea.'

'You have. He's all over last week's papers.'

'What . . . no . . . get off . . . the guy operating from an old fish and chip shop?'

'None other. But it was a fishmonger's. There were no chips.'

Until that moment Tess de Vere had only been half listening. It was a dreary Monday. She was having lunch with Gordon Hayward at the Ming Palace in Hatton Garden, a short walk from where they worked at Coker & Dale, Solicitors, 56 Ely Place, London. Gordon was head of the criminal law department. He was also thirty-nine, single and interested in Tess. Possibly obsessed. Had been since her arrival at the firm four months ago. His latest tactic was to suggest business lunches. On this occasion he'd proposed divine dim sum, a celestial Languedoc and a discussion about a pending judgment from the European Court of Human Rights in Strasbourg. The application was about covert surveillance of legal consultations in a police station. It had some bearing – though tenuous – on a hopeless case of Gordon's. For light relief, Tess had tuned in to a not-so-hushed conversation coming from the table behind. So far it had gone like this:

'The dim-wit sacked me.'

'No.'

'Bloody right. Four days to trial and she pulls the plug.'

'Get off.'

'Picks up the damned phone on Friday night and says she wants out. Doesn't trust me. Says I don't believe her.'

'Do you?'

'No, but that's not the point, is it? You weigh up the evidence. You give your advice. And if you have to, you lean on 'em.'

'Absolutely. Help them see sense.'

'Get the best result.' The speaker had evidently filled his mouth; he spoke while chewing. 'And it wasn't just me. Counsel had a go too.'

'Urged her to plead?'

'Informed persuasion, nothing more. And what do you get for your trouble?'

'A slab of legal aid.'

'Yes, but only for the preparation. I've lost the trial fee.'

'There's other fish in the sea.'

Gordon was having trouble too: with his chopsticks. The dim sum kept slipping away. He was chasing one round the bamboo steamer, his mind on the provisions of Part II of the Regulation of Investigatory Powers Act 2000.

'Of course, intrusive surveillance has to be authorised,' he said. 'You can't just listen in and make notes. You need a mandate. But it doesn't end there. As you rightly said this morning, there have to be *adequate* safeguards to protect the examination, use and storage of the material obtained. That's the key term, *adequate*. I'm not remotely suggesting you're unfamiliar with the legislation' – he managed to trap the dim sum; he raised it, triumphantly – 'but what about the Covert Surveillance Code of Practice provisions? Don't they cover any lacunae in the primary legislation? That's my worry, Tess, and with respect to my – and I have to say very interesting – case . . .' His chopsticks swivelled and the dim sum fell back into the steamer. Tess resumed her eavesdropping:

'I mean she's as guilty as sin. Hasn't got a cat's chance in hell.'

'What happened?'

'She's gets a bit too cosy with her boss. Starts shagging him. Which is fair enough because he's a nice guy and loaded. But . . . have a guess.'

'He's married?'

'That's par for the course.'

'He wants out?'

'That's your birdie.'

'She won't back off?'

'There's your eagle.'

'So she blackmails him? Threatens to tell the wife?'

'You're in the bunker.'

'Kills him?'

'Bloody right. With a broken bottle.'

'Jesus.'

'Right in the neck. Watches the poor sod bleed to death and then walks off as if nothing happened.'

'Diminished responsibility?'

'God no, just passion gone wrong. He held out the good life and then tried to take it back. Sent her over the edge. *Fatal Attraction*.'

'Great film, that. Especially when the dog goes missing.'

'It's a rabbit.'

'Are you sure?'

'It's a bloody rabbit. You couldn't boil a dog. Not on a domestic cooker.'

'Hang on, I think it was a cat.'

Gordon filled Tess's glass, smiling shyly. His soft, blue eyes were defenceless. 'I'm glad you're back, Tess. You've brought some sunshine into a sometimes grey and musty building. I'm sorry, I should have asked. How was Strasbourg?'

'Grey and musty.'

'The symposium went well?'

'Put it this way, a week is a long time to discuss prisoner rights and the limits of rehabilitation. I was ready to break out by Saturday night.'

In truth, Tess had been unsettled. Sitting at the back of the hall listening to a presentation on the lack of clear and constant jurisprudence from Strasbourg in relation to the effect of Article 3 of the European Convention of Human Rights 1950 on UK 'whole-life orders', she realised she didn't want to do this any more. It was incredibly important work, but the required legal choreography had lost its allure. She no longer felt driven to formulate the technical steps necessary to bring a government to heel. With the ache of an exile, she longed to get back to first beginnings. Back to front-line crime, defending people who didn't have a cat's chance in hell.

'My own view is that Strasbourg is losing its way,' said Gordon.

'Really?'

He'd taken to impaling the dim sum – something he'd never have done if he hadn't thought they were approaching the border controls between mere colleagues and friendship. Gordon was increasing his stride, eyes fixed on a greener land.

'Yes. Article Eight of the Convention is all very well – and I'll continue to squeeze it for all it's worth – but who would have thought that "the right to respect for private and family life, home and correspondence" – I omit, with due deference,

16

the masculine pronouns – would stretch to prohibit the interception of criminal communications?'

'It doesn't.'

Gordon tugged a dice-themed cuff-link. 'I was only joking. You know that. Where would we be without Article Eight?'

The couple behind might have given the question some thought, mused Tess, itching to shift tables. The sacked solicitor had moved on to the evidence:

'Her DNA is on the bottle. Her footprints are at the *locus in quo*. She's seen arriving before the killing and leaving afterwards. They catch her at Dover on her way to France with tickets bought the morning after the murder. And when they pick her up, she's got a cut to her hand consistent with a broken glass injury. What do you think she says when they put on the tape recorder?'

'Go on.'

'She cut herself on a tin of tuna. Do you get that? A tin of bloody tuna.'

'John West?'

'Do you know . . . that's the one question I didn't ask.'

'That's why she sacked you. Anyway, what's her defence?'

'Hasn't got one. Just says it wasn't her. That's why I leaned on her. Had to. But she just wouldn't budge.'

'Well, she's stuffed, then.'

'Like I said.'

'Who's picked up the brief?'

'Well, that's your best question yet. Another murderer.'

And it was at this point that Tess sat quite rigid, no longer pretending to listen to Gordon, who'd moved on to *Valenzuela Contreras* v. *Spain*. Because the conversation behind became suddenly charged: she was tingling with intuition.

'Another murderer?'

'Yep.'

'Who?'

'Have a guess.'

'I've no idea.'

'You have. He's all over last week's papers.'

'What . . . no . . . get off . . . the guy operating from an old fish and chip shop?'

'None other. But it was a fishmonger's. There were no chips.'

'You're joking.'

'I'm not. It was only fish—'

'Not that, you prat. Or should I say sprat?'

Tess watched Gordon's mouth moving but no sound reached her.

'I got a call this morning from some market-trader-sprat who calls himself a clerk. Asked me to send over the brief at once.'

'Didn't know he had a clerk.'

'Well, he has. Called himself Archie.'

'What's the brief's name again?'

'Benson. William Benson. Or, as he's known inside, Rizla. Can you get your head around that? A barrister called Rizla?'

'No.'

'Me neither.' The speaker paused as if to wipe his mouth. 'If he hadn't killed somebody, I could almost feel sorry for the clown.'

'Why?'

'C'mon, you're in the sand again. He's not only going to lose, he's going to make a complete fool of himself. This'll be his last case.'

Gordon was looking at Tess, forlorn, wondering what he'd done wrong. He'd shared the best of himself and now he felt naked. Clumsily, he began to cover his embarrassment with *Weber and Saravia* v. *Germany*. The border controls were more stringent than he'd thought.

'Gordon,' she said, 'domestic law will be found wanting next week, in part at least, but the ruling won't help your case. It's critically different. We can't talk now because I have to go. I've got some research to do.'

'Are you free tonight?' His voice almost cracked. His shaved scalp was shining with perspiration. 'Sublime partridge and oak-aged Rioja?'

'I'm sorry. I've got a conference. New work. Cutting edge.'

# 2

'It's him,' said Tess, sipping a Corpse Reviver.

'The guy you banged on about from Paris to Prague?'

'I banged on about the limitations of the jury system. There's a difference.'

'Did you?'

'Yes. I pointed out that a verdict returned according to the evidence can still be the wrong one.'

'Are you sure?'

'Damn it, yes. I was trying to explain a conundrum: the idea of something that's true and false at the same time.'

'I don't recall any conundra.' Sally had gone for a Mojito. A classic Cuban highball.

'You're impossible. Utterly impossible.' Tess shifted back to the present with a suppressed smile. 'He did it. He actually did it. He walked a thousand miles.'

'Where from?'

'Forget it.'

Tess had first met Sally Martindale at university. She'd disappointed her Irish republican parents by favouring Oriel College, Oxford, over Trinity College, Dublin. Given that her father was English, with an ancestry stretching back to the Norman Conquest, and that her mother had taught at the Royal College of Music, the argument – with allusions to the Great Famine and crimes of the Black and Tans – had verged on the bizarre, not to mention incoherent. So Tess had left a rugged stone house overlooking Galway Bay and taken a room with a view on to a trimmed lawn, the sound of the sea breathing through her window replaced, in the first instance, by a quintessentially southern county English voice – polished vowels with crisp consonants – calling out her name:

'De Vere? Where the hell are you?'

Tess had leaned on the sill and looked down to see a girl she'd met in a pub the night before, a History of Art fresher at Magdalen. At that first meeting, she'd been dressed in oversized flannels and battered combat boots (a bid, she explained, to kick-start an Oxford-based grunge revival). For the morning after, she'd plumped for flared jeans, a low-cut white blouse suggestive of lace underwear and high heels (in homage, it turned out, to a seventies *Bazaar* cover photo of Jane Birkin standing on a yacht).

'Help me finish these, will you?' She'd held up a brown paper bag and a bottle with gold foil around the neck. 'The cherries cost more than the wretched plonk. Would you *believe* that?'

Sally could have asked the porter for Tess's room number. She could have looked at the board of names. But no, she had to sail into the quad and call out like an auctioneer at Christie's ignoring the microphone. They'd become friends, their attachment cemented by the mutual disclosure of bruising love affairs, inter-railing (from Paris to Prague), extravagant arguments, tearful reconciliations, shopping, drunkenness and shouting from the cheaper seats at Covent Garden, la Scala, and – only once – the Bayreuth Festspielhaus. They'd been inseparable at Oxford. And they'd been inseparable when they'd moved to work in London, Tess drawn to the world of criminal law and Sally to an assistant manager's desk in a West End art gallery. They'd met every week for cocktails, a sacred arrangement that had only once been broken: when Tess had shocked all and sundry – Sally included – by taking a job in Strasbourg. Having returned to London five years later – only four months ago – the tradition had been quickly reinstated. They'd opted for the Beyond Lounge in Kensington.

'This man got life for a crime he didn't commit,' said Tess. 'He then writes to the parole board admitting his guilt. Next, he signs up for a law degree, gets it after six years, and then applies to join the Inner Temple. Every kind of obstacle is thrown in his way and he just climbs over them, one after the other. As soon as he's released he starts the Bar Vocational Course. Scores outstanding in the final examination. Finally, he gets a pupillage at 14 King's Bench Walk, but only because the head of chambers defended him back in '99. When it comes to an application for tenancy, there's a rebellion. They vote him down. No one else will take him. Not in London, not in the Provinces. He squats here, squats there, picking up bits of work in the magistrates' court, a plea or two in the Crown Court, injunctions in the County Court. They're all just waiting for him to throw in the towel. But none of them spotted what he was doing.'

'And what was that?' Sally had had to squeeze the words in.

'He was building up three years' in practice. That's all you need.'

'For what?'

'To open your own chambers. And that's what he's done.'

'He's going it alone?'

21

'He's no other choice. Maybe it's what he wanted all along.'

Tess had spent the afternoon poring over newspaper articles, columns, blogs, posts. The scandal of William Benson, barrister-at-law, member of the Inner Temple, practising from Congreve Chambers, 9B Artillery Passage, Spitalfields, had blown up while Tess was in Strasbourg. A sympathetic profile published in the *Guardian* on Monday had provoked a savage rejoinder from the *Sun* on Tuesday. Backed by Paul Harbeton's outraged family, an online campaign had been started to shut Benson down. To pass 'Paul's Law'.

'They've collected 218,000 signatures already,' said Tess. 'They want the Justice Secretary to propose emergency retrospective legislation.'

'To what end?'

'Prevent anyone working in the justice system if they've been convicted of certain grave offences.'

'Sounds sensible to me.'

'Sure, but in a civilised society we give people a second chance. That's sensible too.'

Tess wished she'd listened more when she was in Strasbourg. If anyone's circumstances tested the limits of rehabilitation, it was Benson's.

'Well, pardon me for shifting from the depths to the surface, but he is one good looking—'

'Oh, pack it in.'

Sally had been tapping on her tablet. She'd found a photo of Benson standing outside his chambers. He didn't look remotely proud. Just determined. And sad.

'Don't tell me you hadn't noticed,' said Sally. 'Just look at that barely contained suffering. The dark eyes. The shadows in his soul. It's positively Russian. I'd do anything to make him feel better.'

'You're impossible.'

'I'm right. What a paradox. The only way to get anywhere near him is to do something terribly wrong. How completely wonderful.'

Sally now ran the Etterby Gallery in Chelsea. But a second passion was graphology. The study and interpretation of handwriting. As a sideline to selling contemporary black-and-white photographs and English watercolours, she advised companies on staff recruitment and individuals on their relationships – even down to the whether they should start one or not. Her specialism was the art of human relations.

'Do you think he'd be interested in a thirty-something who couldn't care less about public opinion? A brunette of wit and charm?'

'I really have no idea.'

'Would you introduce me?'

'Certainly not.'

Sally swiped her screen with a perfectly manicured thumb. She angled the image towards Tess. She'd found a picture of the Harbeton family. Tess vaguely remembered the three sons, led now by Gary Chilton, Paul Harbeton's half-brother, who dominated the frame. The person she'd been unable to forget was Maureen, their mother. Throughout the trial, she'd sat watching through a haemorrhage of mascara. It was as though the black smudges had never dried.

Sally closed the screen down. 'I couldn't do your job. I couldn't look someone like that in the eye and defend the person she believes killed their son.'

'Someone has to do it,' said Tess.

'Even when you think your client is guilty?'

'I've told you before. On the way to Prague. And since. It doesn't matter what I think. You don't get involved. You don't take sides. All that matters is what the client *tells* you.

23

And if they tell you they're innocent, you fight their corner to the death. It's simple, actually.'

This was the work that had once captivated Tess; work that had gradually been replaced by business-class excursions to the court in Strasbourg. Smiling at Gordon during lunch, she'd felt the old hunger for a fight over the evidence – a hunger similar to indignation, roused into flame by the slacker behind who'd complained about green fees while abandoning his client to the prosecutor. That client would now be represented by William Benson. His long route to this unlikely outcome was a feat of astonishing endurance. And there was more:

'You've got to give it to him. He's accepted the jury's verdict when they got it wrong. And he's done that because he believes in the system that failed him. Can you picture that?'

'Not easily.' Sally took a thoughtful sip. 'How do you know Benson is innocent?'

'He told me so.'

'Ah. That explains everything.'

'No, Sally, this was different.'

'How? I thought you didn't get involved? Didn't take sides?'

Tess reached for her coat. 'Sorry, Sal, I've got to go.'

Sally took another thoughtful sip. Aping mild puzzlement, she said, 'Look at your glass.'

It was almost full. Tess had barely touched her Corpse Reviver and Sally was examining her friend's face as if it were a transcript of their conversation. She was reading the signs. People paid her for what she was now thinking but Sally's expression said you can have it for free. She said:

'Where are you going?'

'I'm sorry,' said Tess. 'I've got a conference. New work. Cutting edge.'

# 3

Tess turned the ignition of her classic Mini and set off for Seymour Road near the Regent's Canal in north London. According to the *Sun*, a gate in the middle of an iron railed fence opened on to a path flanked by trees that led to Seymour Basin, where a barge, *The Wooden Doll*, lay moored on a private wharf. This was Benson's 'exclusive' residence, shared with a cat called Papillon. 'Two strays,' observed the writer.

Tess dropped a gear and a conversation crackled in her memory. It had taken place sixteen years ago in a cramped conference room near the cells in the Old Bailey. The jury were still deliberating. Braithwaite and Camberley had just been called to another court for a mention in a different case. Tess and Benson were alone, sipping coffee from plastic cups. The silence became tense with embarrassment. They were both out of their depth. Their eyes met and locked.

'I didn't do this,' Benson said, very quietly.

'Okay.'

His lips were chapped. Blood had dried on one of the cracks.

'No, I'm telling you as if I was telling the world,' he said. 'You're not my lawyer. You're not on the jury. But you're here. You're a stranger and you've heard it all . . . and I swear I'm innocent. I want you to hear that from my own mouth because when the jury sends me down, I need at least one person I don't know to accept I didn't kill that man.'

'Who says you're—'

'I didn't do it. Believe me. Please.'

'Who says you're going to prison?'

'I do. I can sense it. Tell me you believe me . . . if you believe me.'

'I believe you.'

'Is that pity or what?'

'No, I mean it. I swear.'

They fell silent again, bound by the unforeseen, an exchange of oaths. Benson seemed relieved: he covered his face with his hands, a mop of black hair falling over his fingers.

Aged nineteen, Tess had come to London after the summer term in order to shadow Charles Hutton, a shipping specialist at Hutton, Braithwaite and Jones. They'd been in the Admiralty Courts sitting behind counsel in a couple of trials, the first an action for demurrage under charterparty, representing the plaintiffs, the second acting for the defendants in a claim for damage to cargo, relying upon excepted clauses under the Hague-Visby Rules. It had all been wonderfully civilised. No jury, just a judge. No drama and no appeal to the emotions, just polite intellectual wrangling with occasional lapses from irony into sarcasm. The sums of money at stake had been eye-watering. They'd lunched appropriately afterwards. And then, one day, George Braithwaite – the partner with the smallest office in the building – had said, 'Do you want to see a slice of real life?' She had done, and she'd come to the Old Bailey and met a young man, pretty much her age, facing a charge of murder.

Benson had been so pale he looked sick. And looking sick, he looked guilty – especially when he was in the dock, flanked by guards who'd seen it all before. Only Tess, observing him outside court, had gradually realised that this awful bloodlessness had been fear and anxiety and powerlessness. He'd been overwhelmed by the apparatus of criminal law – until that moment, for Tess, the dry stuff of another textbook, rumoured to be badly paid in practice. The trial itself had profoundly disturbed her. But it had also been riveting. She'd sat, entranced, as the prosecutor span the facts one way and Camberley span them another. The evidence had been *alive*, its meaning moving like a ball off a racket. At times, she'd held her breath: a man's innocence or guilt turned on the bounce. The truth – game, set and match – would only be called when the foreman of the jury stood up to announce a group decision.

'If my future wasn't in the balance, if I wasn't scared to hell, I'd say I've enjoyed this trial.' Benson nodded, contradicting Tess's shake of the head. 'Honestly. If I'd known what being a barrister involved, if I'd realised what happens in a courtroom, this is what I'd liked to have done with my life. It's been a revelation. Like a blinding light. Only it's come too late.'

'It's never too late.' Tess had spoken lightly, but Benson leaned across the table. Those drowning brown eyes were wide with a dying man's hope.

'Are you being serious?'

'Why wouldn't I be?' Tess freewheeled: 'Look, I don't think you're going down. But even if you do, no one can stop you reading law. Sure, they can try and block you coming to the Bar, but you can take them on. There's no law preventing someone with a conviction from starting a legal career. None whatsoever.'

'Are you sure?'

'Absolutely. And barristers are self-employed. They're completely independent. Get yourself qualified and you can do what you damn-well like. Tell the feckers where to get off. You can even operate on your own.'

Tess had made Benson smile; and it moved her. She became emphatic, irresponsibly so, because she was no expert on the Rehabilitation of Offenders Act 1974, or how the Bar worked:

'Sure, it would be a long, bruising haul. You'd have to wear down the establishment, plodding on and taking the knocks until you got there. But if you want it bad enough, you can do it. Do you like the Proclaimers?'

Benson said he did, so Tess went on:

'Do you know that song about what a man will do for the girl he loves? Because a life in the law . . . well, I think it's like a love affair. It is for me, anyway.' She began to sing, her voice low and husky: 'But I would walk five hundred miles—'

Benson took over, his eyes finding hers. They almost threw the words at each other, drawing closer, minutely, until the door opened and George Braithwaite stepped inside, frowning. 'I respectfully suggest we save the celebrations for later. There's a verdict. We've been called back to court.'

Benson glanced at Tess and then he seemed to go under.

He'd been right. The foreman of the jury said the one feared word, 'Guilty'. There was a whoop of triumph from the Harbeton camp and Mrs Benson collapsed. A member of the public caught her as she slumped to one side. Two weeks later Benson was sentenced to life imprisonment. Afterwards, in the cramped conference room, Tess leaned on the chipped wall as Benson told Camberley he'd decided to come to the Bar. With her eyes she told him he could do it, that he could walk a thousand miles, not believing for a moment that he'd actually take to the road. Like Camberley said, the cost was too high, the obstacles too many, the chance of success too small. They all said goodbye. They all felt awkward.

Another conversation now crackled in Tess's memory.

She went up a gear, accelerating, because when it was over, she'd been embarrassed and angry. Back at Hutton, Braithwaite and Jones, again in a cramped (albeit Georgian) room, Braithwaite had given Tess some advice. And a kind of order.

'Take a seat, please.'

'Mr Braithwaite, I was wondering if I might—'

'A word of guidance first, if I may.' He frowned at his tea, observing that the cream had separated from the milk. And then he sighed. 'Miss de Vere, in the criminal courts, one has to be very careful not to get involved with the client. One has to keep some distance in order to remain objective and clear-headed. The work requires a certain personality, or at least a certain discipline. It's not easy to fight passionately on someone's behalf and then walk away afterwards, but that is what we do. It's called professionalism. The detachment is a vital part of offering fearless representation. Down the other road is compromise and complicity. Do you understand?'

'I do.'

'I hope I haven't offended you.'

'You haven't. I take the warning.'

'Good.' And then out popped the order disguised as an afterthought: 'Oh yes, there's just one final matter. Your father is a friend of Charles. And Charles has stood *in loco parentis* while you've been with us. In those delicate circumstances, I think it would be most unwise, not to say inappropriate, if you were to consider visiting Benson. Or writing to him. It's not what Charles expects. Let Benson go, Miss de Vere. He has a long road ahead of him. Yours runs in a very different, and I have to say promising, direction. The twain should never meet. I'm sure you agree.'

Tess nodded.

'You were wondering something, if I recall?'

'It's not worth mentioning.'

Tess had followed Braithwaite's advice. And over the years she'd come to understand, with gratitude, what he meant by the discipline of passionate detachment. She'd also obeyed his order. Which, at the time, incensed her, because – as

Braithwaite divined – Tess had planned to both visit Benson and write to him, as a natural extension of their conversation, and the injunction not to do so brought their association to an abrupt end. He'd separated the milk from the cream. Strangely, she was even angrier now, and ashamed, because knowing what Benson had subsequently done – walk a thousand miles over sixteen years – she felt as if she'd abandoned him. She'd pointed out the difficult road and then gone her own sweet way. She could have helped, and she hadn't done, simply because Charles Hutton didn't want to tell her father that his daughter had taken a shine to a convicted murderer.

Tess parked and cut the engine.

On crossing Seymour Road she saw a bearded man in a leather bomber jacket walking towards her; and he, on seeing her, turned and began retracing his steps. He had a slight imbalance to his gait. Thinking nothing more of him, Tess looked and easily found the entrance in the railings described by the *Sun*, along with the post box without a name, and the bell, which she pressed. Standing by a streetlamp, humming 'Lady Luck' by the Proclaimers, she watched the blue-and-red barge through the bare branches. But no one emerged. There was no movement, save the shiver of the water as it twinkled in the dying light. Looking down, she saw a large cat looking at her through the bars. This, presumably, was Papillon. He purred like an idling HGV.

'Where's Benson?' she said, crouching. 'Where's he gone?'

And in saying those words, Tess realised that she was scared. She didn't know Benson. She'd hardly known him when she was nineteen, and she'd no idea who he'd become now that she was thirty-five. She didn't know where he'd gone, as a man. He'd spent most of his adult life in prison.

The thought unsettled her. Resolved to wait, Tess left Papillon and went back to her car, wondering what eleven years in a cell might have done to William Benson, the student philosopher who'd begged her to believe in his innocence.

# 4

Benson was inexplicably terrified. The last time he'd felt like this was the morning of his trial. It didn't make any sense. *That* had been the Old Bailey. *This* was an old people's home in Shoreditch. Back then, he'd faced a judge and jury. Now it was a ninety-five-year-old pensioner with his pensioner daughters.

The situation would have been comic if a serious question hadn't been in play. Benson had just finished renovating the ground floor of the building that was meant to function as his chambers. He'd furnished three rooms. He'd unpacked two thousand books. He'd placed a name board by the door. He'd authorised modest publicity. He was up and running. And now, at the last moment, he faced eviction two days before a major trial, just when the Secretary of State for Justice was hoping to shut him down. This wasn't a good time for a breach in landlord and tenant relations.

'You'll be okay, Rizla,' said Archie, leading Benson along a gloomy corridor to the chosen parlour. 'Just answer the questions to the best of your ability.'

'You sound like Camberley. And stop calling me "Rizla".'

'Sorry. It's just a habit.'

'This is your bloody fault.'

'I know. I'm sorry again.'

'You should have explained my situation.'

'I did.'

'You didn't. You left out the one bit that mattered. That I'm trapped.'

They'd reached the parlour door. Archie flicked some dust off Benson's shoulder. 'If he says, "Call me CJ", you're home and dry.'

Benson entered the room, leaving the door slightly ajar behind him. His mouth went dry. 'CJ' Congreve, in his wheelchair, was positioned behind a long, bare table. On his right sat Dot and Joyce Congreve; on his left, Betsy and Eileen Congreve. Archie, the only boy in the family, didn't have a place. He was somewhere behind Benson, who sat down on a wooden chair facing the tribunal. None of the would-be judges were smiling. CJ had put on a tartan tie for the occasion. His white shirt and diamond-patterned tank-top hung loose on a shrunken frame. Bald and milky-eyed, he banged the table with the knuckle of a bony hand.

'My father opened Congreve's in Artillery Passage in 1892. In those days, Spitalfields was like a village. There were tailors on every corner. Locksmiths. Grocers. Pawnbrokers. Alehouses. But there was only one fishmonger. And that was Charlie Congreve.'

'Get on with it, Dad,' said Betsy.

'I had two brothers. Both of 'em died in the Great War. One on the Somme. The other on the Menin Road. Serving their country. I was born in 1919—'

'Dad—'

'And I took over Congreve's in 1946. I'd served in the Royal Signals. I was at El Alamein with General Montgomery. We showed Rommel—'

'God almighty,' said Joyce.

CJ hit the table again. 'That's two world wars and Congreve's never shut down once.'

Eileen spoke: 'Dad, Mr Benson isn't interested in—'

'I'm talking about the Congreve name. And there was no dishonour in this family until our Archie went daft and fiddled his tax returns. He didn't tell us the business was failing. He didn't tell us our Patsy was dying—'

'That was Archie's wife, Mr Benson,' said Joyce, as if Benson didn't know already. 'She had cancer and our Archie looked after Patsy on his own when he should have asked for help.'

'And after she died, he held his hands up,' said Eileen.

'And Congreve's had to close,' said CJ. 'After a hundred and seventeen years.' He squinted at Benson. 'And now there's more trouble.'

Benson had shared a cell with Archie in HMP Lindley. And it was Benson, an old hand at thirty-one, who'd showed Archie the ropes, a grieving widower at fifty-six. Archie hadn't wanted help caring for Patsy, and he hadn't been able to tell CJ that Congreve's was up against the wall; he'd thought he could turn things round with a few big contracts – supplying Harrods and a couple of Michelin star restaurants – but that had all fallen through. By trying to keep everyone's world normal, free from worry, he'd sunk not only himself but a family tradition, for which he'd received a two-year jail sentence. Benson had pulled out some hooch and they'd both drowned their sorrows.

They were released within months of each other, Benson to finish his legal training, successfully, Archie to seek work, in vain. No employer would touch him. Living on the dole, he'd set up the 'Tuesday Club', a weekly gathering of ex-cons who met (still) at the Pride of Spitalfields on Heneage Street. The idea was to offer mutual support in a world that – by and large – wouldn't give offenders a second chance. And it was there, on a Tuesday night, that Benson, shown the door by his most recent set of chambers, wondered if now was the time to tell the feckers where to get off. Archie had agreed. He offered Benson the old shop premises in Artillery Passage at a peppercorn rent, subject to CJ's approval; and that approval was granted, all the more so because Archie, at sixty-two, would become a barrister's clerk. But now there was a problem. CJ hit the table.

'I let you into Congreve's because you were good to our Archie. And because he told me you were innocent. And what did I read in the paper last week? That you were guilty. That you'd admitted it after your trial. In writing.'

'That was my fault, Dad,' said Archie. 'I should have—'

'Belt up, son. Come here, young man. Give me your hands.'

Totally bewildered, Benson came to the table, offering both his hands. CJ leaned forward and grabbed them with a weak but sure grip.

'People are talking. About you and about the Congreves. Now, they can say what they like if they've got it wrong, but if they've got it right, you aren't staying in Artillery Passage. Do you understand?'

'Yes.'

'So, tell me, if you're innocent, why say you're guilty?'

Benson croaked from lack of spit. 'If I didn't accept the verdict, I wouldn't have got parole. And I could never have worked as a barrister. The authorities would say I'd refused to accept what I'd done. So I'm trapped.'

CJ tried to squeeze harder, putting on the pressure, but he'd no strength left.

'I have to admit that I killed a man,' Benson went on. 'It's crazy, I know, but if I said I was innocent, they'd say I lied to the parole board, the Inns of Court and the Bar Council. I'd be out on my ear.'

'Meaning?'

'The Bar Standards Board wouldn't let me practise.'

CJ leaned forward from his wheelchair and yanked Benson closer till their faces were inches apart.

'Did you kill that poor man?'

'No, I did not.'

CJ examined Benson's complexion as though he wanted to know if he'd been freshly caught. If he'd had gills, Benson was sure that CJ would have pulled them open to see if they were nice and red. He began to panic. Those watery eyes, unable to focus properly, were looking beyond appearances. For a long time he seemed to waver, but that could have been the trembling of old age; and then, at last, he leaned back.

'You can call me CJ,' he said.

'That means you can stay at Congreve's, Mr Benson,' said Eileen, standing up. 'Would you like a cup of tea?'

# 5

Benson began the short walk back home to Seymour Basin. The day was fading, and with the encroaching darkness, he felt the onset of a depression. Not the beginnings of an emotional collapse – where he'd be stranded, unable to move because of the shapeless weight blotting out his mind – but rather a dimming of the lights, giving rise to a general sadness he wouldn't be able to shift; a sadness he'd have to put up with until something bright came along. He tried to think of the coming trial – he'd only read the brief once and there was a lot of material to master – but he couldn't focus his thoughts. He couldn't shake off his conversation with the Congreves.

Archie had only done a year inside – and that was a Cat D. An open prison. Home from home. Benson was the real thing. He'd done time in those high-walled Victorian dungeons. Dot Congreve, who'd said nothing during the appeal hearing, had been full of embarrassment and questions afterwards. Like a voyeur, she wanted to know what prison was really like . . . did he have a TV? Were the screws on the take? Had he been gang-raped in the showers? Benson didn't know what to say. Even as she spoke, he found himself wanting to scream out the scream he'd learned to suppress, a scream that was still buried deep in his subconscious. What could he talk about? Yes, there were friendships, robbed of depth by constant transfers to another prison. There was solidarity. But these were hardly redeeming features. HMP Anywhere was a hothouse of deeply human problems without adequate resources to treat them; a self-enclosed universe of boredom, shattered self-esteem, remorse, depression, drug addiction, illiteracy, mental illness, abandonment, sorrow, self-harming and suicide. At least, that had been Benson's experience. When his parents came to visit this faraway cosmos, they left the visiting hall in pieces, overwhelmed by the ear-splitting kids and crying mothers, choked by the conversation that hadn't happened, because Benson had vanished inside his head in order to survive. He was still in there somewhere. He'd never made it back to the normal world. What was he to say to Dot, pouring the tea, and Betsy, all excited, who'd opened a packet of ginger biscuits? Ordinarily, he'd have sidestepped the conversation, but he owed the Congreves. They'd given him a break, for a peppercorn. He had to give them something of himself in return, and at cost.

'Have you ever been stuck in a lift?' said Benson.

'Yes,' said Eileen, turning to her sisters. 'Do you remember that time in Clacton? The ghastly hotel? That tiny box for three people? We overloaded the bloomin' thing and it got jammed between floors.'

CJ had fallen asleep, but his daughters were very much awake. They forgot Benson was there, recalling how they'd been cramped, breathing over each other, sweating in the dark, crying out for help with no one responding. Betsy had started banging on the wall, and Joyce had thought she might go mad or die, and Dot had started moaning, sucking at the slit between the lift doors. As Eileen observed, none of the Congreve girls could have auditioned for *Pan's People*. They were too ample. 'It's the steamed puddings and the pies, Mr Benson,' admitted Eileen. 'We were jammed in like four lumps of melting lard.'

'And then that bloke came along,' said Betsy, blinking erratically. 'Said we were lucky he'd heard us because normally he'd have gone home half an hour ago. We could have been stuck there all night.'

'Well, I was in that lift for up to twenty-two hours at a time,' said Benson. 'On average, it was sixteen. For ten years. Then I went Cat D. I thought I'd die, too. That I'd suffocate . . .'

In a way he had done; the twenty-one-year-old philosophy student had died gasping for air. He'd come to life again, obscurely, with the law, the rules and penalties that had put him behind a locked door; the self-enclosed universe that governed freedom and responsibility in the world he'd left behind. Or, rather, the world that had moved on, leaving him behind, because in HMP Anywhere, there was no such thing as ordinary time. Time was only something you did.

'I tend to leave doors open these days,' said Benson. 'Otherwise I get jumpy. And I can never find my keys.' He wondered if he should tell the four sisters what really happened when he found himself in a small room with a closed door; and that he'd been in therapy for years, and couldn't imagine it ever ending . . . but he changed his mind. 'Can we stop there? I've got to get back to work; back to Congreve's . . . and I don't usually talk about prison for long.'

'In case it all comes back?' said Betsy.

'Sort of, yes.'

The four sisters looked at each other while CJ snored quietly.

'And to think,' said Dot, appalled, 'you'd done nothing wrong.'

Benson rounded the corner into Seymour Road. And sure enough, he couldn't find his damned keys.

# 6

Something wasn't quite right.

Tess let her eyes drift along the fence, past the adjoining buildings, up to the end of the road and then back again to the fence and the gate.

And it clicked.

Someone else was waiting. About a hundred yards away, at the junction with Wenlock Street, stood the bearded man wearing a leather bomber jacket. He'd turned around on seeing Tess approach Benson's gate, but he hadn't gone anywhere; he wasn't doing anything. He was just lingering, looking down Seymour Road, rubbing his hands.

Waiting.

But for what?

Darkness was falling fast. Misty orange light spread from the streetlamps. Tess shivered. There was no point in hanging around. Benson wasn't at home and there was no guarantee that he'd be coming home. She slotted the key into the ignition, and just as she was about to give it a turn, there was activity.

A car door had opened on Tess's side of the road, much further up. A man got out and crossed over, striding quickly, thick arms held wide from his body. He was heading down the street, now, so Tess turned, and there was Benson, smartly dressed in a dark suit, coming from the opposite direction, tapping his pockets. He was shaking his head and talking to himself, not looking where he was going. She sensed something was going to happen . . . and it did: when the man reached Benson, he coughed, gathered in his mouth, and spat straight into Benson's suddenly upturned face.

Benson recoiled in shock. But he didn't retaliate. He just looked up to the dark sky and then began tapping his pockets again – presumably trying to find a tissue – as the man backed away down Seymour Road, his hands inviting Benson to bring it on. Tess threw open the car door and reached Benson in seconds, offering a handkerchief.

'Thank you,' he said. 'That's very kind.'

'Are you okay?'

'Yes, fine. It's nothing.'

'It's something.'

Despite what had happened, Benson looked extraordinarily calm. 'Something best ignored,' he said, as if in fact, he'd won some kind of point. 'He'll be bragging in the pub tonight; but he's lost something of himself.'

A car growled into life. It pulled away, roaring towards the end of the road, where it picked up Benson's aggressor. When Tess turned back, Benson was examining her features.

'I think I know you,' he said, slowly.

'The Old Bailey, Court One. Nineteen ninety-nine.'

After that, Tess was tongue-tied. She gestured for the handkerchief and then threw it into a waste bin. When they were back eyeing each other, Benson began to sing:

'"And I would walk five hundred miles . . ." It's you, isn't it?'

'It is.'

'I can't remember your name, I'm sorry.'

'Tess de Vere.'

'That's right . . . I knew it was a de – something. You did a placement with George Braithwaite.'

'That's right.'

'Oxford?'

'Yes.'

'Shipping law, wasn't it?'

'Yes. But no.'

They shuffled in the cold, their talk coming through bursts of fog, Tess distracted, because Benson's appearance was very different from how she remembered him; and very different from the photograph in the *Guardian*. The youthful fear had been replaced by that distinctive melancholy; and, in the flesh, it was strangely appealing. He was a strong man who needed something.

'I took your advice,' he said.

'So I hear. I'm impressed. Very.'

'I told the feckers where to get off.'

'In style.'

'Yes. Would you believe it, I practise from an old fish-monger's?'

'I know. It's brilliant.'

They stalled. And Tess wished she could reach for that Corpse Reviver. All she could do was take in Benson's dark-brown eyes – they wouldn't rest on her for long – his short, jet-black hair, and that sadness which was calling out for something. He spoke:

'Don't get me wrong, but what brings you here?'

Tess held up her hands. 'I'll be honest: I didn't think you'd actually make it. If I'd known you'd start the long walk I'd have helped.'

'I don't think George Braithwaite would have approved.'

'No, he wouldn't. But that was then and this is now.

You're here. And I'm here. And from what I've read, I think you could do with a helping hand.'

Benson scratched the back of his head. 'Do you want a drink?'

'I need a drink.'

He finally found his keys in the side pocket of a rucksack. Unlocking the gate, he turned to Tess and nodded at her car:

'Is that yours?'

'Yes.'

'It's beautiful. Really stands out. There's nothing else like it.'

'She's a classic.'

'What's the make?'

'Austin Cooper S. Nineteen sixty-four. Cherry red.'

'Hard to come by, I suppose?'

'Very.'

'Do you want to keep it?'

'Sorry, I'm afraid I do.'

'Well, you'd better shut the door and lock it up, then.'

Tess had been so engrossed in Benson's humiliation that she'd left it wide open. Crossing over, she looked up towards Wenlock Street. The darkness had become sharp. The clouds of orange mist had turned to pools of stage light. But the bearded man in the bomber jacket had vanished.

# 7

Benson was surprised. Tess had taken one look in his drinks cupboard, then, unimpressed, she'd gone to the local off-licence, returning with a bottle of cognac, a bottle of calvados and a bottle of sweet vermouth.

41

'Have you got a cocktail shaker?'

'No.'

'An egg cup and a jug?'

'Yep.'

She got busy, hardly looking at Benson.

'You made it into shipping?' he said, arms folded.

'No. I got knocked off course.'

She'd spent seven years at Hollingtons doing general crime but had drifted into technical waters – Human Rights Act stuff – which eventually took her to Strasbourg. After five years – four months ago – she'd come back to London and a one-year consultancy at Coker & Dale. She had a roving brief to develop human rights law across the firm. 'I can do what I want,' she said. 'Which is great.' But what she really wanted was ice cubes, so Benson showed her the freezer. His mind, however, was on the stern door. When Tess had returned, she'd closed it and flipped the lock.

'Have you got a sieve?'

Benson hadn't so he gave her a tea strainer.

'Stemmed glasses?'

'Sorry.'

She settled for porcelain teacups and began filtering the mixture.

'This, Mr Benson, is a Corpse Reviver. It changes your outlook on everything.'

Tess was shorter than he remembered; and slender. Her movements were slow and naturally elegant. The burst of freckles had faded somewhat. The sandy hair had darkened to the colour of a beach in late afternoon rather than morning. Her eyes were remote, with flashes of green and blue. Benson had seen the loneliness of the sea. He wanted to trail his hand in the water, to feel the breakers around his ankles.

'The Ministry of Justice may be able to shut you down,' said Tess, walking to some crowded bookshelves that ran the length of the boat. She put her cup down and began examining the titles, one finger stroking the spines.

'I'm not so sure,' said Benson.

'Neither am I; but I'd be worried if I was you.'

'I'm always worried.'

Benson looked at his hands. He was beginning to fidget.

'Richard Merrington is a populist,' said Tess, taking down a volume. She opened and flicked through the pages. 'He's tough on crime and the causes of crime and so on, but you represent a unique chance: his chance to be tough on a criminal. You represent his chance to dominate the media. He's the Lord High Chancellor now but he wants to go a lot further. You're a rung on the ladder. So is Mrs Harbeton.'

'I'm not backing down.'

One of Benson's legs was bobbing on its toes. He glanced at the door, imagining the lock mechanism in operation. Tess had given it a turn. But why?

'If Merrington brings forward legislation to ban a certain class of ex-offender from holding positions in the legal system, you'll be up to your neck in injunctions, judicial reviews and appeals – every kind of legal spitting. He'll do whatever he can to keep you out of court. And by the time you get your case to Strasbourg – if you *have* a case – it'll be too late. It takes years and years, you know that.'

'So what do you suggest I do? Give up now? Because I won't.'

'No. The opposite.'

'What do you mean?'

Tess closed the book, slid it back on the shelf and turned on Benson as if she was ready for an argument:

'If this is Merrington's opportunity, it's also yours. The spotlight is on you like no other barrister in England. It's your chance to make a strong impression. Stun your critics and it will be a lot harder to pass "Paul's Law".'

Benson's mouth was caked with panic. The symptoms had come on fast: his stomach was gaping. His skin was itching. Sweat had gathered on his back.

'Do you mind if I open the door?' he blurted out.

'No, sure.'

'Can I smoke? I know it's disgusting and causes cancer but—'

'Don't worry. It's not a problem.'

Benson quickly opened the door and sucked in the cold air. It came fresh off the canal like the kiss of life. Trembling violently, he knocked a Gauloise from a crumpled packet and lit up. Slowly the shake in his limbs subsided. Papillon slinked in and Tess spoke quietly:

'Have you ever conducted a Crown Court trial?'

'Unfortunately not.'

'I understand you've landed the Hopton Yard killing.'

'I have.'

'Sarah Collingstone?'

'Yep.'

'It's listed for Wednesday morning. The day after tomorrow. Court One, the Old Bailey? Where you were tried and sentenced?'

Benson didn't answer but the receding panic rose like an angry wave. Tess said:

'Have you met her?'

'Last Friday. We had a brief talk, nothing more.'

'What are her chances?'

'Slim to non-existent. Her defence hasn't been investigated. The prosecution have an open field.'

Benson breathed in more chilled air. The itch had gone. The hole in his stomach had closed over. The sweating had stopped. Only an anxious catch remained in his lungs. 'I'm okay, now. Thanks. I'm really sorry . . . but can I leave the stern door open? Just a smidgen?'

Tess was seated at the dining table. Benson joined her and their eyes met, like they'd done sixteen years earlier, when the jury had been deliberating for four hours. His Honour Judge Rigby had said he'd take a majority verdict if they couldn't reach a unanimous decision. The tension had been unbearable.

'Will, we both know a barrister can't investigate a case. So let me help. A lot can be done between now and Wednesday. Without committed representation from the defence, the police may have cut corners.'

'They have done.'

'Your opponent at trial might well be overconfident. It's your chance to surprise them.'

'What with?'

'If this woman isn't a liar, then there has to be more evidence out there. It's axiomatic.'

'I agree.'

'Someone has to find it. You can't. I can. But the way I can help you most – and your client – is by changing how *you* are seen.'

'And how would you do that?' Papillon came between Benson's feet, leaning on his legs, purring like a diesel-driven dredger.

'Simply by coming on board,' said Tess. 'With Coker and Dale you've got some serious backing. You're no longer someone they can joke about. Even Merrington will hesitate. Do you think Collingstone would be prepared to instruct me?'

Benson was sure she would. Ordinarily, he'd have asked Archie to call on his behalf. But given the pressure of the moment – a conference the next morning at the client's home address – professional courtesies were an extravagance. Every minute counted. So Benson stepped outside, on deck, and called Sarah there and then, explaining that things were already turning for the better. A solicitor of significant standing with international experience had volunteered to join the defence team. Would Sarah accept her services? And, as Benson expected, she most certainly would, but on one condition.

'I want you to represent me in court, Mr Benson. No one else.'

'Of course. Miss de Vere wouldn't have it any other way.'

Stepping back into the galley, he paused, surprised at the look of hope in Tess's face. She really wanted this. It wasn't pity. This was as much for her as it was for him.

'Welcome aboard, Tess,' he said. 'We're a team.'

Tess smiled; and those far-off green-blue eyes flashed with something like sunlight.

They talked for a long while, Benson relieved that Tess didn't ask about prison. She already seemed to know and left it alone, as if it were an open sewer. Instead they went over the long haul: how Camberley, of all people, had been an endless source of encouragement and support; how Braithwaite, for all his frowning, had been a guide and friend. And all the while Papillon weaved his way between Benson's legs, causing endless moments of confusion, because once or twice Tess and Benson's feet collided under the table, prompting the usual apologies, waved away with the usual embarrassment.

'Sorry,' said Benson. 'It's pretty tight in here.'

'If you hadn't said anything, I'd have thought it was the cat.'

They covered a lot of ground, only it was Benson who did the talking. Tess asked the questions but she didn't give much away. And just as he was about to launch his own enquiry, she rose, saying it was time to go. She took a set of disks disclosed by the prosecution and they agreed to meet the next morning at a Tube station near Sarah Collingstone's home.

'If we are to work together,' she said, 'we're equals. But you are the person who will stand up in court. So don't hesitate to tell me what you need or tell me what to do. I won't think you're ordering me around. Just say please.'

'Agreed.'

Tess took a moment to admire the boat's fittings – the curved oak beams, the wooden Hobbity windows, the racing green Aga cooker – and then she opened the stern door, pausing on deck by the garden table and chairs, the pots of plants:

'Earlier tonight. The assault. Has that sort of thing happened before?'

'Frequently.'

'Because of the *Sun*?'

'No. It started the day after my release.'

'That's five years of provocation.'

'On and off. They work in twos and threes. One of them does something. The others watch. If I hit back, they'll say I started it. If they're believed, I end up back inside. I got a life sentence, remember. I'm only out on licence.'

She nodded and Benson helped her on to the wharf. For a moment he touched her hand but then she was suddenly out of reach. Again, she looked around approvingly, and made her way towards the gate. Papillon brushed along Benson's legs again, and he called out as Tess vanished into the darkness among the trees:

'Tess, thanks . . . but I'm not sure being seen with me is a good idea. It's hardly a career-building move.'

She replied without stopping, a dark figure shifting among orange light and shadows. 'It is actually. It's new work. Cutting edge.'

\*　　\*　　\*

When he was quite sure she'd gone, Benson went to Seymour Road and retrieved the handkerchief. He'd seen the lace trim. He'd seen the sewn initials, 'T de V'. When he stepped back on board, he came to a halt as if he'd walked into a brick wall: his depression had gone. Normally it hung around for days, like rain in Lancashire, lifting only gradually; but the clouds had been blown away without him noticing. That had never happened before, never once since his release. He put on the Proclaimers – 'Sunshine on Leith' – and went to the shelves where Tess had been browsing. She'd walked straight past the history of Western philosophy, blithely ignoring everyone from the odd and important Heraclitus to the oddly important Sartre. She'd only stopped when she reached the *poetry* . . . the section devoted to Edward Thomas, Robert Frost, Andrew Young and W. B. Yeats: Benson's cellmates, who'd conjured up blue-winged swallows, snowy woods, dust on nettles; sudden and shocking impulses of delight. He was desperate to know which collection she'd touched, but he couldn't find it, not for sure. What he did find was a teacup; and he had to smile.

'What do you make of Tess de Vere?' he said to Papillon, who'd appeared between his legs. 'After all that faffing around, she didn't drink her Corpse Reviver.'

# 8

'I had this cellmate in HMP Stonton,' said Benson. 'He was called Jaffa. And when he cased a joint, he always checked the back garden, never the front. He reckoned it was a good way of finding out what someone was really like. Whether they were careful or not.'

'Why was he called Jaffa?' said Tess.

'Because his scalp looked like an orange. He'd upset a smack dealer, so the muscle poured boiling water over his head . . . having added sugar to raise the temperature and make it stick.'

They walked down a broken path skirting a block of terraced houses near Mogden Sewage Treatment Works in Hounslow.

'This is it,' said Benson, pointing.

Sarah Collingstone's back garden was neat and tidy. The old wooden fence had been repaired with new nails. The grass had been trimmed even though it was October. The windows to the house were clean. There were no net curtains. On either side the story was very different. The grass was ragged and long from the summer. In one, a mix of beer bottles were piled in a couple of soaked cardboard boxes. In the other, the shell of a car had been stripped beside a greenhouse with barely any glass.

Benson humphed. 'No one ever listened to Jaffa.'

Sarah Collingstone led Benson and Tess into the entrance hallway. Passing the sitting room, Benson looked inside and halted. He'd seen a teenager in a wheelchair, his body folded, one wrist twisted on his chest, his head leaning to one side, and all at once Benson was back home in Brancaster Staithe looking at Eddie, his younger brother, a few years after the bike accident. He'd sit for hours in his wheelchair looking out at the sea, unable to speak or move with ease, his mouth half open. Once he turned to Benson and said, sluggishly:

'I'll never go to sea with Dad.'

Benson was standing in the corridor, grass stains on his trousers, a batch of top marks in his school bag.

'I'll never bring in the lobster and the crabs.'

Benson screamed inside. He'd have done anything to trade places. He'd said it over and again though no one really

49

believed him. But they didn't know what had happened. Even Eddie didn't know. He couldn't remember anything about the accident.

'I'm sorry,' said Sarah. 'This is Daniel, my son.'

Benson snapped back into Hounslow, but it was too late. For he recognised in Sarah's eyes the years of rejection, prejudice, embarrassment, disinterest and pity that had tainted too many relationships. Benson was just another nice guy who'd flinched at her son.

'Don't say sorry,' said Benson. He'd read that her son 'had a disability' but he hadn't appreciated to what extent. He crossed the sitting room and took Daniel's hand. 'I'm pleased to meet you. I'm Benson. Will Benson.'

Daniel's head tilted slightly but there was no pressure from his fingers. The nails were beautifully clean and trimmed. He was smiling, but not at Benson's greeting: his expression hadn't changed; this was how he looked normally. Was it paralysis or joy? At any given moment it would be hard to know, unless you were Sarah.

'I'll stay here with my grandson, Mr Benson,' said Ralph Collingstone. 'You can talk to Sarah next door. Would you like some coffee?'

'Please.'

They gathered around an oval dining table, Benson facing Sarah, and Tess to one side. On the pale yellow walls were posters of great stage plays. *The Crucible. The Importance of Being Earnest. The Seagull.* On the shelves were books and audio CDs, some of them read by Ralph. He'd been going somewhere, once. Benson pulled at the bow of the pink cotton tape tied around *R v. Collingstone.* He opened the back sheet and laid out the papers in front of him in piles: witness statements, forensic evidence, photographs, ground plans, police interviews . . . all the while sensing the tension in the defendant that no one believed. She was – Benson had to acknowledge – particularly attractive. It wasn't so much the full lips or the shining, auburn hair, the pencil-line bones. It was the transparency of expression. The unprotected vulnerability. She was thirty-four with the fragile beauty of old age. Andrew Bealing can't have failed to notice.

'I forgot to ask,' said Benson, after Ralph had brought the coffee and tiptoed out of the room, 'does Daniel like music?'

Sound and rhythm had been an important part of Eddie's recovery, insofar as he'd recovered.

'Oh yes,' said Sarah, suddenly animated. 'We turned it off when you arrived. He loves sounds and rhythms and—'

'Please turn it back on.'

She quickly left the room. Moments later, Benson heard Coldplay. First track on *Ghost Stories*. A song he loved: 'Always in My Head'. When Sarah resumed her seat she wasn't quite relaxed. But at least she was smiling.

# 9

The case papers prepared by Trevor Hamsey, the solicitor sacked by Sarah Collingstone, contained a brief client biography, later supplemented by notes from Diane Wendling, the barrister she'd sacked the same day. It made sad reading. Tess had drawn up her own chronology:

| | |
|---|---|
| 05.10.1981 | Born in Brampton, Cumbria. |
| 05.1993 | Parents (RALPH and JANET) separate. SARAH (aged 11) lives with mother. |
| 07.1997 | GCSEs (9 fails). Mother dies of cancer. Sarah (15) lives with father. |

| | |
|---|---|
| 15.12.1997 | Fatal car accident.<br>Driver: ANTHONY GREENE (18).<br>Passengers: Sarah (16) and PAULA RYAN (17)<br>Greene and Ryan killed.<br>Greene at fault. Jumped lights. Collision.<br>Sarah hospitalised. Two months pregnant. |
| 12.05.1998 | Birth of DANIEL 5 weeks premature. ?Because of accident? |
| 25.05.1998 | Daniel admitted to hospital. Brain damage. |
| 08.1998 | Ralph and Sarah move to London. Ralph teaches at Eva Moore School of Drama. Richmond. |
| 26.06.2014 | Sarah (32) meets ANDREW BEALING<br>Entrepreneur: Hopton Transport Ltd<br>Hopton Imports Ltd<br>Hopton Residential Holdings Ltd |

Tess had the document in front of her. Benson had nothing. He began with the birth of Daniel.

'He just stopped breathing,' she said. 'I was holding him in my arms and I saw his lips had turned blue.'

'How old was he?'

'Just ten days. I called for an ambulance but they couldn't get him to hospital quickly enough.'

By the time Daniel was on life-support he'd sustained irreparable brain damage. The cause of the crisis was never nailed down because the bombardment of antibiotics that saved his life had removed the explanation. They'd taken advice, wondering if the original respiratory condition was linked to the car accident. There'd been years of hedging legal opinions and medical reports before the case was dropped.

'We'd moved by then. I wanted a new start, away from the north-west, away from everything that reminded me of my mum, and the accident. And Anthony, Daniel's father.'

'You came to London?'

'Yes. My dad took a part-time job. I dropped out of school. We had to manage.'

'I don't suppose you were overwhelmed by support?'

'No. We'd imagined there'd be more facilities, but there weren't. It was hard.'

Together they'd handled the demands of twenty-four-hour care. With the sale of the house in Brampton, they modified a property in Hounslow. After that, all they had was Ralph's reduced income and a handful of benefits. Which wasn't enough. It still wasn't.

'To meet the needs of someone like Daniel, you need a fortune,' said Sarah. 'An absolute fortune.'

And then, having teased out a motive for murder, Benson jumped sixteen years of round-the-clock nursing:

'How did you meet Mr Bealing?'

'I went to the Alington Trust. They'd opened a new state-of-the-art project for children with disabilities. The Sandridge Centre. I'd seen an article. When I turned up I discovered they did much more . . . they worked with other charities, employers, individuals . . . giving people a fresh chance, or a break . . . and the assessor told me about Hopton's Imports Limited. She told me the company was looking for an assistant manager for three shops. That I should give them a call. I'd done part-time work at the Co-op, so I thought I wouldn't have a chance, but the assessor told me Mr Bealing was really kind. That he'd been through the Trust himself. That I had nothing to lose. The Trust would help with day care and the income would buy additional help. She said it was important I get out of the house and build a future of my own.'

'What was the assessor called?'

'Paula O'Neill.'

Tess wrote the name down.

'You went to see Mr Bealing on Thursday the 26th of June last year?'

'Yes. I had an interview and he gave me the job. I wasn't adequately qualified but he said he couldn't care less.'

'On the 18th of September – three months later – you sent Mr Bealing an email saying, "You've changed my life. Thank you." What did you mean?'

'I meant what I said. Everything was better. For Daniel. For my father. My life was like it had never been before . . . not since Daniel's birth. I was grateful. I thanked him.'

Tess watched Sarah carefully. She seemed to be hiding nothing. She seemed oblivious of any second interpretation of her words, even now, when the prosecution were suggesting she'd started an affair with her benefactor.

'Tell me about Anna Wysocki,' said Benson.

'She's the manager of a shop specialising in Polish food. She was putting me under pressure to get health and safety manuals up to date, training courses organised . . . all sorts. But Mr Bealing kept putting me off.'

'I mean her character. What's she like?'

Sarah hesitated, frowning.

'Don't think,' said Benson, 'just speak the first words that come into your head.'

'Aggressive . . . jealous . . . strong-willed . . . ambitious . . . efficient . . . I'm sorry, I can't think of anything else.'

'Younger than Mr Bealing?'

'Yes.'

'Attractive?'

'Very much so. She'd modelled in Paris and Milan.'

'Why end up managing a shop?'

'She'd never made it big. Like so many others.'

'Single?'

'Yes.'

Again Benson wrote nothing down. But Tess was sure it was all being filed somewhere in his mind. A trial strategy was emerging.

'Did you ever meet Debbie Bealing, Andrew Bealing's wife?'

'No.'

'Did you hear any gossip about her?'

'Lots.'

'To what effect?'

'That she was unstable. She'd had problems with depression. At one point she'd worked with her husband, but then she'd had to pack it all in. I was told a nurse came to see her three times a week, just to make sure she was okay.'

'People rarely gossip with sensitivity. What did they say?'

'That she was crackers.'

'Anything else?'

'That the nurse serviced her . . . you know, because Mr Bealing certainly didn't.'

'You held back a detail.'

'With a thermometer.'

'What was his name?'

'Darren Weaver, a guy from Edinburgh.'

'Anything else about Debbie? A nickname used by those close to Mr Bealing – behind his back, of course?'

'Yes. Screwball.'

Benson paused. 'Sarah, have some coffee. Relax. You don't have to do anything tomorrow. I do. And I'm not worried. Okay?'

'Okay.'

He restarted his questioning before her cup had touched the table.

'You arranged to see Mr Bealing on the night he was

murdered. A Saturday. You arrived at the Hopton Yard premises in Merton at about 6 p.m.'

'That's right.'

'Why see him on a Saturday night?'

'To get the manuals sorted out, once and for all. He always worked late on a Saturday, organising the driving rotas and other business. I thought that was the best time to get him alone, and when he couldn't find excuses and head off somewhere.'

'Was Mr Bealing drinking from a bottle of beer?'

'No.'

'Did you drink from a bottle of beer?'

'No.'

'Did you tell any other employee in advance about that meeting?'

'Yes. Anna Wysocki.'

'Why?'

'I told her I was going to get the manuals sorted out. She'd made me promise.'

'You say you left about half an hour later?'

'I did.'

'How do you explain being seen there at 11.35 p.m.?'

'I can't. It wasn't me. I was at home. Here with my dad and Daniel.'

'What were you doing?'

'Listening to a story.'

'Which one?'

'*The Longridge File*. My father had just recorded it.'

'Did you ever go into the warehouse at Hopton's Yard?'

'Yes, but only once or twice.'

'Why?'

'To speak to Andrew . . . Mr Bealing.'

'You can call him Andrew. Did you ever handle any of the foodstuffs stored on the shelves?'

'No?'

'Are you absolutely sure?'

'Yes.'

'You never touched a beer bottle in a crate? Take one out just to look at the label?'

'No, never. That wasn't my job. I was always on the road, visiting the outlets . . . checking how things were going, taking orders. I touched nothing. Not even in the shops.'

Tess was intrigued. Sarah had turned down several chances to lie. Turned down the chance to explain away a critical piece of evidence. An explanation the prosecution would be unable to contradict. Benson sipped his coffee and said:

'Your DNA is on the bottleneck that killed Andrew Bealing.'

'But it can't be.'

'It can, and it is.'

'Couldn't there be some mistake . . . at the laboratory or something?'

'No. This isn't a case of sample contamination. Your DNA is there.'

Sarah didn't reply. She covered her face with her hands. Benson sipped more coffee.

'Why the last-minute holiday to France?'

'I needed a break.'

'From Daniel?'

'No. Anna Wysocki.'

'Andrew Bealing helped you, didn't he?'

Sarah sniffed. 'Yes.'

'He made your life easier? A life that's been hard, at times?'

'Very hard, Mr Benson. But I'm not complaining. I have a wonderful—'

'He changed everything overnight.'

She nodded. Benson handed her a tissue, pulled from his pocket.

'Did you ever kiss Andrew?'

'No.'

'Hold his hand?'

'No.'

'Fall in love with him?'

'No, no . . .'

'Did you ever – just once after a bad day when you should have known better – did you ever have sex with Andrew Bealing?'

'No, no, no.'

'Are you single?'

Sarah, for once, laughed, but not with pleasure. 'I'll always be single, Mr Benson.'

But Benson fired back: 'On Wednesday the 14th of January of this year – that's a month before the murder – you wrote another email timed at 4.46 p.m. You wrote, "Remember your promise." What promise?'

'To speak to that damned Anna Wysocki about the damned manuals and about damned training days, about a slippery floor in the storeroom, about the low lighting in the corridor, about a mat for the entrance, about . . . O god, I just can't remember it all any more.'

For the first time Benson opened his blue notebook. Rather than write anything down, he detached a page, careful to follow the line of perforations.

'I've prepared a series of questions, Sarah. I'd like you to write down the answers and scan them to me by tonight. Is that possible?'

She nodded. She was exhausted.

'Try not to worry,' said Benson, bringing all his papers into one pile – papers he hadn't touched and which had functioned like a low wall between him and the client; papers he'd memorised. 'Remember, it's my job in court, not yours.'

\* \* \*

Tess and Benson scouted round Sarah Collingstone's part of the world. They paused to look at the sewage works. And Tess rehearsed Sarah Collingstone's remark that she'd always be single. Because it underlined the Crown's strongest point. If someone with a history like Sarah Collingstone latched on to a person, they might never let go. And if it turned out that she'd been used and abandoned, she wouldn't just go for a cocktail. She'd boil a dog.

For completeness, Tess didn't agree with Benson on the merits of Jaffa's advice. Taken with other data, back gardens were a useful tool of analysis. In Tess's experience, neat and tidy people could be exceptionally violent. The order was just a desperate attempt to control their emotional instability.

# 10

'I know the DNA isn't going to go away,' said Benson.

'Doesn't that tell you anything?' Tess was insistent.

'For the moment, no. We can't explain how it got there, that's all. As a matter of logic, it doesn't follow that she killed Bealing. That's an inference—'

'A powerful inference.'

'And as long as we're dealing with inference we have a chance.'

'A sliver of a wafer?'

'Something like that.'

He was standing by the window looking through the blinds on to Artillery Passage. People were lingering to read the new sign on the wall, a blackboard with lettering in white paint: 'Congreve Chambers. Mr William Benson Esq. Clerk: Mr A. Congreve Esq.' These were the only barrister's chambers in England where it was absolutely clear who worked for whom. Archie was the boss. Sort of. Encouraged by the curious faces, Benson said, 'We can't just say she didn't do it. We've got to find another candidate. Give the jury someone else to blame.'

'What do you mean?' said Archie. Like his four sisters, Archie's frame showed an obdurate affection for pies and puddings. Not to mention biscuits. And Mr Kipling's cakes. His sleeves were rolled up, revealing arms like boiled hams. 'We've run out of time.'

'No, we haven't,' said Benson, leading the way into his study. 'All we have to do is find a passer-by in the trial, someone with a close link to Bealing. We don't have to prove anything. All we have to do is point the finger.'

No one visiting could ever have guessed that seafood had been sold from these premises for over a hundred years. The steel counter had gone. So had the chalk and blackboard. And the smell of salt. And the chill from the ice. All that remained were the old ceramic wall tiles, glazed white squares with blue drawings, handmade in Portugal. Roman blinds covered the shopfront windows. There was a tatty school-master's desk for Archie and creaking wooden chairs for any clients. The only throwback to former days was Harold, a 125-year-old Atlantic lobster in a large tank of water. He'd watched over the premises since the very beginning, when Charles 'Bobbie' Congreve – 'CB' – had first opened his shop. CJ wouldn't hear of his eviction. And neither would Archie: they were childhood friends.

The back room – where the gutting and scaling had taken place – was now Benson's study. Layers of paint had been scraped off the ornate plasterwork. The oak floorboards had been scrubbed and sealed. Another desk – a damned expensive relic from a ship captain's cabin – underlined the period charm. Books filled the arched alcoves. *Halsbury's Statutes. Archbold. The All England Law Reports. The Weeklies.*

Journals on this. Textbooks on that. And more. The lot. All a barrister would need to practise on his own.

'I'll check Sarah's story with the Alington Trust,' said Tess, dropping into a worn-out leather armchair.

'And let's get on to the local haulage competition,' said Benson. 'They're all after the same work. They know if someone's running a scam. They know if someone's rubbed someone up the wrong way. There are two outfits nearby, Felbridge Logistics and Winchley Transport Limited—'

'I'll contact them,' said Tess.

'Archie, any progress on the names?'

'Not yet. I've made calls. The Tuesday Club is on to it.'

Tess frowned so Archie explained, hitching baggy brown cords to sit on a large iron radiator. 'It's a private members-only club of highly skilled people . . . specialists in computers, business management, finance, forgery . . .'

Benson took over: 'Discreet surveillance, background checks, home security.'

'All sorts have joined,' said Archie. 'Doctors, dentists, street cleaners.'

'Even fishmongers and students of philosophy.'

'All unemployed. They meet every Tuesday to solve the world's problems.'

Tess, smiling wryly, got the message, so Benson moved on, pointing to a row of ring-binders on the floor: 'Bealing had three companies: Hopton Transport, Hopton Imports and Hopton Residential Holdings. The files contain the numbers. Sales and purchases. Expenses. Tax returns. Contracts. Everything. This is going to be a ball-breaker, Archie, but you've got to go through the lot with a tooth-comb.'

'Looking for?'

'Unpaid debts. Enemies. A reason to kill.'

Archie nodded.

'Look for any dishonesty, too. The Crown's case theory is that he was a good guy killed by a poor woman. It might help if we found out he was a charlatan. Charlatans have—'

'Enemies.'

'Exactly.'

'What about Debbie Bealing?' said Tess.

'We've got to speak to her,' said Benson. 'The Crown can't call her because she doesn't agree that her husband was having an affair. I'd like to call her if we could. There's Roger Grange as well, Tess. Bealing's financial manager. Claims to know nothing about anything. He hardly co-operated with the police. Let's find out why.'

'Okay.'

'What about you, Rizla?'

'Archie, you've got to snap out of it. I'm not even "Will" or "William". In front of the clients I'm "Mr Benson".'

'Sorry. I keep forgetting.'

'And you've got to sound as if you're slightly overawed, all right?'

'I'm trying, honestly.'

'We can't have people thinking I'm going to roll a burn at any moment.'

'No.'

'Read up on Bowker.'

'Who's he?'

'Marshall Hall's clerk. Hall was a giant of the Old Bailey, and Bowker his trusted friend, but there's a touch of willing servant.'

'Forget it.'

'No, seriously. These days senior clerks are managing directors, CEOs . . . it's big business and corporate sheen. We don't want that. We want something of the Bar that's been thrown away – the one bit that every rogue wanted to keep. Strange traditions. Okay. Archie?'

'Indeed, Mr Benson. What will Mr Benson be doing this afternoon?'

'A site visit. I want to see where Bealing was killed. How about we meet back here at seven?' Benson sighed. 'You don't have to bow. This isn't *Bleak House*. And, Archie . . . look the part, will you? Go to Ede and Ravenscroft and get the gear. Striped trousers with front pleats. Black waistcoat and jacket. White shirt and dark tie.'

Ignoring another bow, Benson shrugged on his old blue duffel coat.


# 11


Hopton Transport Limited was situated at Hopton's Yard on Haydon's Road, Merton. From here, starting in 1966, Joe Hopton had built a thriving business. His daughter, Debbie, went on to marry an ambitious driver, Andrew Bealing. With Joe's blessing, Bealing expanded the business into imports and real estate. By the time of Joe's death in 2013, the family net worth was something like £9.8 million. The value of the estate was unknown to Benson because the whole lot had been sold by Debbie Bealing in a rush of grief. Whatever the final figure, the wealth had been generated by Andrew Bealing. And the hub of everything had been here, at Hopton's Yard.

The place had been sold to a developer a couple of months back. All the curtain-siders, artics and flat beds had gone, returned to leaseholders or sold to former competitors. The low buildings had been boarded up. The iron gates were chained together. A guard in heavy black boots ambled around, seemingly led by the whims of an Alsatian on a leash.

'Can I have a look around?' said Benson, through the bars of the gate.

'Sorry, mate.'

'I'm a lawyer who's—'

'Makes no difference to me.'

Benson spotted the crude tattoos on the man's wrists. The pencil-dot tattoo high on the left cheek. 'Look, I'm that barrister Rizla. The one they want to shut down. Give me a break, will you? I'm representing the woman accused of murder.'

'You're the brief who did time?'

'I'm a lifer. I'm always doing time.'

The gates opened and Benson set to work.

He began his reconstruction of the killing in the main office building. First, though, he threw a packet of cigarettes into an oil drum filled with water.

The ground-floor reception room was empty now, but it was here that Bealing's assistants, Kym Hamilton and Tina Sheldon, had handled all the calls and paperwork. Benson looked outside through the peephole in the main door, the way he'd just entered. Bealing must have done the same thing on the evening of Saturday, the 14th of February 2015. According to Hamilton and Sheldon, he wouldn't have opened the door unless he recognised the caller.

Sarah Collingstone's DNA and fingerprints had been found on the handle.

Benson walked from the door, past Kym and Tina's domain, to Bealing's office. It, too, had been cleared. A large window looked on to the reception area. Another window looked on to the warehouse. He closed his eyes, remembering the police photographs. A conversation of some kind had taken place in here. An argument had developed. The theory was that Bealing had told her the affair was over. He'd left the room and Collingstone, in a frenzy of rage, had picked up an open bottle of beer, smashed it on the edge of the desk, and gone after him.

The shattered base, and spillage, had been found on the floor; but no blood. Bealing's DNA and fingerprints were on parts of the glass.

Benson went out of the office, turning left, away from the entrance area. He went down a corridor leading to the warehouse. This was probably where the fatal blow had been delivered, by the door.

The photographs showed blood sprayed upon the left-hand wall. Bloody fingerprints and smudges were streaked across the door. This was Bealing's blood. Fragments of bottle glass had been trodden into the fibres of the carpet. But nothing linked Sarah Collingstone to this specific place, where the attack had taken place. None of her fingerprints or DNA had been found on the wall, the door, or its handle.

So, injured and bleeding, Bealing had opened the door to the warehouse.

Benson followed the imagined figure as he gasped and stumbled away from his attacker. Spilling blood, he'd reeled left and right for thirty-five yards before collapsing between the prongs of a forklift truck, where he bled to death. All that remained, now, were faint traces of a white chalk line, defining the outer limits of where the blood had pooled. The bottleneck had been found on the floor, dropped within a foot of the body, near the head.

Sarah Collingstone's DNA was on that bottleneck.

The floor was made of smooth concrete. It had been dusty from the crates and whatnot. Bealing's footprints had been easily identified. Parallel to them the dust had been disturbed, indicating that a second set of prints had been removed. The killer had followed the bleeding man, intending (it seemed) to ensure that he died. Bealing's mobile phone had been found fifteen yards from the body. His bloody thumbprints had tapped out 999, but the call was never made. The killer must have taken the phone and put it out of reach just after the number had been entered.

Benson slowly retraced his steps, thinking of the required depth of feeling to behave in such a way. It would have taken years to accumulate and it would always fester just below the surface. He had seen many such people in prison. They did dreadful things. But they'd lost something of their free will . . . he came to a halt just before the door to the corridor, where a section of ribbed concrete linked the office to the warehouse. A tiny shred of red leather had been found scuffed on a rib.

The leather came from a shoe belonging to Sarah Collingstone. It had been recovered from her home when police searched the premises on the Monday following the killing.

Benson went outside, retrieved the cigarettes, found a dry one, and lit up. Standing by the oil drum, he smoked for a while, trying to piece together what might have happened if Sarah Collingstone had told the truth . . . but then he spotted the lamppost by the entrance and an intuition tingled in his mind. He went over to take a closer look. Satisfied, he took lots of photographs.

'Good luck, Rizla,' said the security guard, tugging at the dog.

'Thanks.'

Benson had given back the keys. They'd chewed the fat for a minute or so.

'I did time, too,' said the guard. 'Wandsworth. The Scrubs. A few other holes.'

'When did you get out?'

'Ten years back. This job's my first big break.'

His wife did a night shift, so when he got home they only had an hour together before she had to go out. But they were both in work. It was good. He was doing his share. Benson said he was impressed.

'If a wheel comes off, or you need help, just give me a call.'

Shaking hands, Benson told him about Archie Congreve's Tuesday Club and then passed through the gate. As the guard wound the chain through the bars, he said, 'We never really get out, do we? We're always going to be ex-cons. Until the day we die. Make a difference, will you? For all of us.'

# 12

In a way, Tess admired Benson's insistence on cold logic. It was a philosopher's point. But it was also true: Sarah Collingstone's DNA on a murder weapon didn't mean she'd killed Andrew Bealing. But the jury would still want to know how it got there. Without an explanation, everything Benson's willing servants might dig up would be worthless. With that sobering thought, Tess knocked on the imposing Wimbledon door of Debbie Bealing's house.

She'd been crying.

She was pacing around now, like a caged maniac. She was forty-one with hair dyed a sort of purple-black, heavy red lipstick giving the impression of a crushed fruit jammed in her mouth. She wore perilous high heels, a tight white pencil skirt, a tight white blouse and had her pale arms wrapped tight across her flattened breasts. She'd stabbed at the remote control to cut the volume on the television. Contestants were laughing.

'Andrew did not have an affair with that woman,' she said. 'Impossible. I would have known. He was my first and only love. And he loved me. He did. I don't care what they say, I know. He adored me. And now they're going to make a fool of me in public. Humiliate me. Laugh at me. They're going to say he'd gone elsewhere. He'd never do that . . . just look at me for Christ's sake.'

She snapped into a model's pose, one hand on a hip, a coquette pouting at the camera's flash, drinking in the praise.

'I'd have known. I'm a woman. We know these things, don't we?'

She was pacing again, following a precise line directly parallel to the edge of a cashmere rug. The Bealings – or at least Debbie – were into colour. The curtains were burgundy velvet. The sofa was wheat yellow. The plaster cornicing was pink. The pastel wallpaper had fine green lines. The ensemble was quite awful, with the meticulous tidiness of a professionally cleaned home. Debbie probably didn't know where the dusters were kept.

'How can they do this to me? How can they go into that court and tell everyone that Andrew was having an affair? Isn't there a law against this sort of thing? Can they say what the bloody hell they like? I told them, for God's sake, *I told them* . . . but they wouldn't listen.'

'Who wouldn't?' asked Tess.

'The police. A fat oaf in Marks and Spencer's trousers. And her solicitor. He wasn't much better. None of them would listen. Because they think I've lost my marbles. Just because I've been depressed sometimes, just because I've been to hospital . . . that doesn't mean I'm mad. Lots of people have mental health problems. One in three, or something like that. Lots of stars admit it these days. We've nothing to be ashamed of. I'm totally normal. I'm doing well. I've got medication. I never forget to take it . . . But *they'* – she pointed angrily towards a crowd of whispering officials in uniform – 'want to make everyone think I'm a fruitcake. That Andrew had fallen for this woman, felt sorry for her . . . and it just isn't true. Doesn't anyone out there have a heart? Andrew's dead. He's been murdered. Don't they realise I'm in pieces? Anyone would be . . . it's because I take tablets, I know it.'

Tess broke into Debbie's sudden abstraction: 'What did you tell the oaf in Marks and Spencer trousers?'

Debbie came directly to an armchair beside Tess. She dropped her voice, though no one else was near them. 'The Chinese got him.'

'What do you mean, Debbie?'

'A gang. Ninjas or whatever. I don't know.'

'Why would the Chinese get him?'

'Andrew did a lot of work with them. Imports. Mountains of stuff produced in concentration camps or whatever, I don't know how they keep the prices down, but they make everything you can think of and it costs hardly anything and Andrew had lots of contracts with lots of people out there.'

'For what type of product?'

'You name it. Tea. Slimming machines. Car parts. Whistles. Herbs. Circuit breakers. Solar panels. Computer parts. All that Chinese medicine rubbish . . . leaf extract or whatever. I tried some gingko for my depression and it didn't work. I much prefer my little white friends. That's what Andrew used to call them. My friends . . . he'd remind me to take a friend out for dinner.'

After a moment Tess said: 'And the Chinese got him?'

Debbie looked up. 'Sorry?'

'The Chinese.'

She was back on track. 'That's right. But you have to understand how haulage works. The police just wouldn't listen. They think they know it all. But they don't. A haulage company never really knows what they're transporting. Take Hopton's. We'd send a curtain-sider to Heathrow or Ipswich docks or whatever to pick up tons of wrapped crates or boxes or pipes. You don't open them up. You don't look inside. You just check the manifest. And off you go. You drive tons of rubbish from China to Newcastle. That's how it works.'

'And?'

'Andrew had upset one of his clients. A business in Shanghai.'

'How?'

'He'd refused to renew a delivery contract?'

'He told you this?'

'Yes.'

'When?'

'Three days before he was killed.'

'Did he say why he'd refused a renewal?'

'No.'

'But the client was annoyed?'

'Yes, because they'd been safe with Andrew. He'd been their man for years. They didn't want to start all over again with someone else.'

'What was the product?'

'I don't know. But I think it was guns or swords or something. Maybe poison.'

'Why?'

'Because Andrew told me he was frightened. He said they were a gang with a weird name. He said he knew too much. Those were his words, "I know too much, Debs."'

Tess glanced at the television. The audience were clapping. The presenter was wagging a finger.

'That woman is innocent,' said Debbie, nodding. 'The Chinks killed my Andrew, I know it. They didn't want him

70

to go to the police. He knew something. So they sent someone to kill him. Which sent a message to anyone else in the know . . . that you don't mess with the Chinks. That's why I've got a bodyguard. In case they come for me.'

'Where is he?'

'He comes three times a week and today's not one of his days. But he knows his stuff. Ex-SAS. You don't mess with them either.'

Tess agreed, but with compassion. Bodyguards didn't visit their clients, they lived with them. Nurses, on the other hand, came at fixed intervals; and she was sure that this 'bodyguard' was, in fact, Darren Weaver, the nurse mentioned by Sarah Collingstone; the man who 'serviced' Debbie, upgraded for conversations like this, when Debbie, desperate and ignored, wanted someone to take her seriously. 'You're in safe hands.'

'I am. But are you going to tell the court what really happened? So that everyone knows? Will you tell the judge that my Andrew didn't have an affair with that woman?'

'Yes, I will. The court will be told there was no affair.'

'Do you promise?'

'I give you my word.' Tess smiled sadly. If Sarah Collingstone had been let down by circumstances, Debbie Bealing had been let down by something as simple as chemistry. Finding the right medication would have been a really difficult call. Her doctor would have tried everything, switching from this to that, changing the doses, aiming for the right balance . . . and she was now on a relatively even keel, only it hadn't stopped her creating a fantasy to escape the terrible truth that her husband might have been unhappy with her.

'You're selling up, Debbie?' said Tess, conversationally. She'd seen the prestige 'For Sale' sign at the entrance to the property. Copse Hill was a sought-after area. There were no sewage plants nearby. The house and extensive gardens wouldn't be on the market for long.

'Yes. I can't stay here. Not without Andrew. And not after people start talking about an affair.'

Which they would. It was part of the Crown's case. The smear would be all over the papers. Poor Debbie. She lost her father in 2013, her mother in 2014 and her husband in 2015. She had no children. She was all alone with her little white friends and a nurse who came three times a week.

'Where will you go?'

Debbie thought for a long time. She was still sitting on the edge of her seat, close to Tess, examining cracked and brightly painted fingernails. Finally, and with awful longing, she said, 'Somewhere where no one knows who I am, where no one knows about my husband's murder, where I can start again as if nothing ever happened.'

Tess walked slowly down the drive as if she'd left someone to drown. The television was back on. There was nothing she could do but keep her promise.

# 13

Benson put on his duffel coat, locked up Congreve's and bought a packet of Camel. He smoked one, pulling hard on the tab. He then stamped on the packet and threw it in a bin. Twenty minutes later he came to Selby Street in Bethnal Green where he rang the doorbell to the consulting room of Dr Abasiama Agozino, a clinical psychologist specialising in battle stress.

Nothing of substance had been uncovered by Tess and Archie by 7 p.m. The encounter with Debbie Bealing spoke for itself. Roger Grange, Bealing's financial adviser, hadn't answered the phone. The proprietors of Felbridge Logistics and Winchley Transport Ltd had agreed to be interviewed, but only tomorrow, the morning of the trial. And as for Archie's combing of the books, he'd found nothing. After this disappointing review, Tess had gone home, Archie had set off for the Pride of Spitalfields for a meeting of the Tuesday Club, and Benson had ostensibly continued preparing for the trial.

'Thanks for seeing me at short notice,' he said, sitting down in the usual chair.

By agreement, there was no box of tissues between them. Benson had made that a ground rule. Instead, at Abasiama's suggestion, there was a large cactus.

'Has something happened?'

'Yes.'

Abasiama waited.

'I'm back in Court One at the Old Bailey tomorrow.'

Abasiama waited.

'It's where I was tried and sentenced.'

'Yes, I know.'

'Well, quite apart from the stress of going back in there, I've never conducted anything more serious than a burglary. And that was in the magistrates' court. I'm flying by the seat of my pants.'

Abasiama waited.

'I've been instructed at the very last minute. It's a hopeless case. Despite the evidence, I believe she's innocent.'

Abasiama's appearance was often surprising. Today, she'd woven long plaits of yellow and purple hair. There was a wooden bead at the end of each braided tail. She was a walking human festival. But she wasn't saying anything. Benson continued:

'Everyone's against me. The press are on to me. So are Paul Harbeton's family. The government wants to ban me.

People spit in my face. It just doesn't end. That's it. That's everything. I think.'

Abasiama never seemed to breathe. Somehow she drew in the oxygen and let it escape without moving. She was absolutely still, which would have been like death if she hadn't been so alive, in a vibrant, almost threatening way.

'That's it?' she repeated.

'Yes.'

'That's everything?'

'Yes.'

Abasiama shook her head. 'Well, that's just not true. You know you'll cope with Court One. We both do. You've faced greater challenges. Yes, you will shiver and sweat. Yes, you will be sick. But you won't be overwhelmed. You know this. As for your client, you know all about hopeless cases and you know you can handle this one. A great many people have always been against you. Many of them will remain so. And some of them will continue to spit in your face. You know this. I know this. We both know that you are not going to give up. Tell me something I don't know.'

'I've met someone.'

Benson had first come to see Abasiama about two years after he'd been released on licence. He was having trouble coping. The bouts of depression were something he ignored, accepting their arrival as if they were relatives he couldn't avoid. The problem was doors. He kept standing in front of them waiting for someone to bring out their keys. And he could never find his own. He kept losing them. He had to keep doors ajar, regardless of the weather. And he was lonely. He couldn't meet anyone without talking about his past, and his past was a dead place and a place that brought death, for not many people would trust a killer. Not many people wanted to board *The Wooden Doll* for a nightcap.

His best friend was a stray cat. However, within minutes of meeting Abasiama, she'd moved away from everything Benson had raised. She wanted to know about his dad. And his mother who'd died while he was in prison. And Eddie, whom he no longer knew. Blinded by tears, Benson had lunged for a tissue, stabbing himself on the cactus.

'I don't mean romantically,' he said. 'Something else has happened, and it makes me . . . homesick.'

'For the man you once were?'

'Yes.'

Abasiama seemed to foresee everything. Her brown eyes were like windows on to a continent.

'When I first met Tess, I didn't have a conviction. I was an innocent man. And if I'd been acquitted, I'd be an innocent man now. I think we'd have stayed in touch, we'd have become friends, but I was convicted. So in meeting her again after all these years, I'm reminded of the person she knew, the person I might have been . . . and want to be . . . and can't be.'

'No, you can't,' said Abasiama. 'But no one is ever who they might have been. We all think our life is full of graves. But if we were to dig them all up, we'd find there's no one there. We are who we are.'

'But I no longer know who I am. And what I do know I don't like.'

'Well, that's an improvement.'

'Is it?'

'Yes. When I first met you, you said you hated yourself. Do you remember my reply?'

'Sorry, no. Tell me.'

'It'll come back to you when the time's right.'

'You really won't repeat yourself, will you?'

'No.'

She wouldn't budge. She was maddening. And at the same time she was just wonderful. Because it meant recovery was possible. It wasn't a word in the index of a shrink's manual. It was a fruit in a tree. Already within reach.

'A word of warning about tomorrow,' she said. 'Don't fool yourself.'

'What do you mean?'

'Don't think that by winning this trial you'll change your world.' She took one of her dreadful breathless pauses. 'Any number of people can thank you for saving their life, but adulation won't change how you see yourself. It might well change how others see you – and that's all to the good – but you'll be left unchanged. You can't escape guilt so easily.'

'Thanks,' said Benson. 'I feel just great now. I'm really glad I came.'

Abasiama flicked her hair and the beads clinked like a wind-chime. 'Have you had a panic attack recently?'

'Yes.'

'What brought it on?'

Benson sometimes wondered if Abasiama followed him around. She regularly seemed to know what had happened and why. It was unnerving.

'I was talking to Tess. She thought I was worried about the trial or needed a cigarette . . . but it wasn't either of those, and it wasn't the closed door either.' He searched for the right words. 'I don't know this person,' he said, at last. 'I've not seen her for sixteen years. Back then, we only spoke for an hour or so. For her, now, I'm an interesting human rights case. But for me? This is the person who first told me I could make it at the Bar. She gave me the idea, and then she vanished, but she came back, just as I set myself up on my own . . . and I didn't want her to leave again. I didn't want to talk things over with Papillon.'

Abasiama seemed not to have heard. She said, 'Let's talk about your breathing.'

\*     \*     \*

On his way back home Benson found the bin, recovered the packet of Camel and fished out a crushed stub. He lit up and then set off, trying to remember what Abasiama had said to him about self-hatred. He really had no idea whatsoever. When he reached Seymour Road he was still none the wiser. But he sighed. Someone had tipped a sack of rubbish by his gate. Household waste. Half-eaten food, tins, plastic pots, tea bags. The handle of the gate had been covered with something sticky. Papillon was scavenging, disappointed with the selection. After cleaning up the mess, Benson checked his mailbox. There was nothing unpleasant . . . just an envelope marked 'W. Benson Esq. By Hand.' He recognised the handwriting instantly.

It was from Helen Camberley QC, the woman who'd defended him; the woman who'd told him to forget about the Bar; the woman who'd then helped him get to grips with jurisprudence; the woman who'd given him a pupillage against the will of her own chambers; the woman who'd given him a wig and gown, bands and a blue bag; the woman who'd made countless telephone calls to get him work, even as the door was closing. He took out the letter and read it by the streetlamp:

Dear Will,

I'm told you've been instructed in the Hopton Yard killing. Remember what I told you in pupillage: murder is usually a domestic argument gone wrong. It's often very simple. Sift the evidence. Assume nothing. Test everything.

This case is a golden opportunity to establish a name for yourself, different from the one that fate and folly has imposed upon you. All great careers begin with such a stroke of fortune. Seize the day.

I am very proud of you.

As ever,

Helen.

Benson placed the letter in his pocket and made his way through the trees. Once on board, he banged yesterday's leftovers into the microwave and gave Papillon his monthly sardine. He polished his shoes and sharpened his pencils. He placed his blue bag in a cupboard, out of sight. The brief itself had been safely locked in chambers. He was ready for the fight. Leaving the stern door ajar, he went to bed with a volume of poems by Edward Thomas, the one Tess might have touched. For some reason, his mind strayed from the poems, gathering random memories. He thought of Needles, whose seat of power had been a shared toilet. He thought of Jaffa, who'd never learned to go straight, and who'd been killed with a claw hammer; and he thought of the ex-con from Wandsworth and other holes who'd finally been entrusted with the keys to an abandoned building. Benson nodded off, remembering a plea.

'Make a difference, will you? For all of us.'

# PART TWO

## The case for the prosecution

*Benson started shaking. He couldn't control his limbs. He couldn't breathe easily. His lungs were tight. Sweat rolled into his eyes. A scream rose into his throat but it wouldn't come out. There was a hand over his mouth. Needles' hand.*

*'They'll put you in solitary, son,' he said. 'And that's worse. Believe me. Now calm down. Calm down. Shush. You're fine. You're going to be okay. Now, when I take my hand away, breathe in, okay? Just breathe in slowly. Do you understand? You don't want to start shouting, you don't want to be on your own, in the seg. Okay? Are you ready?'*

*Needles slowly took away his hand. 'Good boy.'*

*But the scream was still jammed. Benson was breathing quickly, heaving on the edge of his bunk, but that scream was still there, silent, filling his mind like white noise.*

*'Keep breathing, son. You don't want to be taken off the wing.'*

*A week had passed. And every day, at bang-up – when the door was locked – Benson had watched the door close, he'd heard it slam shut and he'd heard the key turn. And he'd lived clinging on to the edge of sanity, waiting for the sound of the key in the lock and to see the door swing open. The twenty-three-hour gap in between had become a living hell. The panic had been mounting like rising water, day on day, and he'd finally let out a crazed scream, only Needles had quickly intervened, before it could attract the wing officer's attention.*

*'It's time for you to listen to me, son,' said Needles. 'Because you're weak, now. You're ready to make lots of*

*mistakes. Now's the time for you to learn what you've got to do if you're going to survive.'*

*Needles brought over a cup of water. 'Drink up.'*

*Benson didn't calm down. He remained in a panic. But his body began to ease up, separated from his mind.*

*'Okay, now, say "Yes" if you've understood what I'm telling you.'*

*Benson nodded, and Needles began:*

*'You tell no one nothing about yourself. You keep yourself to yourself. Okay?'*

*'Yes.'*

*'If anyone asks how you're doing, you just say, "Fine". All right?'*

*'Yes.'*

*'Don't be needy. Okay?'*

*'Yes.'*

*'Don't do anything that makes you stand out. Don't attract attention. Right?'*

*'Yes.'*

*'Don't make friends. Not for a long while. And when you do, don't make too many. Take things slowly. You've got a lot of time. Yes?'*

*'Yes.'*

*'And lastly, never, ever trust a screw. Got it?'*

*'Yes. I've got to get out of here, Needles. I can't take bang-up. They can lock me in a compound, but I can't cope with being in here, in a cell. I can't—'*

*'There's only one way out, son.'*

*Benson looked up and Needles was tapping his head. What did he mean? Mind over matter? Or something more radical? Unhitching yourself from any relationships, from hope and anger and pain and longing and love? From being an ordinary human being? And Benson realised, with dread, that it was this last, and not the first.*

*Needles was nodding from his chair, his needles clicking as he worked on a yellow woollen scarf.*

*The next morning Benson had a legal visit from Braithwaite. He was brought from his cell to a poky, airless room – the solicitor seemed to thrive in such places. As ever he was immaculately dressed, this time in a dark-blue pinstripe with a red tie. He wore a white starched collar as firm as plywood. But he was more formal than usual. He spoke as if this was a first, reluctant meeting.*

*'How are you, Will?' he said.*

*Needles seemed to barge in: 'If anyone asks how you're doing, you just say, "Fine". All right?'*

*'Fine,' said Benson.*

*'You're sure?'*

*'Absolutely fine.'*

*Braithwaite smiled and, strangely, Benson felt better. He'd passed his first exam. He'd said 'Fine' when he meant the opposite.*

*'Good, because I need your complete and undivided attention.'*

*Braithwaite opened his worn leather briefcase and took out a sheet of paper, folding his hands on top so Benson couldn't read the typed document. Then he said:*

*'I've been instructed to tell you that funds are in place to meet the reasonable costs of any tertiary level studies you might choose to undertake during your incarceration. Do you understand?'*

*Benson was nonplussed.*

*'Please answer,' said Braithwaite.*

*'Yes, I understand.'*

*'Should you succeed in obtaining a qualification, other monies will be advanced to help you establish a career of your choice. Do you understand? I do require a verbal reply and not a nod.'*

'Sorry, yes, I understand.'

'All ancillary costs will be met, their provision dependent upon your progress. We can discuss these at a later date. For now I only seek confirmation that you understand what is being offered.'

'I do . . . I do understand.'

'Thank you.'

'But who's sent you here? Who is the—'

'Please don't ask any questions until I am finished. The aforesaid is dependent upon one condition.'

'Yes?'

'You are never to attempt – either by your own efforts or those of any agent, express or otherwise – to discover the identity of the person who seeks to help you. Do you understand?'

Benson smiled with confusion and gratitude. He began to think of names, but Braithwaite required an answer. 'I do.'

'Are you prepared to sign undertakings to that effect?'

'I am.'

One would have thought that Braithwaite would have been smiling. But he wasn't. He looked profoundly ill at ease.

'I have drawn up the necessary paperwork. Please remember, Will, that I function as a trustee. If the generosity of my client is abused, I have the obligation and authority to restrict or terminate the flow of support.'

With three fingers Braithwaite swivelled the document around and slid it across the table.

'Please read each paragraph carefully. If you are satisfied with the terms, sign at the bottom in the space provided.'

He withdrew a fountain pen from his jacket pocket and unscrewed the lid. Benson signed with a shaking hand. Having retrieved the signed undertakings, Braithwaite said:

'Now, do you have any questions?'

'No.'

'Good. One last matter. Am I right in thinking that you are resolved to study the law?'

'Yes.'

'Then I am also instructed to give you these papers from Helen Camberley. She advises you to read them very carefully.' Braithwaite had spoken while opening his briefcase again. He produced a thick file and said, 'These are transcripts of evidence from various trials that have taken place in the criminal courts over the last century. They demonstrate the art of examination-in-chief, cross-examination and re-examination. In terms of high skill, no comparable examples can be found, save those others which I will bring in due course. Miss Camberley has asked me to say, and I quote, "You can forget about the law, just learn to ask questions". Needless to say, the remark is emphatic in nature, rather than literal.'

Braithwaite remained disconcerted. He was always frowning; but this frown was deeper and darker than usual. Standing up, he said:

'Are you sure you're all right, Will?'

'Yes, I'm fine.'

'Let me know if you need anything.'

Needles made another rasping interjection: 'Don't be needy. Okay?'

'It's fine,' said Benson. 'I can handle this.'

When he got back to his cell he didn't even hear the door close. He didn't hear the lock turn. He didn't hear the clicking of needles. He climbed on to his bed, knowing what he had to do if he was to get through the next eleven years: he had to detach himself from his surroundings; he had to retreat deep into himself, into an inner world, a thousand miles from Needles and the screws and the shouting and the bang of doors before they were locked. And he knew he could make it. Because he wouldn't be crossing this barren desert *alone. He'd met Lady Justice, whose right hand held the sword of retribution and whose left held the scales of justice, equally balanced. She'd come like a ministering angel.*

## 14

Benson just reached a toilet in time and threw up. His stomach had been churning with anxiety. When he came out of the cubicle he saw Winston Corby, another barrister, washing his hands at a sink. He looked at Benson as if he'd found his submission wanting, lacking grace. Hoping that the day's potential for unpleasant encounters would end there, he quickly left the robing room, only to find his way blocked by a silk. A woman was walking slowly towards him. She was Benson's height, slim and graced with eyes as sharp as crystal. They'd been lined black to suggest an Egyptian queen. Other counsel had gathered behind her. There was absolute silence.

'I understand you represent Collingstone.'

The consonants had an edge. But that wasn't the problem. Benson had last heard that imperious voice in HMP Denton Fields when the Inns of Court Conduct Committee of the Inner Temple had travelled from London to hear his application to join the Inn. It had been an exceptional and generous gesture. This, the deciding panel, had been chaired by Rachel Glencoyne QC. Without being a member of an Inn, Benson could not come to the Bar. They'd turned him down.

'I represent Sarah Collingstone, yes,' he replied.

'I trust there won't be any unpleasant surprises.'

'You took the words out of my mouth.'

Benson had appealed Glencoyne's decision to the Bar Standards Board Review. They'd upheld the refusal.

'I may have to serve some further evidence,' said Benson.

'I doubt if I'll accept it. Not this late in the day. You'll have to make an application.'

'I'm familiar with all sorts of applications.'

Benson had appealed the review board's refusal. He'd turned to the Visitors to the Inns of Court, a rarely convened body of Appeal Court judges sitting at the Royal Courts of Justice. Released for the day and handcuffed to a guard, Benson had deployed one argument: the legal profession, in the instant case, had a rare opportunity to demonstrate that very infrequently, in special and perhaps unique circumstances, the scope of rehabilitation should not be constrained, even with a crime as heinous as murder. Having argued over the nature of such an opportunity – whether it was legal or moral (an issue they didn't resolve) – the Visitors had reluctantly agreed.

'You ought to understand something, Benson.'

'Yes?'

'If you think fit to solicit instructions through the pages of the *Guardian* when you lack the required experience, don't think for one moment that the Crown will make any concessions. We won't.'

'Miss Glencoyne, I would expect nothing from you but a performance of ruthless integrity. You can expect the same from me, though I suspect I'm going to be nicer about it.'

When Helen Camberley heard about the Visitors' decision, she'd sent Benson a first edition of *The Life of Sir Edward Marshall Hall K.C.*, by Edward Marjoribanks. A legend until his death in 1927, Marshall Hall had been known as the Great Defender. Volatile and charismatic, he'd infuriated judges, outraged colleagues, mesmerised juries and fought many a hopeless case to a spectacular victory, attracting massive public attention. The inscription from Camberley read: 'The story of a man with a tragic past.' A week later, Braithwaite had informed Benson that upon completion of his sentence, funding would be available from his benefactor for the Bar Vocational Course, should he choose to follow that route.

'Do you have an instructing solicitor?' asked Glencoyne, airily. She'd let herself down. She'd played to the gallery – and it was some gallery. But she'd also broken one of the key rules of cross-examination: never ask a question to which you don't know the answer.

'Yes.'

'I'm surprised.'

'Me too. It's Tess de Vere from Coker and Dale. You've probably heard of them.'

And with that reply, Benson left a stunned Glencoyne to talk to her stunned audience.

On the way to Court 1 Benson breathed deeply, following Abasiama's instructions. But nothing could prepare him for the effect of entering that room. Even the sight of Archie bulging out of a black jacket and dark striped trousers failed to reassure him. The nausea returned – the very nausea he'd suffered aged twenty-one when he first entered the dock where Sarah Collingstone was now sitting. The bile came from the same pit of memory. He tried to calm himself with history. This was the oak-panelled court where Marshall Hall had defended Seddon. Where Cecil Whiteley had defended Bywaters. Where A. A. Tobin had defended Dr Crippen . . . and history wasn't working, because this was where Helen Camberley had defended William Benson.

The court ushers were staring at him. So was the court clerk. So was the shorthand writer. So were the press. So was the CPS representative. He could feel the eyes of the specta-tors looking down at his back from the public gallery behind him. He could hear the whispering. He could imagine the pointing. He opened his papers and lined up his pencils . . .

and the breathing technique wasn't working either. He thought he might be sick again. But then everything happened very quickly.

Glencoyne swept into position along the Bar. There was a loud knock. A door opened. The clerk entered like a minor courtier, his voice loud:

'Court rise.'

Mr Justice Oakshott appeared, dressed in scarlet and black, moving slowly on to the bench. After taking his seat and opening his laptop, he looked up and frowned.

'Mr Benson?'

'Yes, my lord?'

'Who is that man sitting behind you?'

'Mr Congreve, my lord. He's my clerk.'

'Your clerk?'

'Yes, my lord. My instructing solicitor is indisposed. Mr Congreve is here to provide what assistance he can.'

'I think I know him.'

Benson turned around and listened to Archie's whispered explanation.

'Your lordship is quite right,' said Benson. 'Mr Congreve appeared before your lordship following a guilty plea in relation to various charges arising from his tax affairs. Your lordship concluded, with regret, that a custodial sentence was inevitable. That sentence has been served and Mr Congreve and I now work together.'

'I'm lost for words, Mr Benson. Quite lost. Nice to see you again, Mr Congreve.'

The jury were brought in and sworn. The indictment was put to the defendant . . . and Benson noticed his breathing was regular. His skin was dry. He was calm. History came back like a retort. Defence advocates had stood exactly where he would stand, securing spectacular acquittals in the teeth of the evidence. They hadn't always been popular, either as people or advocates. But they had become legends precisely because no one thought they could win. Adrenalin shot through Benson's veins.

*Seize the day.*

Camberley's presence vanished. Mr Justice Oakshott was giving the jury their preliminary instructions. Without so much as a glance towards the Bar, he said, 'You are not here to enter the debate surrounding Mr Benson – as to whether he should be allowed to participate in the administration of justice. You are here to ensure that this defendant gets a fair trial. The same rules apply to this issue as to the case as a whole. Take no account of media reports. Do not carry out internet researches on matters related to the debate, the trial or any issues arising between the parties. Take a moment to look at the defendant, ladies and gentlemen. She asserts her innocence. But she is caught up in a question which has nothing to do with her defence. Give her a scrupulously fair hearing. Miss Glencoyne?'

Glencoyne rose to her feet.

'May it please your lordship, ladies and gentlemen of the jury, I appear for the Crown.'

Benson savoured the introduction. He'd heard it numerous times. But never in Court 1 of the Old Bailey. And never in a murder trial. He listened attentively to what came next, but the words he'd never forget had already been spoken: 'Mr Benson appears for the defence.'

# 15

Tess, briefed to investigate Hopton Transport's opposition, made no progress with Jack Felbridge. Having agreed to be interviewed, he wasn't there when she arrived at the premises of Felbridge Logistics at the appointed time. He'd been 'called out,' explained Belinda, his fidgeting secretary – one of those easily coerced people who are anxious to please.

'When will he be back?' asked Tess.

'I really don't know.'

And she didn't. Because Jack, presumably, hadn't told her. While being struck by this last-minute avoidance, Tess wasn't inclined to chase a reluctant party, so she went to Morden and the run-down premises of Winchley Transport Ltd where Peter Winchley, overweight, red-faced and sixty-something, ushered her into a cramped office made hot by three electric fan heaters whirring on the floor. Winchley belonged to that generation of people who were frightened by people in uniform, and since solicitors made the grade by their association with the police, he eyed Tess as if she might produce a breathalyser at any moment.

'I always had a lot of time for Andy Bealing,' he said, lowering himself behind a large desk stained with coffee-cup rings that Belinda would have wiped away years ago. 'A good lad. Generous. Ambitious. A grafter. Cool head. A good eye for an opportunity.'

'Rich,' said Tess, moving things on.

'Stinking rich.'

Winchley underlined the point with a grimace. 'I don't want to speak ill of the dead, but he was a ruthless bastard. When it came to tendering, he'd outbid his dying grand-mother, just to prove he had the clout. He got a buzz from soaking up the work and watching the rest of us crawl to the bank for an overdraft. But I've got to give it to him. He was a good lad. Generous. Ambitions. A graf—'

'Mr Winchley, can I turn off one of the radiators?'

'Of course. Sorry. I don't feel heat. Unlike the wife. When we drive anywhere, I've got the fan on and she's got her window open. There we go. How's that?'

'Much better thank you.' Tess waited until he was back at his desk. 'This ruthlessness. Did Andy ever go too far . . . push anyone to the wall? Bankrupt them?'

'No, not that I'm aware of.'

'Upset anyone?'

'Well, in this business you're upsetting someone, somewhere all the time. Either you're late delivering or you're not delivering at all or—'

'I mean did he upset someone so much that they might want to hurt him.'

'Well, he wasn't the most careful operator.'

'What do you mean?'

'I wouldn't like to say . . . seeing as I don't know what I'm talking about.'

Winchley reached for a tooth pick and cleared an obstruction towards the back of his mouth. 'Sorry. I had a heart-attack sandwich this morning and a bit of bacon got—'

'Mr Winchley, do me a favour, let's speak ill of the dead. Was there anything about Andy Bealing's private life or working life that might have led someone to stick a broken bottle into his neck?'

'Well . . . somebody did, didn't they?'

'I mean someone else. Not the woman who's standing trial.'

'Ah. Right. Sorry, I was a bit slow there. You're not too cold?'

'No, thank you, Mr Winchley. But I am getting hot under the collar because you're avoiding my question.'

'That's why I'm still in haulage after forty-six years. I keep my nose out of other people's business and only look after my own.'

'You said Andy Bealing wasn't the most careful operator. Was he careless enough to make an enemy of someone capable of serious violence?'

'I wouldn't know.'

'But you knew he was ruthless; and you knew he wasn't careful. And I know people who work for HM Customs and Excise who investigate VAT fraud and when they get up someone's backside they generally wish—'

'Look, I'll break the rule of a lifetime. I'll tell you the little I know. But I don't understand it because I didn't want to understand it, you follow? I didn't ask any questions. Because questions give you answers and answers get you involved in other people's business. And I'm only in haulage after forty-six years because I keep—'

'Break the rule, please, Mr Winchley. Tell me the little you know.'

'Andy Bealing came here last July. Sat where you're sat. He wasn't looking too good. Said he was a truck down and could he borrow one. I said no. Because I'm a ruthless bastard, too. But I wasn't too sure that was the reason for him coming round. He wanted advice, too.'

'About?'

'A dodgy client. Said he'd got himself tied up with some hard-nosed outfit who wouldn't take no for an answer. He didn't want to work with them.'

'Did he say where they were from?'

'Abroad.'

'Anything more specific?'

'No. He just jerked his head back and said, "Abroad".'

'Why come to you?'

'Because after forty-six years in haulage you've seen it all.'

'So what was your advice?'

'I didn't give him any.'

'Why not?'

'Because I didn't ask any questions about the hard-nosed outfit or how he'd got tied up with them in the first place. Why not? Because people like that can be indiscriminate when they turn bolshy, especially if they think you're a mate of the guy they're screwing to the floor. You see, questions give you answers and answers—'

'Get you involved, yes, I'm aware of that. But how did the conversation end?'

'Right there. Just like that. I said everything would come out in the wash. Told him not to worry. He went back to Hopton's Yard as if he hadn't come, and I was none the wiser.'

Tess didn't know what to make of the 'little' Mr Winchley knew. Like the ramblings of Debbie Bealing, he may well have described the expected problems of any transport business. Only there seemed to be something more here.

'I'd like to help more but I can't,' said Winchley, rubbing at one of the coffee stains with a wet thumb. 'But I'll give you some advice. If you want to know what was going on in a haulage business, ask one of the crew, not the management. Hopton's Yard was a big operation. There'll have been a warehouse manager. That's the sort of guy I mean. They know everything – what they should know, and a lot of what they shouldn't. Do you get my meaning? They're like butlers in the royal family. They see everything and say nothing.'

Seated in her Austin Cooper in Winchley's car park, Tess flicked through a file of unused material until she found the name of Andrew Bealing's former warehouse manager: Kingsley Obiora. He'd been sick at the time of the murder, but had still been interviewed as a matter of routine. The statement was only a few lines long, because the investigating officer hadn't asked about Chinese ninjas or hard-nosed outfits from abroad. Feeling faintly ridiculous, she drove over to Mitcham, parked and knocked on the door of Mr Obiora's flat on Thornbury Road. The chances were, he wouldn't be there, it being a Monday. But she was in luck.

'I'd like to talk to you about Andrew Bealing,' she said, after introducing herself.

'Oh yeah. Why?'

Obiora was in his late thirties, heavily built and wary. Unlike Winchley's generation, Obiora's wasn't frightened of uniforms, or solicitors who worked with people who wore them. They were confrontational.

'I understand that you were once employed by Hopton Transport Limited. I've been informed that you were—'

'Hold it. Stop right there. I've got nothing to say.'

The door slammed shut and Tess went back to her car. This sort of thing hadn't happened in Strasbourg. And so far it hadn't happened in London. Working with Benson had introduced her to a whole new world. Pulling out of Thornbury Road on to a roundabout, she nearly struck a motorcyclist. She hadn't been looking where she was going. Her eyes had latched on to Kingsley Obiora running pretty damn fast across Mitcham Common.

# 16

'Murder is always tragic, ladies and gentlemen,' said Glencoyne. The crisp voice had been softened. Her smooth forehead was lined with compassion. 'And among the tragic cases that come before these courts, there are some where the stamp of tragedy marks not only the end of someone's life, but the very life of the person in the dock. This is one such case. And I tell you this right at the outset because you will be moved by pity. You will feel sorry for Sarah Collingstone. But you must examine the evidence dispassionately. You must not forget that a tragic past is not a defence to murder. Andrew Bealing and his family look to you for justice, not pity. Justice for Andrew, and justice for this defendant.'

Glencoyne turned to Bealing's quite extraordinary

background. His parents were now dead. The father a merchant seaman, in and out of prison, the mother an alcoholic who drank herself into a hospice. Andrew (as Glencoyne called him) was in and out of care and foster placements throughout the Portsmouth area. He came to London aged seventeen in 1997. Initially homeless he'd stumbled upon the Alington Trust. Partnered with social services, they not only provided accommodation, they offered him a career – if he was prepared to knuckle down and make a future for himself. And he did. At twenty-one Andrew became an HGV driver. He did a bit of work for various haulage companies before in 2002 meeting Joe Hopton, the founder of Hopton Transport Ltd, who gave him a full-time job. He subsequently married Debbie, Joe's daughter, in 2003.

'Andrew moved from driving to management,' said Glencoyne, leaning on her silk's desk. 'Joe taught him everything he knew. But the benefit was mutual, because this son-in-law had a flair for business. He founded Hopton Imports Limited in the year of his marriage, taking advantage of the influx of EU nationals into Britain. He imported foodstuffs from different countries, selling them through Hopton's own outlets located in areas where national groups had been settling. By 2007, he'd opened three supermarkets: one Polish, one Russian and one Portuguese. Each was managed by a native speaker. The business model was a resounding success. Mr Bealing became a wealthy man very quickly indeed. So much so that his wife, Debbie, was able to stop work in 2008.'

Benson underlined that last assertion in red.

The success, said Glencoyne, was intimately linked to philanthropy, for the people who managed these shops, and the drivers who drove the curtain-siders across Europe, were, for the most part, individuals who'd been referred to him by the Alington Trust. He'd received a great deal himself;

and now he was giving back. In 2008 he'd set up Hopton Residential Holdings Ltd, an impressive-sounding name that was nothing more than a corporate umbrella for several domestic dwellings purchased by Mr Bealing and then rented out to employees at a fair rent.

'This man had come to London with nothing. He'd been sleeping on the street. Within ten years he was a multi-millionaire residing in one of the more desirable parts of Wimbledon.'

But all had not been well at home. Debbie may have stopped work but her mental health was fragile. She'd long suffered from depression. She'd made herself isolated. She'd required hospitalisation on two occasions. A private nurse attended upon her three times a week. Whether Andrew Bealing was able to comfort her on the day-to-day, the court would never know. This much was sure: her former work colleagues certainly couldn't.

Once again, Benson's red pencil flashed across the page.

'So this, then, is the man whom Sarah Collingstone met in June of 2014. He was thirty-four, wealthy but unhappy. And as for Sarah Collingstone . . .'

Benson watched the jurors. His eyes settled on one in particular, a redheaded woman with bold freckles. Glencoyne was right. She did pity her; and so did the others:

'Aged eleven her parents separated. Aged fifteen, the year of her GCSEs, her mother died of breast cancer. Aged sixteen she was the sole survivor of a car crash that killed two of her friends, one of whom, Anthony Greene, was the father of the child she was expecting. That child, Daniel, was born five weeks premature, possibly because of the trauma of the accident. Ten days later Daniel was admitted to hospital after he suddenly stopped breathing. He suffered acute oxygen deprivation, causing significant brain damage.'

Benson had been half listening, cross-referring Archie's

scribbled notes on the witness list with Sarah's answers to Benson's questions (the Tuesday Club had done Archie proud). But now he sat back, living out what happened next to the Collingstone family, because much the same had happened to his own, after Eddie's accident.

At first Sarah was inundated with support. But friends soon dropped off. Relatives became busy at the weekend. Anthony Greene's inconsolable parents – who'd looked forward to Daniel's birth as if, somehow, they'd get their own son back – took the radical step of moving house, far enough away to make it difficult to share in Daniel's upbringing. Because, come the day, while they'd cried at the sight of Anthony's smile and Anthony's nose and Anthony's eyes, he wasn't the boy they'd expected and hoped for. Because Daniel had a disability. (Benson's aunt – Eddie's godmother – had stopped answering her phone. It was a small change, but it had worked; the Bensons had eventually left her alone.) In those circumstances, said Glencoyne, it was hardly surprising that the defendant and her father followed suit. If no one close to home would help them, then why stay at home? Seeking a fresh start, they'd moved to London.

'Sixteen years later, Sarah Collingstone, aged thirty-two, still dependent on her father, still a single parent, heard about the Alington Trust. She went to them seeking support. And if there is a moment when the lives of both the defendant and Mr Bealing changed dramatically, it is now. Because Mr Bealing was looking for an assistant manager and the Alington Trust told the defendant about the post. She got the job.'

Glencoyne was convincing. A rich and lonely man had met a poor and lonely woman. A sympathetic man had reached out to an abandoned woman. They started a secret affair and for nine months they lived out an escape from their circumstances. Only, as with all affairs, there comes a time when they end or endure. And that last option was something Mr Bealing couldn't contemplate. He was bound to Debbie. And he wouldn't abandon her, any more than the defendant would abandon her son. The difference was that the person who stood to lose most was the defendant. Money could not be ignored in this case. Because Mr Bealing's wealth would have transformed the defendant's life and that of her son. Her attachment to Mr Bealing was bound up with the future he represented: affection and security.

'We can't be sure what Mr Bealing was thinking,' said Glencoyne. 'We don't know if the challenge of parenting a young man with special needs proved too daunting; or whether he simply couldn't abandon Debbie, his wife. But this much is sure. In the week leading up to his death, Mr Bealing tried to distance himself from the defendant. On the night of the 14th of February the defendant went to see him at his Hopton Yard premises. Mr Bealing either told the defendant the relationship was over, or he said something else that snapped a cord in this woman's self-control. It doesn't really matter. Either way, the defendant seized a bottle, smashed it, and chased Mr Bealing down a narrow corridor, stabbing him as he tried to escape. He bled to death, ladies and gentlemen.'

Benson felt a light tug from Archie. He passed a note forward. Benson opened it. 'A genie that comes out of a can. 6 letters.' While in prison, Archie had killed time doing puzzles and crosswords, only he could never find the answers. His endless questions had driven Benson mad. He turned the note face down. Glencoyne was dealing with a weakness in her case as if it was a strength.

'Debbie Bealing has lost the man she married twelve years ago. She cannot accept that Andrew had an affair. But we cannot shrink from telling this court about it, even though it grieves Debbie all the more. The media reports will wound her deeply. They will humiliate her. We wish we could spare her the pain, but we can't. Because we owe it to the one person who isn't here to tell Debbie the truth . . . her murdered husband.'

'Thank you, Miss Glencoyne,' said Mr Justice Oakshott. 'I take it your first witness is ready?'

'Yes, my lord. I call Kym Hamilton.'


# 17


Kym Hamilton, aged forty-seven, had been with Hopton's since she was sixteen. She'd been handling phone calls and faxes before Andrew Bealing had even come to London. She later moved to accounts. She'd had a desk right by the large window that brought natural light into Andrew Bealing's office. Her mouth dipped at the corners and her voice had the colour of cheap tobacco. Benson listened with growing distaste. She'd started crying even before she took the oath.

'Well, Andrew had been unhappy for a while.'

'Do you know why?'

'I do, yes. You see Andrew had always been easy-going. Full of confidence and smiles. Chirpy. But he lost it very gradually. And that was because of poor Debbie's condition. The more Debbie went downhill, the more Andrew sort of followed her. His mood was tied to hers. I felt so sorry for him . . . and her.'

'Did you know Debbie?'

'Of course. She worked in the office with me for something like seventeen years. She began young like me, and she carried on after her marriage to Andrew. She'd always fret about the haulage work and she was anxious about Andrew's ventures, even though they were successful. She was cautious, you see, while Andrew didn't mind a risk. He liked a risk.'

'What do you mean by "Debbie's condition"?'

'Depression. She'd go under and couldn't work. And things got a lot worse after her dad died. She'd adored him.'

'When was that?'

'Sixth of April, 2013. That's when dear Joe left us. His heart just gave out.'

Benson circled the name with his red pencil.

'Which would be a year before the defendant came to work for Mr Bealing?' said Glencoyne.

'That's right.'

'A year in which Debbie struggled?'

'Oh yes. She was hospitalised. Twice. Andrew would talk about it when he was in the office. Said he couldn't keep an eye on her all the time so he'd employed a nurse to come round three times a week. He still does, I think.'

'Who's that?'

'Darren Weaver.'

'How would you describe Mr Bealing's relationship with his wife?'

'Well, it was strained. It had to be. You couldn't help but feel sorry for the two of them.'

Glencoyne turned a page.

'Were you present when the defendant came to the Hopton Yard premises for an interview?'

'I was.'

'And?'

Benson frowned as he wrote. Hamilton hadn't read Brontë. Her description of that first meeting came straight from Mills and Boon. There'd been a quiver of tension in the air. She'd felt the jolt herself. Even Glencoyne blenched. But this is what the witness had seen and remembered. These were her words. She'd told her story to the police and the police had written it down.

From that first meeting, Andrew had changed. He'd become secretive. He'd go out not saying where he was going. Sarah Collingstone would arrive at the Hopton Yard premises when Kym was leaving. When she'd come during office hours, Kym had seen them speaking earnestly in Andrew's office. And Andrew was always reaching out and Sarah was always stepping back, as if to say no, not here. And then, at the Christmas party, they crossed a line in public. Glencoyne tied down the detail:

'This was December 2014, a Friday night, two months before the murder?'

'Yes. They went into the warehouse.'

'Where were you?'

'In the front office, but there were windows on either side of Andrew's office, and I could see straight through.'

'Was the warehouse well lit?'

'No. But light fell on them from Andrew's office. This time Sarah let Andrew hold both her hands. She tugged and stumbled back and he pulled her towards him and he kissed her. We're not talking a peck. They lingered, with Andrew sliding his hand towards her bottom. Then they'd come back inside and Sarah was all red and shining. She didn't know we'd seen them. And even though they were apart, Andrew kept following her around, accidentally brushing against her, accidentally touching her hand.'

'Where was Debbie?'

'She'd stayed at home. Darren, the nurse, called in to say she couldn't make it.'

Glencoyne moved forward two months, to the week leading up to the murder. It seemed there'd been a sea-change in the relations between Andrew and the defendant. For a while, there'd been no meetings in the evening. And during this last week, the defendant had taken to ringing the main office, because Andrew wasn't answering his mobile. There'd been several telephone calls a day, some of them minutes apart, but Andrew wouldn't take them. He'd said, 'Tell her I'm out, Kym.' And then he'd put his head in his hands and said, 'Why did I ever let her get anywhere near me? I can't give her what she wants.'

That last conversation had taken place on Friday, the 13th of February, at about half-four in the afternoon, the day before the murder. The defendant had sounded tense and desperate. Hamilton had gone home at five and never seen Andrew Bealing again.

# 18

Benson rose to cross-examine. He waited until Hamilton had finished dabbing her eyes and taken a sip of water.

'Who is Screwball?'

'I'm sorry?'

'You're unfamiliar with the term?'

'Well, yes.'

'Let's talk about Dave, then.'

'Who's Dave?'

'Your husband Dave. The one with a conviction for careless driving. The one who spent three months in HMP Bexley for criminal damage. The one sacked by Andrew Bealing in 2006 for hitting a client. Do you need any further clarification?'

'No.'

'You married him a year before Debbie married Andrew Bealing?'

'Yes.'

'Dave was an HGV driver, too?'

'Yes.'

'Employed by dear Joe before Andrew Bealing had even seen Hopton's Yard?'

'Yes.'

'Why did you call him "dear Joe"?'

'Everyone did?'

'You too?'

'Well, yes, why wouldn't I?'

'Because dear Joe had favoured Andrew Bealing over your husband. He's the one who was groomed to take over. He's the one who ended up in a nice pile in Wimbledon.'

'That's rubbish.'

'Is it? But you were part of the family. You're Debbie's cousin. Dear Joe had married your mum's sister. You'd worked in the firm for eighteen years before Andrew Bealing turned up. You'd married a driver. And you expected Dave to take over, didn't you?'

Hamilton pulled at an earring. 'That's rubbish.'

'But then Andy Bealing went and married thirty-year-old Debbie. No one expected that, did they?'

'No.'

'And all at once Andy Bealing became the apple of dear Joe's eye. Is that rubbish, too?'

'Yes.'

'And your Dave went downhill. Just like Debbie. Because he'd lost the game of thrones. Or is that rubbish, as well?'

'Okay, I admit it. I was upset. He was upset. We'd given years to that firm and Joe took it all for granted.'

'Is that "dear Joe"?'

'Yes.'

'Let's return to Screwball. Have you remembered who that might be?'

Hamilton sipped more water. And Benson praised the genius of the architect who'd designed Court 1. The witness was almost within touching distance of the jury. They could hear her breathe. They could see her sweat.

'Well, that's what some people called Debbie.'

'Screwball?'

'Yes.'

'It wasn't some people. It was everyone. You called her Screwball, didn't you?'

'Well, in a friendly way.'

'Friendly? You call that friendly? Did you visit Debbie Bealing when she was hospitalised in 2013?'

'No.'

'But her father had just died.'

'There were only two of us in that office and I was run off my feet.'

'Did you visit her after work?'

'No.'

'Give her a call when you heard she was on a downer?'

'No.'

'But you'd known her all your life. This is "poor Debbie". Why didn't you reach out to her?'

Hamilton fiddled with a ring, turning it round on her finger. Benson lightened his voice:

'What about when your aunt died of a broken heart in 2014? That's Debbie's mum. Did you check up on Debbie afterwards, to find out if she was coping?'

'I should have done, I suppose.'

'That's not what I asked you. We're not here to find out whether you should have helped Debbie Bealing. We're here to find out if you can be trusted. To find out if you're a liar.'

'Well, I'm not.'

'Mrs Hamilton, you've come to this court crying about "dear Joe" and "poor Debbie" and "chirpy Andy" and you couldn't care less about any of them. That's why you never went to visit Screwball.'

'That's untrue.'

'You're seething with thirty years of resentment.'

'That's untrue.'

'And you resent no one more than Chirpy Andy, who kicked your husband out of the business.'

'That's untrue.'

'You're unemployed now, aren't you?'

'Yes.'

'Why's that?'

'Well . . . Debbie's sold up everything.'

'She's loaded, then?'

'Yes.'

'It's not easy to find a job at forty-seven, is it, Mrs Hamilton?'

'No.'

'What about David? Is he working?'

'He's on the sick.'

'Are you broke, Mrs Hamilton?'

'That's none of your business.'

'Where were you on the night Andrew Bealing was killed?'

'At home.'

'With Dave?'

'Yes.'

'Anyone else?'

'No.'

'So we've only got your word for it?'

'And Dave's. You can ask Dave.'

'That was DCI Winter's job, not mine.' Benson watched her, pondering his next words. 'Mrs Hamilton, before you came into court, my learned friend Miss Glencoyne warned the jury not to have pity on people when tragedy leads them into wrongdoing. Lying in court is wrong, Mrs Hamilton, and I have no pity in telling this jury that you can't even be trusted to tell us who Dave might be.'

Glencoyne was on her feet. 'Perhaps my learned friend might restrict himself to questions. The speech can come later.'

'Certainly,' said Benson. 'Mrs Hamilton, would you agree that sex is a bit of a struggle?'

'I beg your pardon.'

'All that writhing around. Unless you're involved, you wouldn't know if someone was having the time of their life or being tortured?'

'I suppose so.'

'The same can be said of a Christmas kiss, can't it? They're not always wanted.'

'That one was. She was all red and shining.'

'Because she'd been humiliated.'

'I wouldn't know.'

'Precisely, Mrs Hamilton. You just don't know what happened in that warehouse.'

'I saw what I saw.'

'Would you take a look at this plan, please?'

The court usher took a diagram prepared by the Crown and handed it to the witness.

'Please mark with a cross the place where Mr Bealing and my client were standing at the time of the embrace.'

Mrs Hamilton did so. The diagram was shown to the judge, the jury and Glencoyne.

Benson fixed Hamilton with a long stare. She looked away. She was beaten and ready to be compliant. Or at least he hoped so. He moved to what seemed like a trivial subject.

'Mr Bealing was pretty relaxed on health and safety issues, wasn't he? There were no up-to-date manuals setting out correct lifting procedures and so on.'

'No. He found all that stuff boring. He was always putting it off.'

That was the answer Benson had wanted. He let the reply linger before asking his last question:

'Did you ever consider that when Mr Bealing said "I can't give her what she wants", all he meant was a load of manuals?'

'That never entered my mind.'

'Thank you, Mrs Hamilton, I've no further questions.'

Glencoyne had no re-examination. As Hamilton left the stand, Benson turned over Archie's note asking what kind of genie came out of a can. He wrote 'Sprite' and turned to hand it back, glancing up at the public gallery. Instantly he was AC1963 again. He felt the suffocation of a locked cell. He sensed Needles, knitting on his throne. He could smell the corruption. In fact, Benson had made a mistake . . . but for a second, he thought he saw his brother Eddie sitting at the back of a packed public gallery. The brother who'd never believed that Benson was innocent. The brother who knew too much.

# 19

Tess couldn't understand it. According to Archie, Benson had savaged one witness after the other, and none more than the stunning Anna Wysocki, the one employee who'd made Sarah Collingstone's life a misery. It had felt like a score was being settled: Sarah Collingstone's big brother had gone round to Anna Wysocki's to sort her out. It hadn't taken long. Within minutes she was dazed, bleeding admissions.

She'd never made a single work-related complaint prior to the appointment of Sarah Collingstone. She'd never raised any of her concerns with Andrew Bealing, despite a stream of worked-related emails, letters and calls. And then it had all come out: yes, she'd been jealous of the defendant's appointment as assistant manager – she'd applied for the job too; yes, she'd considered the defendant to be out of her depth; and yes, she'd tried to break her spirit.

'Shaw called that the devil's work, didn't he?' Benson had wondered.

Wysocki didn't know, because she hadn't read Shaw.

'I commend him to you.'

She knew the defendant would be seeing Bealing on the night he was killed. She knew that Bealing always worked late at Hopton's Yard on Saturday nights. She retracted the assertion that Bealing had favoured the defendant, given that she, too, as an Alington Trust referral, had received generous support from him. Yes, she'd sent him grateful emails. Yes, he'd changed her life. No, she'd discussed none of this with DCI Winter. He hadn't asked. Finally, Benson seemed to relent.

'Do you have an overcoat, Miss Wysocki?'

'Yes.'

'A hat?'

'Yes.'

'That coat. Has it got more than one colour?'

'Yes. Same for the hat.'

'Where did you buy them?'

'Krakow.'

'Winter wear, would you say?'

'They are, yes.'

'Did DCI Winter ask if he could borrow them?'

'No.'

On that strange note, Benson had let her go, and Tina Sheldon was called into the ring. Twenty minutes later she left the court in tears, admitting that she'd come up with 'Screwball' as a nickname for Debbie Bealing; that she was the one who first suggested Darren Weaver serviced her three times a week.

'Don't be modest. This is high invention. Take all the credit.'

'I don't know what you mean.'

'What about the thermometer?'

'No, no, that wasn't me. That was Kym, that was.'

Then Ricky Warton took the stand. He'd been the last person to see Andrew Bealing alive.

Warton was a driver. He'd turned up at Hopton's Yard on Saturday night at 6.10 p.m. to hand in his time sheet. Standing in the warehouse he'd looked through the office window to see the defendant and Mr Bealing having what seemed to be a stand-up row. Mr Bealing was trying to take the defendant by the arms, but she pushed him away. She was in floods of tears. At that point, Mr Bealing turned and saw Warton, and came into the warehouse. When asked if he was okay, Mr Bealing made a grimace and said, 'It's nothing. She's got her teeth into my arse and she won't let go.'

The phrase could have meant anything.

According to Glencoyne, this was a reference to the final throes of an affair. Benson scorned the idea, seizing on the coarse wording: it didn't belong to a sympathetic man who'd once fallen for an abandoned woman. It belonged to a boss who was sick of being pestered by an employee. Warton agreed.

By the time the court rose for the day, the notion of an affair turned sour had been seriously challenged. Of course it was still possible – the affair had been secret – but Benson had exposed so much gossip, jealousy and ambiguity that there was growing room for reasonable doubt: and that was all the defence needed.

So Tess was surprised to find Benson abstracted when he should have been thrilled. He kept glancing towards Artillery Passage from their corner table in Grapeshots Wine Bar. He'd kept his duffel coat on; and she had seen a book peeping out of a pocket. He was reading Robert Frost. Tess liked Frost. Especially the 'snowy wood' one. Something about promises to keep and miles to go before I sleep.

'She's hiding something,' said Benson. 'I think Hamilton was right. There was a fling between Sarah and Bealing and they both got burned.'

'Who cares?' said Archie. 'The jury's no longer sure, that's all that counts, isn't it?'

'No. If one part of her story is false, then the rest might be. If she loses the jury later, she'll lose them for good.'

Benson's gaze drifted to the entrance.

'Debbie Bealing may be fragile,' said Tess, drawing him back, 'but she's given us a lead. She's not the only one who thinks the ninjas killed her husband.'

Tess had got some corroboration. And she wasn't referring to Felbridge's no-show or Winchley's reticence or Obiora's flight. She'd contacted Roger Grange, of Wellborn and Grange, Solicitors and Financial Advisers.

'I rang him at work. Wouldn't see me. Ten minutes later I get a call-back from his wife, Amanda. She's also his secretary. She wants to see me later in the afternoon when she can get away from her husband.'

Tess met her in a coffee shop in South Wimbledon. She was pretty damn scared. In April 2014 Roger's business partner Hugh Wellborn had been killed in a car accident on the A4. He lost control on a bend and hit a lamppost. It was heartbreaking. He left a wife and four kids behind. But Hugh liked fast cars. His licence was at the limit on points. He wouldn't heed a warning. Amanda and Roger hadn't thought there was anything more to the accident until Andrew Bealing came to see Roger in September that year.

'According to Bealing, Wellborn's death had been no accident,' said Tess. 'He'd been murdered for trying to void one of Bealing's contracts. It was a professional hit.'

'Who was the contract with?' Benson was focused now.

'Some European company operating as a front for Chinese interests. Amanda didn't know which one and neither did

Grange. Bealing hadn't said; and they didn't want to know.'

Benson turned to Archie. 'You've got to go through the files for 2014 again. Examine every client. Untangle their corporate structures. Check them out. If needs be, get the Tuesday Club on to it.'

'Okay.'

'We're not talking hard-nosed punters,' said Tess. 'Those Chinese interests weren't legitimate. Bealing was talking about a gang. Gang interests in the UK. Based here in London.'

'And according to Debbie,' recalled Benson, 'he'd been moving their stuff around.'

'So it seems.'

'Contraband. Only we don't know what.'

'No. But I'm sure Obiora knew.'

'We've got to find him.' Benson tapped the table. 'So what have we got? Bealing was the lynchpin of a distribution operation. It's criminal and probably international with Bealing handling the UK side of things. He's got a good name so he's unlikely to attract the attention of the police or customs. And if he does, he'll just plead ignorance. The truth is, to quote Debbie, the drivers don't open the boxes. They only check the manifest. But once those shops start bringing in the money, Bealing wants out. He wants to go completely legit. So he asks Wellborn to get him out of the contract. Wellborn contacts the client. The client wraps him round a tree.'

'Lamppost,' said Archie.

'It doesn't make sense,' said Benson. 'Why kill Bealing? He'd got the message. He'd carried on making deliveries.'

'He knew too much,' said Tess. 'That's what he said to Debbie.'

Benson was frowning. 'But why tell Grange nearly six months after Wellborn was killed?'

'Because he wanted to make sure that Debbie was okay

for money if anything happened to him. He wanted to make Grange a trustee to manage the estate. He didn't think Debbie would be capable.'

'So?'

'A trust deed was drawn up, but Bealing never signed it. He left it too late. That's why she's probably undersold the Hopton portfolio. There was no one to stop her. She got rid of everything within eight months.'

Benson was drinking Spitfire from a pewter mug. He gave it a swish and lined up the dates: sometime in early 2014 Bealing tells Wellborn to get him out of a contract. Wellborn is killed in April. By July, Bealing is turning to Felbridge and Winchley. He's floundering. In September he blurts it all out to Grange. By February of the following year, he's dead.

'This has nothing to do with Sarah Collingstone,' said Benson. 'She turned up in June. It's pure coincidence. Bealing was already looking at his grave.'

'But we have no evidence,' said Tess. 'No one would believe Debbie Bealing. Amanda Grange only spoke off the record because her husband's got lung cancer. Chemo and the rest. They don't want me adding to the pressure. So she won't make a statement, and neither will her husband. Neither will Felbridge and Winchley. Neither will Kingsley Obiora. They're all scared and they all want nothing to do with the trial.'

Benson checked Artillery Passage again, his eyes scanning the windows and entrance.

'We can't let them go,' he said. 'We've got to get them into court.'

For a long while they pondered that unlikely outcome in silence. Tess was uneasy. She might have raced around London, hunting the reluctant and the scared, but she'd kept her eye on the ball.

'Collingstone's DNA is on that bottle,' she said.

'So you keep saying,' said Benson.

'And it doesn't matter if the Triads, the Yardies and the Hamilton family were after Bealing. Collingstone could still have got there first.'

'She could and maybe she did, but she says she didn't.' Benson finished his beer and checked his watch. 'I'm off to chambers. Don't worry about Sarah's DNA. Just find a way of getting Grange to swear and sign a statement. And the others. And while you're at it, check out Wellborn's death.'

Tess watched him thread his way to the door in his worn blue duffel coat. He then threaded his way back, and said, 'I meant to say "Please". I'm sorry.'

On leaving Grapeshots, he looked left and right and then moved quickly on.

'He's out of sorts,' said Archie. 'Has been all day.'

Tess fished the lemon slice out of her gin. 'He can't even walk down the street without thinking someone might whack him. Do you know he gets assaulted by these mindless thugs and he never retaliates?'

Archie said he did; and Tess remarked that it was strange that Benson never seemed to *want* to hit back. That he accepted the abuse as if it were a kind of unofficial punishment. Something he deserved. Archie didn't pick up her lead. He remained hooked on his own preoccupation. 'Something happened today,' he said.

'What, exactly?'

'I don't know for sure. Maybe it was Court One. Maybe it was the memory of Paul Harbeton. But he turned round, totally at ease, and then, bang. I've never seen him look so spooked.'

Archie went back to Congreve's and the ring-binder for 2014. Tess, on the other hand, drove over to Seymour Road by the Regent's Canal. The street was deserted. The orange light from the streetlamps gave a soft sheen to the uneven paving flags, the old brickwork and the iron railings. It was a charming spot. One of those hidden corners of London. As she had expected, more rubbish had been dumped at Benson's gate. Gingerly, she gathered up the mess and threw it in a waste bin.

# 20

At Glencoyne's request the court usher took a long coat out of a transparent plastic bag and laid it on the exhibits table before the jury. He removed a hat from an identical bag and did the same thing. Each item had a card attached to it. On each card was a number. The hat and coat belonged to Sarah Collingstone. They'd been found by the police during a search of the defendant's property on Monday, 16 February 2015.

'Mrs Jonson, would you kindly come out of the witness stand and take a careful look at the clothing on the table, please.'

Mrs Jonson did as she was asked and then resumed her place. Glencoyne continued her questioning. This sprightly, blue-rinsed, diminutive seventy-six-year-old in thick glasses had an excellent memory. Everything she said tallied with her statement. She was precise and confident. Benson wasn't sure who was in charge, Glencoyne or Mrs Jonson.

'That's what I said, Miss Glencoyne. I said six o'clock because I meant six o'clock.'

'Of course, I apologise.'

'I looked out of my window and I saw a woman walking towards the main entrance of Hopton's Yard. She was wearing a multi-coloured coat. She was also wearing a hat.' Jonson

# JOHN FAIRFAX

pointed towards the exhibits table. 'That is the precise style of coat she was wearing, and that is the precise style of hat.'

'Could you be mistaken?'

'No, Miss Glencoyne, I could not.'

'Why?'

'Because it is a distinctive coat. I have never seen anything like it. In my view it is gaudy. It's red and blue and green and yellow and orange. There's every colour under the sun. It is altogether memorable.'

'And the hat?'

'The shape is nondescript. But again, the colours are numerous. I recognise it without any doubt whatsoever.'

'I'm grateful, can we just linger a while on what you saw?'

'Well, of course, that's why I am here.'

'What was the weather like?'

'It had been snowing. There was a well-trodden path to the main office building, and tyre tracks, too, of course, from those infernal wagons and what not.'

'Was the street lighting on?'

'No, but the area was exceptionally well lit. Mr Bealing had the most awful bright lights installed. The sort of thing I remember from my childhood during the war, to spot the bombers. The Germans would have seen Hopton's Yard from Berlin if they'd only looked. It was a safety measure, according to Mr Bealing. The whole entrance was lit up.'

'Thank you. My lord, the position is this. The defendant has served written admissions as to the following: the coat and hat belong to her; she attended Hopton's Yard at about 6 p.m. wearing both items. In her defence statement she states that she left the premises at about 6.30 p.m. The Crown does not accept this last assertion.'

'Thank you, Miss Glencoyne. The defendant's case, then, is that the person who killed Andrew Bealing must have come to Hopton's Yard after she'd gone?'

116

'Precisely.'

'Please continue.'

'I'm grateful. Miss Jonson—'

'Mrs.'

'I beg your pardon. Mrs Jonson, at what time did you go to bed?'

'Eleven p.m. As always.'

'Please tell the ladies and gentlemen of the jury what subsequently happened.'

Mrs Jonson had been about to draw her curtains when she saw movement down in Hopton's Yard. This was at roughly 11.35 p.m. The woman she'd seen arrive was now leaving. Mrs Jonson watched her walk all the way to Haydon Road. Some thirty-five yards in distance and, at one point, about twenty yards from her window. It was lightly snowing. Glencoyne said:

'My lord, at this point I remind the court that Mr Bealing was attacked some time prior to eleven twenty-two in the evening.'

'How do you arrive at such precision?'

'That is the time when Mr Bealing attempted to make a 999 call. It seems the bloodied mobile phone was taken from his hands and put out of reach before it could be sent. The timing is consistent with the pathological evidence. It is not contested by the defence.'

Glencoyne reiterated the Crown's case: Sarah Collingstone had arrived at 6 p.m. to talk things out with Bealing. They'd had a row. She'd stabbed him prior to 11.22 p.m. and left the way she'd come at 11.35 p.m. Mr Justice Oakshott noted the times, and said:

'In effect you are saying that the person seen by Mrs Jonson is almost certainly the person who killed Mr Bealing?'

'I am, my lord.'

'Is that the end of your examination-in-chief?'

'It is.'

'Mr Benson?'

Benson had slipped his moorings. He couldn't stop thinking about his brother. His mind kept straying back to the accident when they'd been inseparable, and to the trial when they'd become strangers. The impression of having seen Eddie the day before had been so real that he'd sat in Grapeshots half expecting to see him at the door in his wheelchair. He'd barely slept. Throughout the night, like now, he saw Eddie on his bike shifting like a rocket towards the main road, head down, while Benson screamed.

'Mr Benson?'

He turned a page to mask his confusion. Then he rose, with a flap to his gown.

# 21

'You are wearing glasses?'

'I am.'

'Were you wearing them on the night in question?'

'I was.'

'Would you be offended if I said your prescription must be on the strong side?'

'Certainly not. I'd go further, without them I couldn't see the nose in front of my face.'

'And with them?'

'I can see as far as . . .'

'Berlin?'

'Don't be facetious, Mr Benson. My eyesight is not in issue.'

'I'm afraid it is. Can you confirm that you were wearing them at 6 p.m. and at 11.35 p.m.?'

'I can.'

'You didn't change them for reading glasses?'

'I wasn't reading.'

'Do you clean your own windows?'

'At my age? No. Mr Sullivan comes round on Tuesdays.'

'Four days before you saw that unforgettable hat and coat?'

'Yes, that must be right.'

'The windows can't have been clean. Those infernal wagons send filth everywhere.'

'They do. But you haven't seen those big lights at Hopton's Yard. It's like a stage when they're lit. I saw your client, Mr Benson.'

'I know you did. We're agreed on that. What time do the bomber lights go off?'

'Nine p.m.'

'Thereafter the entrance to Hopton's Yard is covered by street lighting?'

'That's right.'

'Would you take a look at these photographs, please?'

Benson handed enlarged images to the clerk, who gave them to the judge, the jury and Glencoyne.

'Can you confirm that this is the streetlamp at the entrance to Hopton's Yard?'

'That's the one. It's been there for years. It was there when George and I bought our house. And you ought to know, Mr Benson, that it throws a strong, bright light. We can see it through the curtains.'

'I'm sure you can. Just out of interest, do you know Kym Hamilton?'

'Yes. Since she first came to Hopton's.'

Benson checked Mrs Jonson's witness statement. A lot rested upon the questions he would now ask, and the answers he'd receive. He took a sip of water, and mentally he fell

119

on his knees hoping not to strike a mine . . . one of those spiky things that floated in the Channel when Mrs Jonson was a little girl.

# 22

Tess began her day with a cold call to Felbridge Logistics. But fidgeting Belinda said Jack was away for the week. So Tess left her contact details and went to the main office of the Alington Trust in Camberwell.

Paula O'Neill confirmed Sarah's account in every detail. She'd first approached the Trust in May 2014 and they referred her to Mr Bealing. It was all part of a well-established routine. Mr Bealing would ring up if he had a vacancy and the Trust, subject to the Equal Opportunities Act, would offer a candidate to fill it. Mr Bealing had been looking for an assistant manager. Sarah got the job.

Tess then contacted Luke Baker, the accident investigator who'd been brought in by the police to examine the death of Hugh Wellborn. She'd tracked him down after tracing the officer who handled the case. They spoke on the phone.

'Sad case,' he said. 'But not that surprising.'

'Why?'

'The *locus in quo* was a death trap for anyone speeding. Still is. There's been lots of accidents there. You'll see signs and chevron barriers and flashing lights, but the problem is the camber. It tilts the wrong way . . . ever so slightly . . . so if you fly into it, you spin over. Nothing you can do to prevent it.'

Tess tried to get foul play off the ground. She really did. But Luke Baker had no doubt this was an ordinary accident. Nothing suspicious. Nothing mysterious. If Wellborn had been chased off the road, the chasing car would have gone flying as well.

She hung up and went back to Thornbury Road, and the flat of Kingsley Obiora, hoping to bring him round. The door was opened by a young woman in her teens chewing gum. She was Kingsley's daughter, it turned out. Her name was Abigail. She made coffee in a tiny, spotless kitchenette.

'Ma mum's gone, right. Found another fella. I've only got ma dad and I want him back, okay?'

'I just want to talk to him for a short while.'

'Well, he doesn't want to talk to you. Do you want some sugar?'

'No thanks.'

She lit up, blowing smoke out of the side of her mouth. Purple lipstick had stuck to the filter.

'I don't know anything, okay. All I know is ma dad won't come back until this trial is over. He says it's best for him and best for me, and he told me to tell you to leave us all alone.'

'Abigail, have you ever been accused of something you didn't do?'

She thought for a minute, chewing and smoking at the same time. 'I've got away with things and I've been done a few times, but I know how to look after myself.'

'Well, not everyone does. And Sarah Collingstone is a mother, only she hasn't gone off with another fella. She's stayed with her son, who's sustained brain damage, with only her dad for help. And now she's in court for a crime she says she didn't commit. On my own I can't help her. But with your dad I might be able to. Give him this, will you?'

Tess handed over her business card.

'He can call me night or day. I'm not going to force him to do anything. But what he tells me might help all the same.

It's urgent. This trial will end in a few days. If my client is convicted, I don't know what will happen to her son. Unlike you, he can't look after himself. Think about it, will you? Talk to your dad.'

Abigail bit the chewing gum and stretched it with the hand that held the cigarette. She was thinking. Weighing things up.

'Look, it's not what you think, okay?' she said, chewing again. 'Nothing's illegal. It's cool. Hopton's looked the other way, that's all.' She flicked ash into the sink. 'Hopton's were shifting legal highs, that's it.'

'Come on, I need more.'

'This is between us, okay? I don't want ma dad going down or anythink. Ma mum's gone, okay?'

'Okay.'

'Ma dad was shelving some boxes, right. At Hopton's. And one of them fell off the forklift. It split open and these little plastic bags fell out. They were meant to be herb tea. That's what was written on the box, right, but they were Spice.'

Tess understood instantly. Abigail's dad had probably helped himself to a handful. And every time the boxes of tea were delivered he'd take a few more. Never too much. Just enough for personal use.

'He didn't give any to you, did he?'

Abigail ran the tap to clean away the ash. 'They were legal, okay?'

'Did your dad's boss know about these wrongly marked boxes?'

'Yeah. He was there when it fell off the forklift. Told my dad to tape the box and forget it.'

'When was this, Abigail?'

'Last year, like.'

'When?'

'January or something.'

'Did your dad know where these boxes came from?'

Abigail shrugged and ran a tap on the cigarette stub. 'Will you leave ma dad alone now? He's done nothing wrong, okay? Everything was legal. But if he gets lifted he could be done for theft, right? And he's looking for work, okay? He's been on the dole since Hopton's closed.'

'Abigail, your dad wouldn't be done for theft. Tell him to call me, will you? I won't force him to do anything.'

Tess climbed into her Mini and checked her mobile. There was a text from Gordon Hayward: 'Douglas Coker wants to see you ASAP.'

Douglas was the senior and founding partner of the firm. He'd lured Tess back to London from abroad and given her a dream job that many would die for. He was also her godfather. But, being absolutely professional, he hadn't contacted Tess directly, but gone through a department head. Which meant it was professional and not personal. And since Gordon was head of the criminal law department, she could easily imagine what Douglas might want to talk about. She switched on the radio and caught John Humphrys chairing a discussion on a news item that Douglas had probably tracked already. She listened for a while, before pulling away, intrigued.

A second online petition had been started in relation to William Benson, though not linked to any newspaper. It was called 'Everyone Deserves a Second Chance'. There were 3437 signatories already. Which was quite low, really, observed Mr Humphrys, when you considered that 9.2 million people in the UK had a criminal record, with 85,000 of them presently incarcerated.

Tess had a sudden intuition. If the sleeping giant woke, Richard Merrington MP might have to think twice about his emergency legislation.

## 23

'Mrs Jonson, you were a primary school teacher for forty-three years, is that right?' said Benson.

'Forty-three wonderful years, thank you.'

'Did you ever do experiments mixing colours?'

'Year in year out.'

'With paint?'

'Yes.'

'What about light?'

'Well, of course I did. How else do you learn about the colours of the rainbow?'

'Take a look at Sarah Collingstone's coat of many colours. Where were you first asked to examine it?'

'At the police station with Detective Chief Inspector Derek Winter of the Merton CID.'

'Can you tell us exactly what happened?'

'I was shown into a large room. Fifteen different multi-coloured hats and coats had been laid out on three tables. I think they were worried, Mr Benson. They all thought I might get confused. But they were wrong. With these glasses I can see anything. And I picked out the hat and coat immediately.'

'So the record demonstrates. Was the room well lit?'

'Perfectly . . . with natural light.'

'Mrs Jonson, would you look at the photograph of the streetlamp at the entrance to Hopton's Yard. Do you know what kind of light that lamp emits?'

'Well, I should do, given I've lived right by it for most of my married life. It's sodium.'

'That's right. Would you explain to the jury what that means.'

'Certainly.' Mrs Jonson turned to them as if they were a

class of nine-year-olds. 'If you take all the colours of the rainbow and mix the light all together the colours vanish and you get white light. It's like magic. You can't see them, but white light is full of colour. But *sodium* light is very different. It's simply *yellowy-orange* light. There's no other kinds of light in there.'

Benson intervened. 'And what happens when you look at multi-coloured objects in that kind of light?'

'Well, that's getting complicated, Mr Benson. I didn't do that with the children. That's for secondary school.'

'Would you do it with the jury, please? I think DCI Winter might be interested, too.'

'All right, then. Here we go. When *sodium* light falls on an object with lots of colours, some of the colours will *absorb* the yellowy-orange light, and since there's nothing left to reflect back, those colours will look all wishy-washy.' Mrs Jonson paused to check she hadn't lost her class. 'Now, some colours will *reflect* the sodium light . . . but all they can reflect back is the yellowy-orange, because, remember, there's nothing else in that kind of light.' She paused again, only resuming when she'd received a wave of nods from the jury. 'That's it. Nothing could be simpler. When sodium light falls on a multi-coloured hat and coat all you'll see are shades of yellowy-orange and shades of wishy-washy. Now you know why everything looks vaguely the same under a streetlamp.'

There was a pause of appreciative silence. Mr Justice Oakshott broke it. 'Well, I never. I have to say, Mrs Jonson, I've never understood why that's the case. Perhaps I'm not the only one who's learned something today. I'm most grateful.'

Benson was, too. 'Mrs Jonson, when you looked out of the window at 6 p.m., you saw a coat that was red and blue and green and yellow and orange. I never doubted your vision. I never doubted your memory. You are a careful and impressive witness. You saw my client arriving to see Mr Bealing.'

Mrs Jonson was looking at Benson in horror. 'I've made a fool of myself.'

'No, you haven't. You just made a mistake. Because when you looked out of the window at 11.35 p.m., you couldn't have seen a coat that was red and blue and green and yellow and orange. Or a hat that was multi-coloured.'

'No, I couldn't.'

'Because the bomber lights had been turned off. The sodium light was on.'

'It was, yes.'

'So while you certainly saw someone leaving, you don't know the true colours of their hat or coat.'

'No, I don't.'

'You *couldn't* know if it was the same hat and coat you'd seen earlier that evening.'

'No, you're right, I couldn't.'

'That individual could have been wearing any of the fifteen hats and coats Detective Chief Inspector Winter showed you.'

'Because they all would have looked much the same. I wouldn't have been able to see the difference. Oh dear, how could I have made such a mistake. I'm so very sorry. I should have known better.'

'There's no need to apologise,' said Benson. 'It's not your job to ensure that the evidence put before this court is reliable. That duty falls on Detective Chief Inspector Winter and my learned friend Miss Glencoyne.'

'It's a basic error.'

'It is. And it is upon such evidence that my client faces a charge of murder. Can we just review your testimony?'

'Of course.'

'You have no idea if the person you saw leaving Hopton's Yard was wearing the hat and coat on the exhibits table?'

'None whatsoever.'

'You don't even know if that person was a man or a woman?'

'No, I don't.'

'For all you know, it was Kym Hamilton?'

'Absolutely.'

'Or Dave, her husband?'

'Yes. It could have been anyone. This was February. It had snowed. Most people were wearing a hat and coat.'

'Mrs Jonson, you ought to know that my learned friend will shortly tell this court that my client cut her right hand when using a broken bottle as a weapon upon Mr Bealing. Please think very carefully. Was there any indication that the person you saw had sustained a cut to their right hand?'

'None.'

'Please reflect longer. Was there anything odd about the way they walked or held their right arm?'

'Absolutely not. The person was sliding their feet through the snow, so they wouldn't slip, and they had their arms by their side. If there'd been a cut, there'd have been blood on the snow . . . and I saw no blood.'

'Thank you, Mrs Jonson. I've no further questions.'

# 24

Glencoyne was calm and collected, her gestures slow and deliberate, but she was rattled. Benson knew it. One of the things he had learned in prison was how to read people's behaviour. Apart from books, there was nothing else to pore over. Nothing else to do. He'd studied the likes of Needles and Jaffa for hours on end. So he wasn't fooled by Glencoyne's casual announcement that she wished to recall Kym Hamilton. She was worried. Holes were appearing in her case.

'I'd like to ask you some questions about Mr Bealing's attitude towards security.'

Hamilton nodded but she was looking at Benson, scared of what he might do next.

'Why had bright security lights been installed?'

'Firstly to help the drivers when they were coming in and out of the yard, but also because Mr Bealing was worried about trespassers . . . people who might try and break into the warehouse.'

'How did the lights operate?'

'The front ones were on a timer, but there were others at the back, and they came on if anyone approached the building.'

'As regards the front door, there was a mortise lock?'

'Yes. And a peephole.'

'Was there anything distinctive about Mr Bealing's work habits on a Saturday?'

'Yes, he always worked on his own.'

'Did he take any personal security measures?'

'Oh yes, he'd lock the door and he wouldn't open it to anyone, unless he knew them. That's why there was a peephole.'

'So in relation to the Saturday when Mr Bealing was killed, if someone had knocked on the door late in the evening, Mr Bealing would only have let them in if he recognised them?'

'Yes.'

'Any doubt about that?'

'None. The stock in the warehouse was very valuable.'

Glencoyne sat down. Hamilton was staring at Benson as if he might throw a brick across the courtroom.

'Let's stay with the evening when Mr Bealing was murdered,' he said, staring back as if she was right.

Hamilton nodded.

'Let's imagine it was you who knocked on that door. Mr Bealing would have opened it, wouldn't he?'

'Yes . . . but I was at home.'

'So you say. With poor old Dave.'

# 25

Douglas Coker was a graduate of Trinity College, Dublin, and Downing College, Cambridge. Upon qualifying as a solicitor, he'd worked for five years at Freshfields and then set up his own firm with Maurice Dale from Slaughter and May, after which he hadn't looked back. Tess had looked to Douglas when arguing with her parents about England over Ireland, saying she only wanted to follow in the steps of her godfather. He'd backed her argument, saying he'd look after her. He was wonderful and tweedy and adored. His eyes twinkled and his silver, untrimmed eyebrows curled up to his forehead suggesting optimism and – obscurely – mischief. His defining fault was fascism on questions of food. He'd chosen the restaurant. He'd chosen the wine. He'd have chosen the fish if Tess hadn't put her foot down.

'Tess, the partners and development committee wanted you at C and D because of your human rights track record. They asked you to review our team structures and our research systems, to be an adviser on new and existing cases . . . and now they find the firm's name being dragged through the gutter.'

The last phrase was true. The rest was only half the story; a loving story. Sure, the partners and development committee had made the decision to recruit Tess, and their current displeasure was no doubt genuine, but it had been Douglas's proposal, and it had concealed another objective – one that hadn't even been mentioned to Tess herself, though she'd seen through his flannelling. He'd engineered a one-year consultancy with her specifications in mind because he'd learned that Peter Farsely, her former boyfriend, had finally quit London for New York. Douglas had told Tess, in code, it's time to come home, if you want. He continued:

'They imagined C and D as a meaner outfit, better organised, better coordinated, better informed, with an enhanced reputation. Instead the firm is locked into a tawdry murder where counsel himself is a killer. They're not pleased, Tess. This isn't what they expected.'

'It's not what I planned,' said Tess. 'But this is a significant issue. Merrington wants to stop Benson from practising at the Bar. Okay, there's a growing petition to shut him down, but human rights aren't determined or protected by petition. That's why we have a law. If Benson presents no risk to the public – and he doesn't – preventing him from pursuing his chosen career might well be in breach of Article Three. This is the sort of thing the partners wanted, Douglas. It's not popular. But it's right. And . . . I just don't want to do this any more.'

Douglas wiped the corners of his mouth and said, 'I beg your pardon?'

And Tess explained. She had to tell him, honestly, that she'd tired of this very type of struggle, important though it was.

'I went to Strasbourg last week and I realised I didn't belong any more. And then, by chance, I heard about Benson, and meeting him has brought me back to where I began all those years ago. It's hard to explain, but I've sort of gone astray. I really want to come home, now, Douglas. I want to come back to basic crime.'

Douglas was the only person who knew why Tess had quit London for Strasbourg, and she hadn't told him. He'd found out. Things had ended badly between Tess and Peter; it had become very . . . complicated. Shortly afterwards, Douglas had flown to Strasbourg with a string of leading questions – questions which contained the answer, seeking merely a 'Yes' or a 'No' response – and Tess had answered none of them . . . confirming what he'd learned. It was their secret, a secret that permeated everything they said to each other.

'You urged me to come back to London to rebuild my future, and I did. You told me to take my time until I found out what I really wanted to do . . . and I have done.'

He'd imagined something in human rights, possibly academic. So had Tess, though without much enthusiasm. But hearing about Benson, and meeting Benson, had changed everything. She'd felt young and foolish again. It had felt great to shake off all that acquired prudence. She'd glimpsed who she'd once been, before Peter Farsely came along. She'd heard the Proclaimers belt out some passion.

'You want to join the crime team?' asked Douglas.

'Yes. As and when I can; if I can. If not, I suppose I'll have to go somewhere else.'

A waiter poured the Sancerre and retired discreetly. Douglas had chosen Dover sole. He'd urged the same on Tess. She'd chosen the sea bass.

'There's room,' he said. 'We're planning to recruit next year. But it goes without saying you'd increase your chances if you were to distance yourself from Benson.'

'I can't do that.'

'Why am I not surprised?' He thought for a while. Then he said: 'I can't guarantee you a future at C and D, you know that?'

'Yes.'

'You'd have to finish the consultancy on a high note.'

'Obviously.'

'And then apply for the job like anyone else. So let me nudge you again. After this trial, don't you think you could find other counsel to instruct? Separate your name from his? If only to ease the fears of the partners?'

'No. Because of Article Six. People have a right to choose who they want to represent them. You see, Douglas, this is nothing to do with me. Sarah Collingstone picked Benson. There's no stopping him, now. He's out there, with his name on a board. If he wins this case, against the odds, people are going to start asking for him, regardless of the partners and the development committee, regardless of the profession, the press and Richard Merrington.'

It went without saying that if Benson was victorious, Coker & Dale would share in the credit. And so would Tess. In a peculiar way, her future prospects were now intimately linked to Benson's. If a pariah becomes a celebrity, so does his champion.

'I've never told you this, Douglas, but it was my idea that he come to the Bar.'

'Really?'

'Yes. I told him to go for it; and he did.'

'And now you feel responsible? You feel you should help him get established?'

'No. A bit. Maybe.' She moved her food around her plate. 'But I'd be misleading you if I didn't admit that I want to work with him. I think he has something . . . special.'

'I know you do.' Using his fish knife, Douglas carefully lifted the soft white flesh, exposing the bone underneath. 'This is a really delicate situation, Tess. Not just for the firm, but for you. You're putting yourself on the line because you're convinced he's innocent, am I right?'

'Yes.'

132

'But what if he isn't?'

'But I believe he is. I felt it, viscerally. I was there.'

'Let's imagine he isn't. Let's imagine that for whatever reason – shame, or not wanting to shatter his parents, his girlfriend, his friends, or whatever – let's imagine he fooled you.'

'Okay.'

'That makes him, eventually, a pathological liar.'

'Oh come on—'

'I don't mean back then, I mean now. If he told one great lie for the trial, because he couldn't face what he'd done, then he has to lie for the rest of his life. There's no way back. We've both seen this in the courts, Tess. A witness gets saddled with something they said under pressure, they've made a sworn statement, and years later we pull them apart because we've found some evidence that shows they've been less than honest. Benson is no different. Unless he came clean at the outset, he has to lie endlessly. Every day, just like you brush your teeth. It could be bitter in his own mouth, but there's nothing he can do but keep up the brushing. He's trapped.' Douglas paused to examine the spine, wondering how best to remove it. 'A lie like that, left deep in your life, well, it becomes a kind of cancer. It's a disease that works itself right into the bone.'

Tess swished the wine in her glass, spilling some on the table.

'And what makes Mr Benson different if not unique among the world's liars, if he is one, is that he's managed to swing it both ways. He's only lied in private. He's told the world the truth. He came clean, after all.'

'So what are you saying?'

'He's not straightforward, Tess. If he'd admitted his guilt before trial, I'd have felt differently – Jaysus, I'm a lapsed Catholic, we don't forget the big stuff – but he didn't. You don't know who you're dealing with. You don't know if you can trust him.'

'You're still not saying what you really mean. I know you.'

'And I know you, Tess.' Douglas lifted the spine with the edge of the blade, gently levering the finer bones away from the lower fillet. 'And I'm worried for you. Honestly, I am.'

'But why?'

He put down his knife and fork. 'Look, you're thirty-five, this is nothing to do with me. You make your own decisions and I'm here whatever happens, you know that . . . but I didn't urge you to leave the continent so you could come home and, God, I don't know . . . I just don't want to see anyone breaking your heart again.'

Douglas had always been a sort of watchman in Tess's life. He'd guided her career. He'd seen opportunities and risks, vaguely nodding towards the better path, leaving her free to choose. But since that flight to Strasbourg, when he'd become the keeper of unspoken secrets, he'd turned into a special kind of friend. He knew things known to no one else: not her parents, not even Sally.

'Peter didn't break my heart, Douglas,' she said. 'Meeting him was the worst thing that's ever happened in my life. Leaving him was the best. Strasbourg was simply a circuit breaker. And I'm not drawn to Benson in that way. I'm not sure I want to feel that way ever again.'

Douglas's pained eyes said, *Of course you will* . . . and then he spoke: 'Every once in a while there's something special about meeting someone we knew when we were younger. Before things got complicated, all round, for everyone. There's a kind of sigh, Jaysus, how did we get from there to here . . . and all I'm saying, Tess, is be careful. Watch over your heart. Hearts are restless and foolish. At least mine is, and I'm seventy-four. God, you'd think we get wise . . .'

'He's someone I admire, nothing more.'

Douglas said nothing, but Tess almost heard herself say, *I know . . . I said that about Peter, too. You were right about him.*

And Douglas, seeming to read her mind, spared her a knowing nod, because he'd tried to warn her; and now he was warning her again: 'I have this fear he might be exploiting you . . . your name and reputation. That's he's drawing you into a complex world of . . . deceit – a deceit he can't control, because—'

'No, no, no. I went to him. He didn't even know I was in London.'

Tess had lost her appetite. Her mind was clouding.

'How do you know?'

She didn't.

Douglas ordered more wine. 'There was an announcement in the legal press. There was talk. He remembered you, like you remembered him. He'll have checked you out, like you checked him out. He'd have seen your photograph, like you'd seen his. He knew you were back in London, Tess.'

'But why lure me of all people?'

'Because you've believed in him from the beginning. He knows that. And he also knows that Tess de Vere is compassionate and wouldn't count the cost . . . and that she happens to be a hot-shot at Coker and Dale. I suspect Mr Benson could do with someone like that at his side, given that no one with clout is prepared to instruct him.'

Throughout the meal, Tess had grown increasingly uneasy. Her simple view of Benson had been shaken. Her mind began crawling over a small detail that, at the time, had pleased her: Benson had used the word *fecker*. That was her word. It was an Irish word. And used by him, it referred back to their first meeting; and that strange exchange of vows. Douglas approved the new wine and said:

135

'You should know that the Harbeton family came here this morning. They wanted you sacked which, ironically, might help you in the long run, because no one here wants to be seen as bending to outside pressure. We said no. Politely.'

Tess replayed Benson's look of dawning surprise when he'd recognised her . . . it had been utterly convincing . . . if it was a performance.

'Apparently, Merrington informed them he intends to revise the scope of his legislative proposals.'

'In what way?' She was fully present now.

'His target is to exclude from the legal profession anyone who is still serving a sentence.'

Tess had to think for a moment before she understood.

'Benson is only out on licence,' she said. 'He's still a lifer. He'll always be a lifer.'

'Behold, my dear, the agility of the political mind. And I have to say that Maureen Harbeton was pleased. Pleased that something might yet be done to protect the memory of her son. Strange, isn't it? There's nothing much in the Human Rights Act for grieving mothers and angry sons.'

# 26

If Douglas was right about Tess being exploited – which was a strong way of putting things – it would mean that Benson had planted that article in the *Guardian* in order to attract her attention. At least in part.

And she'd come running.

The thought wouldn't go away. She arrived at the Old Bailey in time for Benson's cross-examination of Dr Henry Lucas, the lean, spectacled Home Office pathologist who'd examined Andrew Bealing's body for the Crown. She slipped into the solicitor's benches and sat beside Archie.

There wasn't much to argue about. Historic injuries were related first. Two scars on the right forearm. Surgical scarring from an appendectomy. A nick on the chin from shaving. The human body really is a kind of diary. Dr Lucas moved on to incidental markings: a bruised big toe. Five scratches to the back. He then addressed the injury that had brought about fatal consequences: a jagged curved wound measuring 60 mm by 25 mm on the left side of the neck, 31 mm below the angle of the jaw. Surrounding abrasions and lacerations were superficial in character . . .

*If Douglas was right, it would mean that Benson had pretended he couldn't quite remember her name. He'd sung, 'And I would walk five hundred miles', as if reeling in a fish.*

The jugular vein and carotid artery had both been totally severed. There would have been swift and heavy bleeding. Within a matter of minutes Mr Bealing would have suffered . . .

*It would mean that Benson feigned anxiety, gasping for air, because he knew that Tess de Vere had felt sorry for him once and might well feel sorry for him again.*

Dr Lucas would have none of it. The injury was the result of a stab and not a fall. The injury was inflicted from behind, with Mr Bealing turning to face his attacker. He was being followed down the corridor towards the warehouse. Considerable force had been applied. There was no sign of hesitation, as one finds with prodding or scraping, for example. There'd been a single thrust deep into the left sternomastoid musculature. Blood would have sprayed from the open wound. The injury could have been inflicted with either the right or left hand.

*And if Douglas was right about Benson exploiting Tess, he might be right about Benson having lied.*

While this was an assault more commonly associated with men, Dr Lucas had been instructed in many cases where the assailant was a woman. No method of attack was gender specific.

*It would mean that Benson was diseased. Which was barely credible; only Tess couldn't uproot the seed of doubt that Douglas had planted. It was quietly germinating in a dark part of her mind.*

Benson left matters there. The court was adjourned until the next morning and he convened a conference in a side room with Sarah Collingstone, her father, Archie and Tess. She was totally thrown, however, when he asked her to explain developments. Speaking through a kind of fog, she told a wide-eyed audience what she'd learned in four days of research.

'But you must understand, we've no evidence. People have only explained why they're not prepared to make a statement. But it does seem reasonably clear that Andrew Bealing had become involved with the distribution of legal highs, at least, and that when he attempted to extricate himself from the arrangement, he became scared for his life, almost certainly with good reason.'

Ralph Collingstone's mouth had fallen open. 'You've no evidence?'

'None.'

'Can't you tell the court?'

'No. What I've been told is hearsay and double-hearsay. For me to repeat it would be double-hearsay and triple-hearsay. It's useless, evidentially. I am not the witness. We need someone to say, "This is what I know, saw, said and heard." Nothing else counts.'

'But Sarah's totally innocent.'

Tess played safe. 'Sarah faces a raft of evidence that Mr Benson and I seek to discredit. If we succeed, Sarah will be acquitted.'

'No, no, sorry, that's not good enough. Sarah didn't kill Andrew Bealing, you know that, we all do. The man with cancer has got to pull himself together. He's got to say what he knows. So does the warehouse manager.'

'I am working on them. There's no point in twisting arms. The best way to handle frightened people is to keep a low voice. I'm trying to lure them out with gentleness and an appeal to conscience.'

'And if they don't respond?'

'Then they don't respond.'

'But the police must know about these gangs. Don't they watch them?'

'Probably, yes, but it's irrelevant to Sarah's case. It only becomes relevant when we demonstrate the link between one of those gangs and a threat to kill Mr Bealing and when we find a witness who is prepared to explain that link to the court without reference to hearsay, or with elements of hearsay introduced by notice with the judge's approval, with or without screens, maybe by videolink . . . it's complex, Ralph. You have to trust us.'

'I didn't kill him, Miss de Vere.' Sarah's quiet voice broke the tension. 'I didn't do this. I promise. I'm innocent.'

'Then please help me,' said Benson. He waited for the raised feeling to subside a little. 'So far, we're not doing too badly. The suggestion that you had an affair with Andrew Bealing is looking pretty thin. The jury are prepared to accept that someone else could have come to Hopton's Yard after you say you'd gone. This is good, Sarah. We've made ground. The jury will be asking themselves who that someone might have been, and we've given them three names: Kym Hamilton, David Hamilton and Anna Wysocki. The police should have investigated them and they didn't and now it's too late. We're in a good place. But you have to help me. Otherwise, everything can fall apart.'

'How, what do you want me to do?'

'Just be brutally honest.'

'What about?'

Benson leaned forward, as if to exclude everyone from the room. 'Your DNA is on the murder weapon. That's not good. Tomorrow morning I cross-examine Dr Elaine Gooding who found it there. I need an explanation.'

'But I don't have one. I swear I never touched that bottle. There wasn't even a bottle on the table when I was in that room. I don't know where he got the bottle from. What else can I say?'

'Who said there was a bottle on the table?'

Sarah's face collapsed. 'You'll always be able to trip me up, Mr Benson. So will Miss Glencoyne. But it changes nothing. You must understand, I only care for Daniel. I *can't* go to prison. Don't you realise, I'd do anything to help you defend me? But I didn't touch that bottle. I didn't.'

'Okay, fine. But returning to another question in the trial. Your relationship with Andrew. Are you sure you didn't get close to him? He'd been kind. It would be natural and normal.'

'No. I didn't.'

'Not even once?'

'Not even once.'

'Fair enough. I'll do what I can tomorrow with Dr Gooding. It's going to be a decisive moment. I'll do what I can to advance your best interests.'

Tess thought that last statement rather strange. It was more like an explanation or a warning. The conference ended and Sarah Collingstone and her father left to collect Daniel from the Alington Trust day centre.

'Does anyone fancy a quick one at Grapeshots?' said Benson, awkwardly. 'Or somewhere else?'

'No, thanks,' said Tess. 'I've already got something planned.'

She avoided his attention.

'Archie?' Benson ventured.

'Sure.'

'Good. I'll just get changed.'

After Benson had left the room, Archie said, 'He's brilliant. I'm no lawyer, but he's taken control of that court. It's extraordinary. He's a fisherman's son from Norfolk, a simple lad, but he sounds like he was born into a wig and gown. He's made for this . . . he's—'

'Archie, does Benson read the legal press?'

'He reads everything.'

'Whose idea was it to speak to the *Guardian*? You know, the article on Congreve Chambers.'

'His. Why?'

'Just wondering. It made him a lot of enemies. But he won some friends, too. Do you think he saw that coming?'

'Of course he did. You should watch him in court. He's one step ahead of everyone.'

Tess went along Ludgate towards St Paul's. On the way she picked up a copy of the *Evening Standard*. The Hopton Yard killing dominated the front page, with detailed reference to Benson's dismantling of key witnesses. The outcast had thrown his critics into disarray. But the item that caught her attention the most related to Debbie Bealing. She'd been hospitalised under Section 3 of the Mental Health Act 1983. She'd smashed an aquarium at the Bamboo Terrace Takeaway in Wimbledon, screaming, 'It's the Chinks who killed my husband.'

## 27

'But you've always been impulsive,' said Sally.

'No, I haven't.'

'Tess, you have. You think that just because you're a lawyer, you must be cool-headed, analytical, measured, all that stuff, and you aren't. You're bloody Irish, for God's sake. You've got freckles. You're a Banshee. You fly off the handle and even you don't know why, but you're clever enough to find the sort of reasoning that got you a First.'

'Nonsense.'

'Remember that warlock at Balliol? The one with spells?'

'Sally, don't be so—'

'And the playwright? The one who wrote that dream-state crap about Gandhi and Che Guevara waiting for the same bus.'

'You're being—'

'No, I'm not. I still don't know why you went to Strasbourg. You came up with all that twaddle about the Centre of International Something or Other but you made the decision overnight. You hadn't really thought it out. You'd been over-whelmed by a whim. And it's the same with this Benson. You meet him in court, you're convinced he's innocent, your freckles light up, and you talk of nothing else from—'

'Paris to Prague. I've heard that one.'

'Well, here's another. You overhear a conversation in a restaurant and by the time you go to bed you're aligned with a convicted murderer. Not privately or secretly but in public. That's what I call fast. It's not cool-headed, analytical and measured. It's impulsive. It's why I like you. You bring colour and chaos into the world.'

They settled on a kind of speakeasy in north London: The Bar With No Name on Colebrooke Row. Inspired by Matisse,

Sally had dressed in yellow and red. Dashes of blue. She was drinking a French 75. Tess, wanting to get a long way from London, had plumbed for a Mai Tai. The location was apposite. Benson lived five minutes away on foot.

'This isn't something romantic,' said Tess. 'It's—'

'Professional?'

'Yes, actually. But it's also personal, you're right. I'm shifting tack, Sally. I'm moving back to what people call "bog standard" crime. It's where I belong. And it's inevitable that I'll be working with Benson. I want to work with Benson. But I saw Douglas today, and he shook me. He thinks Benson might be using me to help neutralise the outrage against him . . . make himself marketable.'

'So what . . . if he's innocent?'

'Exactly. I was troubled at first but then I thought about it: if you've been to prison for years you might learn to dodge and weave, rather than ask for help. You're slow to trust. You do desperate stuff to survive. I can live with that.'

'But if he's guilty?'

'Exactly, again. It would mean he's drawing me into something very different.'

'A couple of days ago, you told me you believed he was innocent because he said he was innocent. What's changed?'

'I wasn't involved, I suppose. And now I am. Back then, nothing hung on it. Now . . . there's a lot.'

And if she was absolutely honest, regardless of Douglas's reservations, and those of Braithwaite before him, Tess was drawn to Benson. He was a man of so many contradictions. His books were ordered, but there'd been one volume of philosophy among the poetry (by Wittgenstein: she hadn't understood a word). He reached out but he was withdrawn, not wanting anyone to approach him. He kept leaving doors open but was always looking for his keys. The inconsistencies made him oddly vulnerable and Tess felt vaguely protective.

More deeply, she'd been moved by the epic scale of his choices. Not many men would enter a courtroom if it meant they'd be spat on when they left it. Moreover – which moved her even more – he'd no appreciation of what he'd achieved: he was oblivious to its scale. But there was another reason for this growing attraction. Tess had felt a shiver of excitement during Benson's routine cross-examination. Archie was right. There was a kind of electricity in his voice and bearing; even the gesture of a hand. He had the one thing that can't be learned. Talent shows called it star quality. And, once again, Benson hadn't the faintest idea that he possessed it. Tess had to sigh: it would be magical if he was innocent, rejected, self-effacing and brilliant. But if he wasn't?

'Take a look at this,' she said, changing the subject. She removed a sheet of paper from her briefcase on which she'd pasted photocopies of certain paragraphs taken from Sarah Collingstone's replies to Benson's questions. The content was innocuous and couldn't be linked to the trial. 'Look at the answers. What do you make of the handwriting?'

Sally was gracious. She confined herself to the text. She made no reference to the previous history of snorting ridicule.

'It's not an exact science,' she said, flute in one hand, papers in the other. 'The upstrokes are all clean and tidy, all the letters are well formed . . . the capitals are precise . . . there is almost total uniformity—'

'What does it all mean?'

'The writer is probably a woman. She's hiding a great deal. The order is a front. No one is that tidy without effort. In my experience people usually hide two things. Guilt and shame. The large lettering here and there is like a burst of colour to liven up the monotony. But it's a choice. They're not instinctive. She's had years of practice . . . the swift formation of words suggests someone who's got used to what she's doing . . . being someone different to whom she feels herself to be. You can't trust her, I'm afraid.' Sally handed back the papers. 'People like that can be stubborn. They stick to their cover story, even when it's obviously not in their best interests.'

Tess thought for a while. 'I've never heard such a load of bollocks in my life.'

'I just knew you were going to say that.'

'But it is. You described yourself. You always do.'

'I just knew it.'

'And a good half of what you said is me. And everyone in this room.'

'Don't ask again.'

'Do you really get paid for saying stuff like that?'

'Yes. And they come back for more. Because it works.'

'What do you mean it works?'

'It's confirmed by later experience. You'll see. For what it's worth, while the writing couldn't be more different, whoever wrote the questions has a similar profile.'

'Really?'

Tess had an idea. She finished her Mai Tai and said, 'C'mon. Let me cook you dinner. My place. I've something else to show you.'

Tess lived in Knightsbridge. Ennismore Gardens Mews. A two-bed refuge from Coker & Dale and everything her profession represented: the fight for an outcome where no one agreed on what that outcome should be unless the Supreme Court had considered the matter. Or, in relation to human rights, Strasbourg. It had been the London pad of her paternal grandparents, when they weren't in Warkworth, Northumberland, and then her father when he'd done his Ph.D. at the LSE. The family joke was that Tess's mother had fallen in love with the mews, and not her father. The irregular, cobbled lane; the heavy wisteria above the arched, dimpled windows; the cracked earthenware pots with shrubs . . . they'd have won over any Irish rebel.

'Cast an eye over this one,' said Tess.

'No.'

'Please. I'm interested.'

'I refuse. Pass the Chianti.'

'No.'

'God, you're childish.'

Sally snatched the page of A4.

'This is the same person who wrote the questions,' said Sally. 'The writer is a man.'

Tess nodded.

'Which was written first?'

'The one in your hand.'

Sally began to read. 'The open, round letters are rather closed. Ms and Ns are difficult to distinguish. The horizontal strokes on the Ts and Fs rarely touch the vertical stroke. Curiously, he doesn't write on the line. He writes above it. The capitals are—'

'Cut the crap. Do your stuff.'

'Like the woman, he's got a great deal to hide. He can turn himself into different people depending on who he's with . . . because he's fragmented . . . keeps different parts of himself in different drawers. He daren't pull them out at the same time . . . because he can't face the totality of himself. That's why the horizontals float free of the verticals. He's a rebel, too. Refuses – literally – to sign on the dotted line.' She handed back the paper. The content spoke for itself. 'I'd be slow to trust him, I'm afraid. This is William Benson, isn't it?'

'Yes.'

'Well, what I've just said tells you about him in 1999. He's deteriorated since then. That later handwriting shows someone who's even more closed and fragmented. How did you get the early stuff?'

'I kept a copy of the trial brief.'

'That's pervy.'

On returning home with Sally, Tess had taken the brief out of its storage box for the first time in sixteen years. It lay open on her desk as if the statements and notes were a fresh set of instructions.

'What are you going to do?' Sally was holding the empty bottle up to the light of a chandelier.

'I need to know if he's innocent or not.'

'Well, no one's going to tell you, are they?'

'No. Which is why I'm going to have to find out for myself.'

'Oh no. What are you planning?'

'I'm going to find out who killed Paul Harbeton. This is no whim. It's a cool-headed, analytical and measured decision. Will you help me?'

# 28

'I turned around, and it was as if Eddie was there, sitting at the back of the public gallery.'

Benson was on the phone to Abasiama. He was lying on his bed aboard *The Wooden Doll*. It was dark. The stern door was open. A cold breeze came off Seymour Basin.

'I even looked out for him afterwards.'

'It's been a very long time, hasn't it?'

'Sixteen years.'

Benson had last seen his brother on 4 July 1999, the day before his trial. By that stage, Eddie had broadly stabilised. After extensive and varied therapies, he'd recovered the use of both his arms, though one was stronger than the other; he could speak, but slowly, which gave his words a strange emphasis and power; his memory was intact, save for the accident itself and the weeks that followed; his mind was sharp; but his legs remained paralysed: useless attachments to his body. Ordinarily someone charged with murder would have been remanded into custody. But exceptionally – and largely because of Eddie's condition – Benson had been granted bail so he could help out at home. Which was why he'd been with his brother, the day before his trial. They'd had a brief and unforgettable conversation looking over the salt marshes at Brancaster Staithe. And every time Benson had been alone with Eddie, he'd said much the same thing, only this time he'd gone one step further.

'I don't believe you, Will.'

'I'm innocent, Eddie.'

'You're not. We both know you're not. Stop all this screwing around.'

'I'm innocent, Eddie.'

'I haven't given a statement to the police, Will, because if I did, you would be convicted. You can't put me in this position. You've got to put your hands up and take the consequences. There's a bigger story here, and it has to come out. You're locking me up, here, Will, and I want to be free. God, I've had it bad enough, don't make it worse.'

'But I'm innocent, Eddie. What else can I say?'

Eddie had spoken to the gash of crimson cloud above the sea. He'd rolled forward in his chair, getting some distance from his brother. 'If you go ahead with this charade, I'll never speak to you again.'

Abasiama seemed not to be there, but then she said:

'You looked for him in the public gallery once before, didn't you? On the day you were sentenced.'

'Yes.'

'And he wasn't there, was he?'

'No. But he couldn't be. There's no wheelchair access. But I still looked.'

'Because you don't accept he can't walk.'

'No, I don't. It's crazy. He does, and I don't.'

'Do you ever see him elsewhere, in other circumstances?'

'Yes. Often. Every time I see a kid on a bike. Every time I see a wheelchair. And then there are times when I just see him in someone else.'

Abasiama waited a very long time before she next spoke. 'What would you say to Eddie if he rose from that chair? If he stood up, his legs restored, and he walked towards you?'

If words could kill, Benson would have died from these. He felt like he was Andrew Bealing lying between the prongs of a forklift truck, watched by his killer; or Paul Harbeton lying in a Soho gutter, blood pooling around his head. These would be Benson's last words. 'I'm so sorry.'

'That's not enough,' said Abasiama, after a minute or two. 'When are you going to tell Eddie the truth?'

'I don't know.' Benson closed his eyes, seeking darkness within darkness. 'I can't imagine that day ever dawning.'

'Then the sun will never set on your guilt. You will remain a haunted man.'

Abasiama waited, but Benson didn't reply. With his free hand he stroked Papillon; Papillon who was always there, no matter what he said or didn't say. No matter what he'd done or failed to do. Twenty minutes of silence later, Abasiama said:

'That's a choice, Will. Things needn't be that way. You just have to face reality. Face what you have done.'

'But I can't. That's why I came to you.'

'And I can't help you live a false life. I can listen. I can help you relax and breathe. I can prescribe medication. But I can't take the fruit from the tree. You have to reach out for yourself.'

'Goodnight, Abasiama.'

# 29

Not wanting to pressurise Abigail Obiora, Amanda Grange or Jack Felbridge – at least not just yet – Tess went to the Old Bailey the next morning, leaving Archie free to study Bealing's business files. Glencoyne called Dr Stuart McDonald to present the forensic evidence relating to blood, finger-prints, footprints and a shred of scuffed shoe leather. Benson's cross-examination was like an illusionist's trick. It was all in the structure of the questions and order in which they were asked. Tess had the impression of walking through the crime scene while he magically erased Collingstone's presence.

Her fingerprints were only on the front door handle and on the edge of Bealing's desk. Nowhere else. Not on the bottleneck. Not on the door handle that led to the warehouse. Not on Andrew Bealing's telephone.

None of her blood was found at Hopton's Yard at all.

None of Andrew Bealing's blood had been found on the defendant's coat, even though blood had sprayed from his wound and the assailant must have been standing within arm's length of his victim.

Two of the defendant's footprints *were* found at the front entrance, where snow hadn't gathered, but nowhere else. They tied in with the fingerprints on the door handle. And yet, whoever killed Bealing had wiped the interior floors clean before leaving. Just as they'd disturbed any footprints in the warehouse. The impression created by Benson was of *someone else* being present at Hopton's Yard on the night of the killing. They'd cleared away any trace of themselves, leaving behind apparent 'clues' that now pointed to Sarah Collingstone. In fact, they meant nothing. Except to DCI Winter and Miss Glencoyne.

But what of that shred of red leather scuffed on to a rib of concrete, thirty yards or so from the body? Dr McDonald confirmed the shred had been found at the exact spot where Kym Hamilton had seen Sarah Collingstone stumble over a Christmas kiss. Had other scuffed material been found? Yes. Had it been traced? No.

Tess needed a sip of water. But for the DNA evidence, Sarah Collingstone seemed to be walking out of the court-room; and this, when Benson was conducting his first criminal trial, opposed by a silk of considerable experience and renown. The dominant presence in Court 1 was William Benson, not Rachel Glencoyne. He'd impressed his audience, sure, but now the show was over. Because Dr Elaine Gooding had taken the stand and was about to explain that Sarah Collingstone's DNA was on the bottleneck that had severed Andrew Bealing's left jugular vein. No one could upset that evidence. Not even the Great Defender, Marshall Hall. It was infallible.

# 30

'I take it you are familiar with the work of van Oorschot and Jones?' asked Benson after Glencoyne had surrendered her witness.

'I'm sorry?'

Benson gave a pointer. 'The study published in *Nature* on secondary DNA transfer.'

'That's some while ago.'

'Nineteen ninety-seven. Have you read it?'

'Yes, I think so, but that's hardly recent scholarship.'

'It's an important piece of work, isn't it? Because this was the first time that forensic scientists explored the possibility

that an innocent person's DNA could be inadvertently transferred to a surface or object – I'm thinking of a bottleneck
– which that person has never touched. It would mean, for
example, that my client's DNA could be transferred on to
the bottle by someone else, if she came into contact with
them, and that person then handled the bottle.'

'Mr Benson, I'm afraid you are very much behind the
times. The issue of secondary transfer has been discussed by
the forensic science community for many years. My view is
that it remains a theoretical possibility. Later work replicating
real-life conditions didn't support the thesis.'

'I imagine you're referring to Carll Ladd and others?'

'They weren't alone.'

'You've read the Technical Note published by Ladd et al.
in 1999?'

'I will have done, yes. If I remember rightly, laboratory
personnel shook hands and then handled objects for various
lengths of time. Swabs were then taken and tested. No
secondary DNA transfer was observed.'

'Quite right, it wasn't.'

'As I say, there's been other work, and while there's room
for argument, I remain sceptical.'

'So that's your formed, professional view, relying upon
published data?'

'Very much so, Mr Benson.'

Tess felt slightly sick. Benson didn't seem to realise that
science was a living discipline. He'd relied entirely on research
published prior to his imprisonment. She looked at the broken
bottle fragments laid out on the exhibits table, the brown
shards. It was a Bavarian beer. She could see the label: Etaller
Heller Bock. Sarah Collingstone had picked the thing up, but
she wouldn't admit it.

'Do you keep up to date in your reading, Dr Gooding?'

'I do, Mr Benson.'

'Have you read last month's online edition of the *Journal of Forensic Sciences*? It's an American publication.'

'I haven't, not yet, no.'

'Are you a subscriber?'

'No, I'm not.'

'Maybe you've heard the buzz? I'm referring to another Technical Note on secondary DNA transfer, this time by Cale et al.'

'No, I can't say I've heard anything about it.'

'Here you are, Dr Gooding, you can see my copy. I'm a subscriber.'

Benson handed printouts of the article to the court usher. While Dr Gooding, Mr Justice Oakshott and Glencoyne did their reading, Tess, electrified once more, revisited all the conversations she'd had with Benson about this, the central and most troubling issue in the case. He'd known about this article all the time. It had been in his mind when he'd questioned Sarah Collingstone. But he'd said nothing; and he'd said nothing for a reason. Tess took another sip of water. Her mouth was as dry as sandpaper.

'Let's take this in stages, Dr Gooding. DNA amplification technology is now far more sensitive than it was in the past?'

'It is.'

'And in this recent experiment volunteers shook hands and then handled various knives?'

'Yes.'

'The knives were then swabbed for DNA samples.'

'Correct.'

'And Cale et al. discovered that in 85 per cent of the cases DNA from a person who did not touch a knife had been transferred in sufficient quantity to produce a profile. In five samples the main or only contributor of DNA to the weapon was from someone who hadn't touched it at all.'

'That's right.'

'I would call that a profoundly disturbing outcome.'

'It is. As the title of the paper indicates, it means an innocent person could be falsely placed at the scene of a crime.'

'Van Oorschot and Jones were right, weren't they? The risk of DNA transfer through an intermediary isn't simply theoretical at all, is it?'

'No, it's not. And I admit that this is a significant development. I wish I'd seen this article before giving my evidence.'

'There's no harm done, Dr Gooding, because you can still help this court. Do you now accept that even though Sarah Collingstone's DNA was found on the bottleneck, it does not mean she actually touched it? That is only one possibility.'

'Yes, I agree, and I withdraw my evidence on that point.'

'Thank you.'

'But we have to follow the science through, Mr Benson.'

'Please lead us.'

'Given the facts of this case, you are suggesting that your client must have touched Mr Bealing's hands early in the evening, and that he then transferred her DNA on to the bottle when he was drinking from it, presumably after she had left Hopton's Yard.'

Mr Justice Oakshott intervened to help the jury: 'Is that a possibility, Dr Gooding?'

'It is, my lord.'

'Which would mean that later in the evening a third party, presumably wearing gloves, could have entered Hopton's Yard, broken the bottle and used it to kill Mr Bealing . . . but only the victim's DNA and defendant's DNA would be found on the weapon?'

'That is possible, yes.'

Mr Justice Oakshott frowned, tapping a note into his laptop. 'And of course, the use of gloves would also explain the absence of that person's DNA and fingerprints at the crime scene?'

'They would, my lord. It's an ingenious theory, but – with great respect – I'm not sure Mr Benson appreciates the implications of his own argument. He's forgotten something important.'

'What might that be?'

'According to Cale et al., the defendant would need to have held Mr Bealing's hand for at least *two minutes*. That's what was done in the experiment. It's a long time. Think of that song by the Beatles. "I Want to Hold Your Hand" doesn't last much longer. And of course, she need not have held his hands at all. Holding on to his body would have produced identical results. Intimate relations are an obvious mechanism. I understand these are denied.'

Benson sat down. 'Thank you, Dr Gooding.'

It took Tess some while to understand what had just happened. And when she did, she nearly banged the desk with a shout. Mr Justice Oakshott and Glencoyne had got there first, but Tess was now with them. Benson hadn't forgotten anything. He'd pretty well sprung Sarah Collingstone from the dock, using the Crown's star witness and a High Court judge to do it for him.

Benson had forced Collingstone's hand. Literally. If she didn't kill Bealing, she would now have to admit that she'd had intimate contact with him on the night he was murdered – on her account between 6 p.m. and 6.30 p.m. And in doing so, given the already weakened prosecution case, Benson had provided the jury with all they needed to acquit her. All they required now was a good explanation as to why Collingstone had denied having a close relationship with Andrew Bealing. If she could do that, then she was going home to Daniel and her father.

Unless, of course, Sally was right; and Collingstone, being stubborn, maintained her denial.

# 31

Benson joined Tess and Archie for lunch in a backstreet café off Fleet Street. The decor was tired and a grimy air extractor coughed and sputtered but the sandwiches were out of this world. They bought a selection to share. Adrenalin was still giving Benson a good kicking; if anything the kicks were getting harder because the next witness was DCI Winter. And DCI Winter had angered Benson. His short-cuts and assumptions had nearly robbed Sarah Collingstone of a fair trial. He was the kind of officer, Benson was sure, who'd put Needles down for one of the offences he hadn't committed, mindful of the ones he had.

'There he is again.' Tess had spoken. 'Don't look now, but there's someone hanging around outside. He keeps looking in, moving on and then coming back.'

Benson had his back to the window. 'Has he got a beard?'

'Yes.'

'Five foot ten or so?'

'Yes.'

'Bomber jacket? Black leather?'

'Yes,' said Tess. 'I've see him before. The other night at Seymour Road. He was there, hanging around. He was with the others.'

Benson nodded. 'He's been tailing me for a while.'

'Do you want me to land one on him?' Archie had pushed his chair back.

'No, I don't. Think of the media reaction. Anyway, I'm not bothered.'

'Don't you get sick of it?' asked Tess, seeming to check every line on Benson's face; her concentration snapped a thread in his defences. Something gave way:

'Of course I do. But it's worth it. They've only carried on

all these years because I came to the Bar. In return I get to question people who think they know what really happened. I get to question experts who think they know everything in their field. And I get to question police officers who should have done their job properly. I get to fight my own trial over and over again. So that guy out there can follow me from here to Spitalfields. He can tip rubbish at my door. He can spit in my face. But I get to walk into a courtroom. And in there, where he can't reach me, I'm fully alive, in a way I can't explain, he'd never understand and you can't imagine. I'm someone else. I've no more worries, no more fears, no more concerns, only those of a defendant who says they're innocent.'

Archie glanced at Tess.

'Calm down . . . have a radish,' said the clerk.

She looked confused and Benson felt embarrassed, acutely aware he'd made an admission, one he'd rather have kept to himself: that outside court he was barely alive. He'd been planning to show Tess an easy-going guy who was interested in human rights and weird cocktails. He'd pictured himself on the Albert Canal sipping a Body Snatcher or whatever it was called. Instead, he'd shown himself as he really was. Angry and half dead.

'Let's get back to court,' he said.

# 32

It would be right to say that DCI Winter looked uncomfortable giving his evidence. And it wasn't just the inflammation from a hasty shave. Word of Benson must have reached him. He answered Glencoyne's questions as if he was desperate to please. As if he'd done his best. He kept throwing glances in Benson's direction.

In effect, DCI Winter was bringing the prosecution case to a close. He was the final witness whose account brought together any loose ends. Benson watched him, thinking of Sarah Collingstone, scared and out of her depth, frightened for Daniel.

DCI Winter had arrived at Hopton's Yard at 08.00 on Sunday, 15 February 2015. The divisional surgeon, a photographer and the scenes of crime officers were all on site by 09.15. While uniformed officers carried out house-to-house enquiries, he had gone to visit Debbie Bealing, the deceased's wife. He'd found her extremely distressed, speaking of Chinese gangs and apparently hearing voices. He'd contacted Darren Weaver, her nurse, along with Dr Adrian Phillips, her general practitioner. Both parties had attended the premises and taken care of their patient. DCI Winter had then made contact with Kym Hamilton, who'd explained the structure of the various Bealing companies.

The next morning, Gloria Jonson had presented herself at the crime scene and described the individual she had seen arrive and leave. Kym Hamilton had recognised the description of the coat, saying it belonged to Sarah Collingstone. Two detectives had gone immediately to the defendant's premises where her father, Ralph Collingstone, informed them that his daughter had departed for France that morning. She'd bought tickets for the 12.10 ferry. The defendant was apprehended at Dover at 11.15. On being cautioned she'd said, 'I would never kill Andrew, never, never, never.' She'd refused the assistance of a solicitor. The defendant was subsequently transferred to London and was booked into Merton police station at 16.32. She was examined by Dr Faisal Khan, who found a laceration to the right hand. The defendant said she had cut herself the day before when opening a tin of tuna. Dr Khan concluded that the wound was 'not inconsistent with a broken glass injury'.

Trevor Hamsey, the duty solicitor, arrived at 17.20. The defendant was interviewed at 18.00 and made no replies to all questions. After overnight detention, the defendant was interviewed again at 12.00, once again in the presence of Mr Hamsey. And again the defendant refused to answer any of the questions put to her. The defendant was released on police bail with . . .

Benson remembered his own experience.

It had been so horribly similar. And he well knew that something else had happened in Merton police station that simply couldn't be transmitted to the courtroom. And that was the inrush of fear. Your mind can't handle it. You don't know what PACE 1984 is or the Codes of Practice, even after they've been explained. You say things you don't mean. The tape recorder is catching everything. Police officers know this. They know that as soon as the interview procedures kick in, ordinary people start drowning. Some will help you. They bring you cups of tea and a sandwich. They check you're okay. One or two will exploit it. One officer – DC Terry Leyland – had told Benson in a corridor, 'You're a statistic, you murdering bastard. We've got you nailed to the wall.'

Indeed they had.

Like they'd got Sarah Collingstone when all she could think about was Daniel.

# 33

'We've heard a great deal about what you have done, DCI Winter, shall we now have a look at what you didn't do?'

Tess couldn't help but see Benson with insight and clarity. He *was* different in the courtroom. He *was* someone else.

He was *only* there for Sarah Collingstone. And that encompassed Daniel and Ralph, one small family confronting the powerful machinery of the state.

'Did you check if Kym Hamilton had an alibi?'

'No.'

'Were you aware her husband – a man with a record for violence – had been sacked by Andrew Bealing?'

'No.'

'Did you examine their telephone logs, emails, computer hard drives . . . you know the score, everything you did with Sarah Collingstone?'

'I didn't, no.'

'What about Anna Wysocki? I could ask all the same questions all over again, so let's make this brief, did you explore her background and her movements on the night of the murder to find out if she had motive, means and opportunity?'

'I didn't. Her DNA wasn't on the bottle. She hadn't cut her hand.'

'Ah, yes, the DNA. We'll come back to that. What about her coat? Did you check it for blood spattering?'

'No.'

'Speaking of coats, where on earth did you get fifteen overcoats from?'

'The Red Cross shop in Tooting.'

'The Red Cross shop in Tooting? Why not go to Kym and Dave Hamilton's in Mitcham? It's nearer.'

'This isn't a joking matter.'

'I'm being serious. When did you find out that the security lighting at the front of Hopton's Yard only operated on a timer until nine in the evening?'

'During this trial.'

'Did you know that the streetlamp emitted sodium light?'

'No, I didn't. My lord, can I just say something to the court?'

Mr Justice Oakshott sighed. 'You'd do well just to answer counsel's questions. I'm sure Miss Glencoyne will look after you.'

'I just want to say that in a murder inquiry, you have to start with the evidence you find, not the evidence that might exist. Mr Bealing employed over thirty people. Many of them came from different countries. He had contracts with hundreds of clients, here and abroad. We wouldn't interview them all . . . not when we had a prime suspect.'

'Have you finished?' asked Benson.

'Well, no, to be honest, I just want the jury to understand my position.'

'Oh, they will do, DCI Winter, don't worry on that score. Can I just return to what else you didn't do?'

'Sure. Yes. But—'

'You didn't check out if there was any substance to Debbie Bealing's belief that her husband had got on the wrong side of a Chinese gang.'

'I didn't, no. Because Mrs Bealing was sectioned later that day, just like she was yesterday. This is what I mean. An investigation has to be targeted.'

'And your target was nailed to the wall the day Mrs Jonson told you about a coloured hat and coat. The day you caught Sarah Collingstone at Dover. Since that moment, you left this case to the scientists.'

Tess hadn't noticed that Archie had come into court. He leaned close and said, 'I've found something in the files.'

They stood by a wall a few yards from the court entrance, Tess with arms folded tight, Archie bent forward, his voice hushed:

'I think I've found a ghost client. Alan Richard Shaftoe. He runs a consultancy. The company's based in Zurich with an office in London. Advises clients on business opportunities in East-Central Europe and Asia. At least that's what the blurb says.'

The financial routing was complicated, but Bealing, personally and through his companies, had paid Shaftoe Management £3.7 million in the space of six months. 'It's all down as investment, disbursements, loans and fees. Infrastructure across the EU. He's down as planning more supermarkets selling tins of cabbage from Romania. The tax people would find the hole easily enough, and so would the police, if they'd taken a careful look.'

'So what was the scam?' asked Tess.

'It could be money laundering, bringing dirty money into the business through legal highs and cleaning it up through the import business. But I think he was planning to disappear. I can't find anything on an Alan Shaftoe. There are no tax returns. The London office doesn't exist. The business was set up after the death of Hugh Wellborn and without the involvement of Roger Grange. It looks like Bealing shifted a wedge abroad and was going to vanish before the people he'd upset could get to him.'

Tess was making notes, thinking it through. 'But once he'd gone the police would eventually find out that Alan Shaftoe was a fiction. And the tax people would find out they were owed a wedge as well.'

'They would, but first they'd have to look. And even if they did, by then it'd be too late. They'd never find Alan Shaftoe. Shaftoe doesn't exist. He has a Swiss bank account, that's all, and the Swiss aren't very helpful. Their best clients were Nazis, remember. So Bealing gets his money through Shaftoe, but he'll have lived by another name. Far off. Out of reach. That's my guess anyway.'

'Far away from Debbie, too.'

'Yep.'

'And she's part of the problem now. By selling up she's

muddied the water. Makes it difficult to track all the numbers. It's not relevant, of course, but she undersold everything, you know. She sold the lot as fast as she could. I'm really surprised that nurse didn't intervene. He must have seen what she was doing and just looked the other way.'

Tess gave her pen a click and closed her pad. 'Archie?'

'Yes?'

'You look sensational.'

'Really?'

'It's your granddad's watch chain. Very Edwardian. And the silver hair to match. What chambers are you from? I simply have to send you tons of work.'

When Tess got back into court, Benson was winding up. DCI Winter was puce.

'The painful truth, DCI Winter, is that you aren't an old school police officer, are you?'

'And what's that supposed to mean?'

'In the old days, detectives knocked on doors and used their intuition. You belong to the generation that relies on computer programs. The generation that thinks a DNA profile is a magic bullet, and once you'd been told Sarah Collingstone's DNA was on that bottle, you just filled in the boxes.'

'Untrue.'

'You left the basics undone.'

'I did not.'

Benson leaned back and folded his arms. 'What about the tin of tuna? Where is it?'

'I don't know.'

'Didn't you look for it?'

'No.'

'Why not? This was my client's explanation for the hand injury that you say was caused by the bottle even though her blood never dripped on to the floor at Hopton's Yard. It should be on the exhibits table.'

'I suppose it should be.'

'That's your first and only concession, DCI Winter. Am I right in concluding that if you could carry out this investigation all over again, the one difference is that you'd drive over to Hounslow and have a look in Sarah Collingstone's rubbish bin?'

'I wouldn't put it like that, but yes.'

'Thank you. No further questions.'

DCI Winter left court and Glencoyne addressed Mr Justice Oakshott:

'My lord, that concludes the case for the Crown.'

The judge turned to the jury and informed them that it being Friday afternoon, he proposed to adjourn the case until Monday morning, when the defence case would open. After the usual warnings not to discuss the evidence or trawl the internet, the court clerk brought the assembled lawyers and journalists to their feet, and Mr Justice Oakshott retired with a friendly piece of advice:

'Have a quiet weekend.'

Benson swung round to speak to Tess:

'We're in with a shout. It's in our client's hands. Let's have a conference.'

# 34

Benson stood, head bowed, listening to Archie. When the clerk had finished they both entered the conference room. There was a sense of confident expectation made agonising by the fact that the trial wasn't over; and not being complete, anything could still happen. But no one doubted that Sarah was in a very strong position. The jury was with her. There was only one problem. She still needed to explain how her DNA got on to that bottle. Benson put off the question for later.

'There's been a development in what we know about Andrew Bealing,' he said. 'It seems he was planning to skip the country and start a new life elsewhere. He was killed first.'

Ralph Collingstone could barely contain himself. The judge had to be told immediately. And Miss Glencoyne. And the jury.

'It's still not evidence, Ralph,' said Tess. 'This is what we think. We don't know. We're trying to make sense of holes in his business records, and at the moment, all we know for sure is that he transferred £3.7 million out of the jurisdiction. It's suspicious. It's alarming. But it isn't necessarily linked to his death. We still haven't got witnesses who can demonstrate that Mr Bealing feared for his life . . . which would then explain why he might try to create a new identity.'

'Isn't there anything you can do to force them to speak?' asked Ralph. 'Can't you bring them here against their will?'

'What would be the point?' said Tess. She was sympathetic but firm. 'Unless they want to give evidence, they'll just deny everything they've told me in secret. I'm working on them. I've told them special measures can be taken to ensure their protection, but they aren't interested. I'm hoping they'll change their minds.'

Ralph was confused; and Benson understood his anguish: people thought you could come to court and tell the jury anything; and you couldn't. He thought people could be forced to say what they knew, and they couldn't.

'How much did you say?' asked Ralph, reaching for something he could understand.

Benson repeated the figure – £3.7 million. It was a fortune.

'Does the name Alan Shaftoe mean anything to you, Sarah?' he asked.

She was flushed and confused. 'No.'

'Who's he?' asked Ralph.

'On the face of things, he was a client of Mr Bealing. He could be the false identity Mr Bealing was planning to assume. An alternative reading would be that Mr Bealing wasn't planning to leave the country at all. And Alan Shaftoe was someone else's fictional identity – perhaps related to the gang he feared. Perhaps the £3.7 million was laundered money from legal highs. This kind of speculation can go on for ever and it takes the spotlight off the most important issue in this case. It's a distraction.'

Sarah had lost weight. She was drawn and pale and she turned to Benson, as if expecting what he was going to say.

'Even if we could prove that a Chinese gang wanted to kill Mr Bealing, and we could prove that he was planning his escape, Miss Glencoyne would still say this is a very simple and tragic case. That you are the one who killed him. Because you'd been jilted. Because you'd had enough of the loneliness and poverty. There's enough evidence to suggest you had an affair with him. And, most important of all, your DNA is on that bottle. It either got there because you touched it; or you touched someone who did . . . and for quite a long time.'

Sarah closed her eyes – like Benson had closed them the other night to escape the words of Abasiama. Seeking darkness within darkness. Ralph reached over and took her hand as if to stop her falling over the edge into an abyss. Benson felt for him. His own father had done the same thing. He, too, had looked helpless, choked with emotions he'd never felt before.

'Reflect carefully on the evidence of Dr Gooding, Sarah,'

said Benson. 'Have a quiet weekend, like the judge said. Think things through. And if you want to, call me. But remember this. On Monday morning you will go into the witness box. I will ask you to tell your story. And then, I'm afraid, it's Miss Glencoyne's turn. I won't be able to do anything to protect you.' He wondered what phrase to give her that might work like a key. 'Don't be frightened of the truth, Sarah. If you tell the truth, whatever it might be, you'll remain free for ever . . . even if they send you to prison.'

Benson, Tess and Archie braved the cameras outside the Old Bailey. They walked through them, frowning at the flashes of light; they pressed on, until the clamour and scuffling had died away; until the only person with an eye on them was the bearded saddo in the bomber jacket on the other side of the road.

'Can't I land one on him?' asked Archie again, as if they were back in HMP Lindley.

'Not today,' said Benson. 'Not any day. We've moved on, Archie.'

They reached Ludgate. Benson wanted to break out, get away from all that reticence and fear that had been implanted in him by the guilty verdict of a jury. He glanced at Tess. There was a sadness in her that had ignited his attention. He wanted to know how it had got there. Ever since he first noticed it – when she made that Grave Robber thing – he'd been visualising those greeny blue unprotected eyes, summoning them, not voluntarily, but instinctively, against his own need to protect himself. In the café, when he dropped his guard, the words had poured out, but he'd been staring into lonely pools of distant water, knowing she was in there somewhere. He wanted to jump in.

'Does anyone fancy anything to eat?' he said, taking a strange emotional risk; because in prison Benson had learned never to come forward; to move around the wing as if he wasn't there, to never attract attention.

'I'm in,' said Archie.

Tess hugged herself. It was chilly and a wind came whistling along Fleet Street. 'Sorry, boys,' she said. 'I'm already taken.'

She left them standing at a set of traffic lights on Farringdon Street. Benson watched her go. There were hundreds of people on the pavement, all dark figures, jostling in the fading light, but he never lost sight of her once. She got smaller and smaller, until all he could make out was a speck of emerald green, a velvet hat afloat on a sea of strangers.

# PART THREE

'Have a quiet weekend.'

(Mr Justice Kenneth Oakshott, *R v. Collingstone*)

Benson had expected to be moved closer to home, but his application was never processed. His enquiries got nowhere. In the end, he stopped waiting. What was time, anyway? It was a question that had perplexed every philosopher and physicist, and yet Needles knew the answer:

'Time is something you do, son. Do your time and don't think about it.'

Benson had never imagined that he might consider someone like Needles to be a friend, but that is what he became. A sort of friend, anyway. A prison friend, who broke all his own rules – the rules he'd given Benson after he'd wanted to scream his way to freedom. Or at least, he broke them with Benson. Out of the blue, he'd told him about a woman he knew, Carol. They'd had a child. A boy. Larry. There was another child out there, too, Sharon, though Needles hadn't mentioned the mother. He hadn't seen any of them in years. Didn't even know where they were.

'I've been in and out of prison all my life, Rizla,' he said, sitting on the toilet, knitting. 'You lose touch.'

It was a Saturday. Association had been cancelled. They'd been banged-up for twenty-two hours. Benson was reading an abstract on bullet damage to human brain tissue – how the wound was incredibly complex, forensically, containing vast amounts of information about the weapon, the bullet, the calibre, the distance at which it was fired, the angle and more – but this last remark by Needles caught Benson's attention. Needles had said the same thing several times over the past few weeks, 'You lose touch', but each time he'd said the phrase, it sounded like a fresh disclosure.

'But you don't repeat that, Rizla,' he said, turning to look at Benson. 'You don't mention my kids to anyone, okay?'

'Okay.'

He'd said that, too. Several times. And Benson was now fairly sure. Needles had a form of mental illness . . . maybe Alzheimer's or something. Whatever it might be, it hadn't been diagnosed and he wasn't being treated. Somehow or other the ins and outs of prison life – from the routine, through to the structure of the building, where to eat and where to wash – had all remained within his mental grasp, but the rest, his real life out there in the real world, had become floating fragments in his mind, things he recognised, without remembering where they came from. He spoke about them as if they were first sightings after a marine disaster, forgetting that the ship had gone down years ago.

'I've got a boy called Larry. He must be a man now.'

# 35

The brick came straight through the front room downstairs window. Shards of glass showered a handwoven carpet from Inishmore on the west coast of Ireland. Sally screamed. Tess ducked. Suddenly enraged, she ran outside, just in time to see two men heading at speed towards Kensington Gore. A black car was waiting for them, the rear passenger door open. They jumped in and the car pulled away. Back home, Tess surveyed the mess. And she sighed: if the glass hadn't been tough, the brick would have hit the facing wall or the wedding portrait of her parents. Relieved, she called a glazier and fetched a dustpan and brush.

'Aren't you going to call the police?' asked Sally, standing with her back against the wall.

'No point.'

'You're sure?'

'They're gone.'

'But they might come back.'

'Yes, they might.' Tess, on her knees, looked up. 'This is what I've got myself into. If you're involved with me, digging into Benson's past, and Harbeton's, they might do the same to you. Do you want out?'

Sally flinched as if she'd been slapped. 'Out? You must be joking. I haven't had this much fun since we were arrested in Vienna.'

They'd divided the labour. Sally had researched the Harbeton family. Tess had gone over Benson's trial brief from 1998. Sitting at a table in the upstairs drawing room, Sally laid out a number of photos printed off the net, explaining who was who.

Maureen, mother and matriarch, had been through the mill. She was nineteen when Paul was born. The father, Kenny Harbeton, worked for the council. Two other sons followed in quick succession, Stephen and Brian. That made three children between 1965 and 1968. And then, when the kids were six, five, and three, Kenny just vanished. He next appeared on the scene twenty-seven years later, after Paul Harbeton's murder . . . but a lot had happened before then.

Maureen went to work in 1975, when the kids were all at school. Paul did well, but he was left to fend for himself. Maureen had a hard enough time doing night shifts in a clothing factory without having to worry about school exams and the like. So Paul probably didn't fulfil his potential. He left school at sixteen to work on different building sites. The brothers were another story altogether. In and out of trouble with the police. Both Stephen and Brian did stints in young

173

offender institutions. They probably had the sort of friends who chucked bricks through windows.

Then things seemed to look up for Maureen. She met a bus driver. Ron Chilton. Aged forty, she gave birth to Gary. The Harbeton brothers were all adults by then. So young Gary was a sort of only child. Five years later, Ron dies of cancer, and Maureen finds herself – yet again – on her own. She's forty-five, for God's sake. She must have had enough.

'And it's Paul who comes home every weekend,' said Sally, sliding his photograph forward. 'And as you'd imagine, he's very important to young Gary.'

All this was on the internet. Private lives spilled out in detail to the *Sun*, the *Star*, the *Independent* . . . tabloids and broadsheets. Radio interviews, too. And television. Facebook. But it's not Maureen who does the talking, it's Gary. The brothers chip in when they can. And then there's Kenny Harbeton, the father . . . but he's another story.

'So this is the situation in 1998. Paul's twenty-seven, working as a hospital porter. He helps out at various charities.'

'Which ones?'

Sally checked a notepad. 'Leadgate House in Lambeth, Barnardo's . . . don't know where that was . . . and a trauma clinic in Finsbury. He's Maureen's success story. A good guy.'

'Who headbutted Benson when he crossed him.'

'Be fair, Tess. These charities thought the world of him. He volunteered to help and he needn't have done. And yes, he knew how to look after himself.'

Though that didn't help on the 7th of November 1998, when he walked into Soho after the fight with Benson. She didn't voice the thought, but said, 'I'll check out his employment history.'

'Why?'

'It's interesting he stayed at the bottom of the work ladder.

If he had drive – and he did – why not become a nurse? Why stay on the edges?'

'What will a work history tell you?'

'Everything he ever did. Maybe there's a pattern. Maybe the pattern will tell us something.' Tess had had a hunch; and, as with all hunches, she didn't know why it had nudged itself into her mind. 'Anyway, Harbeton was thirty-three at the time of his death which means that Gary Chilton was only—'

'You anticipate me.' Sally slid another picture forward. 'This tough nut lost his father at five and his big brother at twelve. That's two kicks to the goolies before he's even hit his teens. And when he does hit his teens, he hit lots of other things as well, mainly people, but property as well.'

He was in an *awful* lot of trouble. Looking back, he says it's all because William Benson killed his brother. Which is convenient, of course, but it might well be true. His childhood was pretty well trashed.

'Tell me about Kenny Harbeton,' said Tess. She moved away from the angry faces and sat at the piano, an old Steinway recovered from a damp garage in Alnwick.

'I imagine he blames somebody as well. After dumping Maureen he pops up twenty-seven years later out of nowhere. In fairness, his son had been killed. He comes to Benson's trial. He's the spokesman . . . and then he clears off all over again. Fifteen years later, last week, he's back in front of the cameras. He's there standing behind Gary Chilton. You'd think he'd never been away.'

Tess pressed a few random keys. 'And Maureen says nothing.'

'Nothing at all. She's the unforgettable presence in every photograph. The silent force in every interview. You wouldn't want to ask her a question.' Sally had an intuition; and it came like another brick through the window. 'Oh my God . . . you aren't going to speak to her, are you?'

'I think it's inevitable,' said Tess. 'Not today, not tomorrow. But if we find out that someone else killed Paul Harbeton, she will want to speak to us. And who knows, maybe along the road, we're going to need her help.'

Sally tried to imagine the meeting . . . with Stephen and Brian and Gary; not forgetting Kenny. 'I need a drink,' she said, making a pile of the photographs. She went to a cabinet with various bottles clustered on a lace cloth. She was pensive. Finally, she said, 'Can I have the brick?'

Tess was bemused. 'What for?'

'Well, there's a good argument that it's art – urban contemporary, with a certain retro nostalgia – but if someone is going to chuck something at me, I intend to chuck something back.'

# 36

Benson went to sea with his dad. To avoid the press, they got up at five in the morning, setting out in *Dalston's Girl*, a small boat always moored by the jetty at the end of the garden. They went twenty-seven kilometres north of Blakeney Point and twenty-eight kilometres east of Chapel St Leonards. Roughly. There, in the middle of the Wash, they bobbed around in the water. This was Race Bank where Jim Benson used to put his crab pots. Until a High Court injunction stopped him last year. There were plans for an offshore wind farm. Dong Energy, the developers, had been compelled to seek legal redress.

'As soon as those wind turbines get going – ninety-one of them – the sand will disappear,' said Jim, frying rashers of bacon on a Primus. 'And once the sand's gone, the crabs'll go too.'

Overall it was a dilemma. The need for green energy versus an ancient industry, which itself had damaged the marine environment. Naturally enough, Benson had sided with the fishermen, but he couldn't do anything. No one could. The world had changed. The need to save the planet came first.

'I've been worried about you, son,' said Jim. 'All that stuff on the television. The petition. Digging up your trial again . . . everything that happened. I wish I could do something.'

Benson told him not to worry. There'd be no injunction. They couldn't stop him going out to sea. It was a storm in a teacup.

'It upsets me because you've paid the price,' said Jim, angling the pan. He wore a dark blue gansey, knitted by Benson's mother. The thing wouldn't wear out. 'And I know you're innocent, so you've paid a price you shouldn't have paid . . . so I wish they'd just leave you alone. Let you get on with your life' – the bacon sizzled and spat – 'I don't know why people want you to pay for ever.'

'Because Paul Harbeton will pay for ever,' said Benson.

That was the argument. Another hard one. And naturally enough, Jim had sided with his son.

'I know you're innocent, Will. I *know*. You don't have to persuade me.'

He kept saying it. Every time Benson came home he said it. But he always sounded so unsure. Like he just *knew* where the lobster had gone . . . into deeper water. Wherever that might be. Benson took a bacon sandwich and looked out to sea. There was a faint mist struggling with the morning light. Soon it would be sharp and clear. A light wind was rising.

'Eddie's doing well,' said Jim, inviting some reply. When he didn't get one, he said, 'You've got to understand, Will, he's not like you and me. He's not like he was. His brain got damaged. He changed. He's someone else. That's why he won't believe you. It's just something here' – he stroked

177

a temple, gently, as if he were by Eddie's bedside during one of the endless night vigils – 'he knows you got convicted, so that's it for him, you're guilty. It's like maths, one plus one equals two. If there'd been no accident, he'd have believed you . . . like me . . . I'm sure of it.'

Benson nearly laughed. His dad wanted to believe that only someone with a brain injury would have accepted the jury's verdict. But it wasn't funny. Jim said, 'He's beginning to remember the week of the accident, you know.'

'Is he?' Benson made it sound bright.

'Yes. Little bits, here and there . . . he remembers the day before . . . and getting his bike out of the shed. Hopefully he'll get everything back, one day, I'll ask him what the hell went through his mind.'

A couple of miles inland from the family home in Brancaster Staithe stood Lushmead's, a hotel that had once been a stately home. Wooded grounds sloped to an ornamental lake. Benson and his brother used to faff around the winding lanes on their bikes. Out of sight. Smoking. Talking about girls. On the 9th of July 1988, a sunny Saturday – the date, time and weather were burned into his memory – Benson (aged ten), Eddie (nine) and Neil Reydon (eleven) had been playing daredevil. Cycling down a grassy slope as fast as hell and braking before the lake. Getting as close as possible without ending up in the water. Benson had been standing on the edge, waiting and watching. He'd given the signal to Eddie. And then, all of a sudden, his brother had set off in a different direction, head down, pedalling like a maniac, along a path that led to the main road, a path screened from the road by a bank of trees. Benson had already seen a car take the bend, further away. A red people carrier. Citroën. C8. It was out of sight now, but it had to be coming down that road. It had been shifting, too. And Eddie couldn't see it and he couldn't know it was there.

Benson gazed over the Wash. It would soon be a kind of cemetery.

'How's he getting on?' he asked.

'As well as can be expected.'

That was the phrase. The family had been using it for years. They'd never find another one. It shut the subject down and it told the truth; and to Benson, it said nothing had changed. Eddie lived at home in the converted downstairs back room. Neil Reydon came round every day. He took him out every week. They were still the best of friends. Better, ironically, because of what bound them together.

'They're at Neil's door, too,' said Jim. 'The press. They won't leave any of us alone, friend or family. But you've got nothing to worry about. I'll keep on telling them you're innocent, even if you went and admitted everything. And Eddie won't say anything. Not that he has anything to say, but you know what I mean.'

Benson did.

'Maybe one day, we'll be a family again,' said Jim, brusquely, shaking the pan. 'Maybe we'll come out here together, the three of us, and bring in the crab. If only for your mum's sake.'

Benson looked at those old, rapidly blinking eyes. 'I love you, Dad,' he said.

# 37

Tess hadn't noticed it before. But after rereading Benson's trial brief it was obvious. There were a number of striking parallels between his case and Sarah Collingstone's. And their personal circumstances. It was eerie.

Benson accepted he'd had an argument with the murdered

victim earlier in the evening, insisting that they'd parted ways before the killing.

That was Sarah Collingstone's case.

The Crown had said the argument was far from over. That Benson, in a rage, killed his victim shortly afterwards.

Which was the Crown's case against Sarah Collingstone.

Benson denied having any particular relationship with the deceased.

So did Sarah Collingstone.

Benson was seen near the crime scene by a credible witness at the time of the murder.

So was Sarah Collingstone (but for that clever point about sodium lighting).

Benson was said to have followed his victim and hit him from behind, probably lingering while the victim died.

So was Sarah Collingstone.

No one had believed Benson. The circumstantial evidence had been overwhelming.

No one had believed Sarah Collingstone.

Except Benson.

He had refused to accept that she was a liar, even though – to quote her former solicitor – she looked as guilty as sin. Benson had *wanted* to believe in her innocence. He'd seen something in her that had nothing to do with the case, and this was where their personal histories were also strangely similar. They'd both lived with the impact of disability on someone they'd loved. The impact of disability on a family. They'd exchanged a kind of Masonic handshake. Collingstone's son Daniel had suffered a brain injury. So had Benson's brother Eddie. It was all there in the pre-sentence report, prepared for Benson's case. Like Collingstone, he had spent hours in hospitals and clinics. He understood her secret world.

'I don't like this,' said Tess, not understanding why.

Sally was dusting scallops in flour. 'Don't like what?'

'The coincidence. The parallels. It can't be accidental.'

'Well, it could hardly be planned.'

'No, but it could be a reason for why Collingstone instructed Benson. His history was all over the *Guardian* and the *Sun*. Four days prior to trial she sacks her solicitor and barrister. She goes to see Benson the same day, a Friday, with the trial starting the following Wednesday. He doesn't get the brief until Monday morning. He's no experience. Why pick him?'

Sally had no idea. Her world was pictures and prints. 'She wanted someone she could manipulate? Get him to do and say what she wanted?'

Tess rebuffed the idea. It was the evidence that determined what a lawyer said and did.

'Maybe she wanted to exploit the controversy around his name?'

'But why do that?'

'Get the benefit of the doubt – not about her but about him. Maybe she's thinking the jury will let her go because they'll want to show they haven't been influenced by all the mud-slinging. Do you have any lemons?'

Tess went to the fridge. 'But the woman I met wasn't that calculating. That cold.'

'She is, darling. You just can't read between the lines, like me. I did warn you. I did say you couldn't trust her.'

'You said she was stubborn.'

'I said she had a lot to hide. Butter?'

If Sally was right that would mean Collingstone was almost certainly guilty. No innocent person would behave in such a way. It would mean all that 'I just don't know, Mr Benson' stuff was a charade. It would mean the emerging picture of Andrew Bealing's dealings with organised crime was an irrelevance.

181

Sally banged the skillet. 'You're all confused, aren't you?'

'Very.'

'I don't mean about Collingstone, I mean about Benson.'

'I am, yes.'

Tess wanted to believe that Benson was innocent, just as Benson wanted to believe that Collingstone wasn't guilty. She had a great deal invested in his integrity. And the idea that he might have lied to her, like Collingstone might have lied to him, was profoundly destabilising. She wouldn't have given the notion a second thought if someone other than Douglas hadn't mentioned it. But Douglas was wise. He saw things. Like he'd seen the bastard in Peter Farsely. Sally was making a wholly unnecessary racket, banging and shaking the pan.

'You do realise, don't you,' she said, ' that this martyrdom stuff – letting people dump yoghurt over your head while you turn the other cheek – all that makes sense if you killed someone and can't bear the sight of yourself any more? It's *completely* consistent with a totally decent fellow who lost his temper and belted someone over the head with a crowbar or whatever. He was a philosophy student, wasn't he? Well . . . he's simply *got* to have a ballsed-up view of himself.'

'Yes, I know. But you should see him in court, Sally. He's there like some great defender of the little guy, a moral force. His integrity is palpable. He cares about the truth, not just the evidence. He couldn't be all that in court and be someone else outside.'

'Of course he could. That's what it's all about. There are drawers to his personality, remember? He keeps his ethics well away from his logic. And in public, he's recreating himself. He's inventing someone he can never be in real life, because back home, away from the Old Bailey, that possibility's gone for ever. He's got the mark of Cain. He's a fugitive. He's an outcast. Plates.'

'Never sit on a jury, Sally.'

'Why not?'

'You're a fantasist.'

Sally pondered the point. 'My paying clients call me visionary.'

# 38

Helen Camberley called and she insisted. Benson didn't want any help, but the woman who'd once defended him, and who'd given him a pupillage, wouldn't take no for an answer. Call it parental worry. She wouldn't be deflected. In fact, she was a little late in the day. The difficult work had been done. All that remained was the defence case: there was nothing to do but call Sarah Collingstone. Yet Helen wasn't so sure. She'd invited him to have lunch followed by a cigar over billiards in her large Hampstead home.

'That was a neat move with Collingstone's DNA,' she said.

Helen, like Benson's former tutor in epistemology, had always stressed the importance of challenging assumptions concealed in apparently irresistible evidence. 'You were quite right. Collingstone's DNA on that bottle is just another piece of data that requires an explanation. It's up to her now. You've given her a chance. Let's hope she takes it. For her sake.'

Helen's hair had once been light brown (apparently). It had gone silver by the time of Benson's trial, and was now white, cut short. She was seventy-three years old and still haunting the courts with a rich, contralto voice. Diminutive, and dressed in black linen, she drew on her cigar as if she were George Sand worried about Chopin's health.

'Rachel's in a difficult position,' she said, referring to Glencoyne. 'Personally, I think she'd have been better advised to risk presenting Bealing as a bit of a *bastard* who'd used Collingstone and then dropped her – which is what I suspect happened. Instead, she went down the prince and pauper route, not wanting to attack a dead man's character, or present the jury with a man they'd dislike . . . and, inevitably, a defendant they'd pity. But now she's stuck with the fact that the affair looks flimsy. And someone else might have come to Hopton's Yard after Collingstone went home – if she went home. You've set things up very well indeed. It's difficult to believe this is your first Crown Court trial.'

Benson shrugged off the remark. He'd spent eleven years reading transcripts of evidence and articles on forensic science. There was no magic to it.

'I find it delicious that colleagues think you're responsible for anything that's bad, and I must be responsible for anything that's good,' she said, chalking her cue.

'You are, Helen, in every way, and you know that.'

Without Camberley's support Benson would never have made it to the Bar. She'd advised him not to try, but once he'd taken up the challenge, she'd been there at his shoulder, regardless of personal cost. She'd showered him with gifts, some of them humbling, like the wig that had belonged to her grandfather. And someone out there had paid for his legal training, bought him a boat, given him an income for three years and provided a library, all subject to those signed undertakings. But Benson had guessed it was Camberley, even if Camberley would never admit it. Secret patronage on such a scale creates a certain tension between the giver and the receiver, and he had felt that tension from the moment he began his pupillage. Everyone did. Everyone knew that Helen's son had committed suicide. Everyone knew that Benson had appeared in her life like a dead body she longed to revive.

'I met Rachel last night,' she said, lining up her shot. 'I was surprised. She was rather confident about the case.'

So this was why Helen had called him.

'Frankly, everyone thought you'd flounder and drown, but you haven't done. The person who's seen to be sinking is Rachel. So she ought to be embarrassed, given your limited experience. She ought to be worried that Collingstone is going to slip through her fingers. But she isn't worried. I got the impression she's looking forward to tomorrow.' Camberley played a winning cannon but frowned. 'I think you ought to be careful.'

'How?'

'Rachel's got judgement. She's honest. But she's not beyond a shit's trick. She played fast with me once, and I've never forgotten it. So take nothing for granted. She might be planning your humiliation.'

Benson had spent a great deal of his pupillage in this smoky, panelled room. The evenings mainly; and sometimes well into the night. It had all been work. She'd made him question her. Endlessly. Showed him how to dismantle a lie. How to construct a narrative. How to move in for the kill. Showed him when to drop an issue and when to leave it hanging in the air . . . like a noose; or a lifeline, it depended on who you were questioning.

'Don't worry, Helen,' he said, holding his cue almost at a right angle to the table. He was planning a massé. Possibly the most exciting stroke in the game – and dangerous, because with a fraction too much pressure, the strained green cloth would tear. 'I might have a surprise or two for Glencoyne. We're on to Bealing's killer. All I need is the evidence.'

It was late when Benson ambled home along Seymour Road. He was preoccupied, thinking of his dad, alone with five hundred lobster pots. When he left school, Benson had joined the family business, like all the Benson sons before him. He'd become a fisherman. He did his best to learn the trade, and to love it, but after a few months his dad pulled in the nets, so to speak.

'You weren't made for the sea, son,' he said.

Benson was confused, and worried that he'd somehow disappointed his father. He said he'd try harder, he'd work at it, he'd get there one day, and that . . . but his dad cut him short with a fond smile.

'It's not about trying, son. You've done all I've asked and more.'

'Then what's the problem?' Benson replied.

'You've stopped asking "Why?". For years you've driven us mad with your endless questions, and now you don't ask them any more. The sea isn't your home. You don't want to find lobsters. You want to find answers. So go catch 'em, my boy.'

And so Benson enrolled to read philosophy at King's College London. His parents were immensely proud. They bought him the college scarf. After leaving the shop, Jim kicked himself, and went back, insisting that Benson choose a pair of cuff-links to match.

'Trust me, you'll be needing those,' he said, knowledgeably, though he'd never worn such things in his life. At no point did he reveal what must have been pressing on his mind, perhaps even as he wrote the cheques: that with Benson's departure, three hundred years of family tradition would come to an end.

So, thinking of his dad, Benson didn't quite notice the white van parked right in front of his gate, and the three masked men waiting by the open back doors. When he did it was too late. They threw him inside, face down. He was pinned at the wrists and ankles while one of them, or maybe two, set to work, beating Benson across his legs, buttocks and back. They didn't utter a word, just the odd grunt. It was all rather mechanical, businesslike, efficient. When they'd finished, they threw him on the pavement and drove off. The last thing Benson saw before he closed his eyes was the loser in the bomber jacket on his phone. The job had been done.

# PART FOUR

The case for the defence

Benson raised the matter of Needles' mental problems with one of the screws – a screw he thought might be decent – and the screw said he'd mention it to the healthcare people the next day, but even as he was speaking, Benson knew nothing would happen. The screw already knew and he didn't care, or if he did, he knew that mentioning it to the healthcare people wouldn't make any difference. So Benson gave up looking for help, as he'd given up waiting to move. He went back to his cell to do his time with Needles.

'What are you in for, Needles?' he said, after he'd finished an article on fracture patterns in glass and polymers.

'Petty theft, I think  . . . I can't remember, son.'

Benson had already asked him, but Needles had replied as if he hadn't, and with the same resignation. Needles had spent his life coming in and out of prison for minor offences until he couldn't remember what he was in for. He couldn't live outside any more.

'What are you in for, Rizla?'

'Murder.'

'Silly boy.'

Benson began reading another article, this time on the use of non-human DNA analysis in forensic science.

'Hey, Rizla?'

'Yes?'

'You lose touch when you're inside, you know what I mean?'

Benson looked over the top of his magazine.

'Sure I do, Needles.'

And Needles shook his head like a sage defeated by a

*rune. And Benson frowned. The yellow woollen scarf. It never got any longer. Needles kept knitting, but the thing got nowhere nearer to being finished. It didn't make sense.*

# 39

The policeman who found Benson and helped him to his feet got talking about the Hopton Yard killing as soon as decency would allow. And he volunteered that back at the station the lads were split fifty-fifty on whether Collingstone was going to get off. 'My view, Mr Benson, is that Miss Glencoyne is going to eat your client for breakfast,' he said. Which was probably Glencoyne's view, too, because when Benson passed her on the stairs to the robing room – refusing to limp or give any indication of the pasting he'd received – she said, 'Good morning.' Such an outbreak of courtesy could only mean she was bursting at the seams with confidence.

But Benson had a surprise of his own lined up. After declining a lift to the hospital, he'd bought a packet of Sobranie Black Russians, smoked three, run the packet under the tap, thrown it in the bin and gone to bed, lying face down to try and limit the pain. Methodically, he buried his rage. He piled a sort of clay on his longing to hit back. Slowly, he felt a deathly inner quiet like anaesthesia. The call from Sarah Collingstone had come shortly afterwards, while he was reading 'March Hares' by Andrew Young.

'Mr Benson, I'm sorry. But I haven't told you the whole truth. I've lied. And now I want to tell you what really happened.'

\*　　\*　　\*

Camberley's advice had always been let them tell their story. Efface yourself. Let the jury hear the witness as if you weren't there.

So Benson, in constant blazing pain, asked short and simple questions. And Sarah gave an account she'd never told anyone before, not even her father. Yes, she'd got close to Andrew Bealing (taken slowly, it all sounded so natural; Glencoyne had been right). Bealing had been very kind; he'd been understanding; he'd been very attentive. He'd eventually started to pursue her. He'd touched her, frequently, on the arm, the hand, the shoulder. At the Christmas party he'd pulled her towards him and she'd not wanted to resist.

But there was no relationship. No affair. Just these moments when they could so easily go further; much further; only Sarah didn't want to, because of Debbie. She felt confused, not knowing what the future might be, not knowing how to conduct herself. And it had been in this state of uncertainty that she went to Hopton's Yard on Saturday, 14th of February 2014. As she'd always maintained, the reason for the visit was to tie Mr Bealing down in relation to the health and safety procedure manuals for Anna Wysocki. Sarah entered Mr Bealing's office, saying how awfully cold it was outside. She took off her hat and coat and laid them on a chair. She rubbed her hands. When she turned around, Mr Bealing was standing there. He'd come from behind his desk. He cupped both her hands in his, holding them tight.

This was the moment witnessed by the driver Ricky Warton. Sarah's frustrations with Anna Wysocki's demands overwhelmed her and she started crying, with Mr Bealing telling her not to worry, and Sarah saying she wasn't leaving until he'd either called Wysocki or given her the wretched stuff she was after. Mr Bealing left the room to speak to Warton. When he returned, he drew a curtain over the window on to the warehouse. He drew a curtain over the window on to the reception area. And then he wiped a tear off her cheek with a thumb.

Sarah had no real memory of how she lost self-control. Within what felt like seconds, Mr Bealing had lifted her off the ground and brought her to the edge of his desk; they made love, and yes, Sarah gripped the skin on his back. Benson was obliged to ask whether Bealing's hands touched her skin, keeping them there for any length of time, and Sarah, crushed and humiliated, said, 'Yes.' Benson had to go further: 'For how long?' and Sarah told everyone watching what they already knew: 'A lot more than two minutes.'

'Why didn't you explain all this to DCI Winter, the court and your legal representatives?' said Benson, eyes on the jury as if they already understood the answer. 'Why hide so much that was so important?'

'Because I thought I'd be convicted of the murder.' Sarah was holding on to the witness stand with both hands. 'The detective already believed I was guilty . . . if I told him what happened, he'd have used it against me. I was at sea, Mr Benson. I didn't know what to do . . . that's why I said nothing in my first two interviews. I was wondering how much I could say without incriminating myself even more. That's why I said nothing to you, because I was worried you wouldn't believe me when I said I was innocent. I can't go to prison, Mr Benson. I have a son who's totally dependent on me. I have to be with him. I'm the only one who knows what he needs. I can read his mind . . .'

Benson paused there, letting her find a tissue. Mr Justice Oakshott said there was no rush. He suggested to Sarah that she might like a glass of water. When she'd composed herself, Benson tidied up the rest of the evidence as if everything now made sense.

Sarah had left Mr Bealing at about 6.30 p.m. She went home and made a tuna salad, cutting her right hand on opening the tin. She then listened with Daniel and her father to an audio book. She went to bed at 10.15 p.m. The next morning she felt awful about what had happened – because if Debbie found out it could send her over the edge and she'd feel responsible. She wanted to get away, to think and calm down. Impulsively, she bought tickets to France, telling her father she needed a break because of the Anna Wysocki business, which, of course, remained unresolved. She was then arrested at Dover. She panicked. The fear set in. She lied. She made things worse for herself.

'You did,' agreed Benson, in a tone suggesting we've all made that particular mistake. 'Please remain there, Sarah. My learned friend Miss Glencoyne will have some questions for you.'

As he sat down, Benson wanted to scream with agony. He allowed himself a pained sigh, suppressing the rest with the ecstasy of expectation. Because Sarah Collingstone was home and dry. She'd been patently honest. She'd been credible. She was out of Glencoyne's reach.

# 40

Tess had met Rachel Glencoyne socially. She was charming. In a remote, intellectual sort of way. She'd endured a very public divorce from a much-loved judge who sat on the South Eastern Circuit (which encompassed London). Which meant she was not infrequently obliged to appear before him, as long as the client didn't mind. In short, she could never quite escape her past. Her affair with an Australian neurologist specialising in pain control was always being mentioned, usually by understatement or innuendo, and often with some obscure sexual gloss. Such was the Bar's Gossip Circuit, only to be distinguished from Hopton's Yard by the vocabulary. The break-up and flippancy had marked Rachel. She was reserved. Those bright, black-lined eyes could cut you with a glance. Her cross-examinations were sometimes cruel.

'It must be an enormous relief to have finally told the truth?' said Glencoyne.

'It is.'

'To have shifted the burden of lying?'

'I'm not proud of myself, Miss Glencoyne.'

'No, I'm sure you're not. But let's just look a little more closely at what you've just admitted.'

Glencoyne had a habit of standing with one ankle crossed over the other, like someone waiting at a bus stop, the toe perpendicular to the ground. Her expression was of someone who couldn't quite work out the timetable.

'You lied to DCI Winter?'

'Yes.'

'Trevor Hamsey, your previous solicitor, and Miss Wendling, your previous barrister?'

'Yes.'

'The court, in pre-trial hearings?'

'Yes.'

'Mr Benson and Miss de Vere?'

'Yes, I did. And I'm sorry.'

'Your father?'

'Yes.'

'But at last you've grasped the nettle and told this jury?'

'Yes, Miss Glencoyne.'

Glencoyne nodded, still bemused. 'So now your conscience is clear? You've said all there is to say?'

'I have, yes.'

Glencoyne placed a hand behind her back. 'Where is Shinwell Lane?'

'Shinwell Lane?'

'That's right. Where is it?'

'I don't know.'

'That's one lie in the bag. Let's catch another. Where is Felton Street?'

'I'm sorry, I'm not following you.'

'Lie number two. If you won't explain, I'll tell the jury. Both roads are in Portsmouth. Who is Judith Appleton?'

Benson turned to give a worried look to Tess, wondering if she knew where this was going; but she'd no idea. Sarah Collingstone did:

'She was my aunt.'

'Your mother's sister. And where did she live?'

'Portsmouth.'

'Fifty-six Shinwell Lane?'

'Yes.'

Glencoyne nodded, no longer puzzled. 'She's dead now, isn't she?'

'Yes.'

'Two thousand and five. But her next-door neighbour Karen Brookland is very much alive. Do you remember her? Is it all coming back, Miss Collingstone?'

Sarah Collingstone nodded but Mr Justice Oakshott made her reply for the record.

'Karen Brookland remembers you very well,' said Glencoyne. 'And she remembers your aunt very well. More to the point, she remembers you going to the Clayhall Youth Club. Is she right about that?'

'Yes.'

'Do you recall where it was located? Sorry, speak louder please.'

'Felton Street.'

'Exactly. Round the corner from where your aunt lived. And where you lived between July and September of 1998 after your mother had died. Am I right?'

'Yes.'

Glencoyne waited for the wave of surprised whispering to die down.

'You'd had a difficult year. You'd failed your GCSEs in June. Your mother had died of breast cancer in July and to all intents and purposes you'd been homeless. Because you refused to go and live with your father, didn't you?'

Sarah Collingstone nodded and again she was made to reply.

'Because – to call a spade a spade – you'd sided with your mother after the separation in May of '93. So when you found yourself having to move in with your father, you called Aunt Judith in Portsmouth.'

Glencoyne filled out the picture with small brush strokes. The defendant had moved to Shinwell Lane in Portsmouth. She'd planned to re-sit her exams at Newtown College. She'd planned all sorts. Only she hadn't gone to Newtown College and she hadn't stayed in Portsmouth. Glencoyne took a step to one side.

'Now that your memory's coming back, tell the court who lived at 17 Shinwell Lane?'

'I can't remember their names.'

'Mr and Mrs Newland. But you remember their house, don't you?'

'Yes.'

'Because you were never out of it. And do you remember who'd been placed there by Portsmouth Social Services? Tell the court, please.'

'Andrew Bealing.'

'Who you claim to have met for the first time on the 26th of June 2014, having been referred to Hopton Imports Limited by the Alington Trust. That was another lie, wasn't it?'

Glencoyne left the witness hanging in silence, and Tess almost heard a rope creak, but Mr Justice Oakshott eventually said, and kindly, 'You must answer the question. Have you lied again?'

'Yes.'

Glencoyne placed her hands behind her back. 'Where, in fact, did you first meet Andrew Bealing?'

'At the Clayhall Youth Club.'

'On Felton Street. That's right. Why didn't you stay in Portsmouth?'

'Because my aunt changed her mind.'

'Oh, Miss Collingstone, please. Let's stop beating round the bush. Your aunt rang your father, didn't she?'

'Yes.'

'And she rang him to say that looking after Sarah as a schoolgirl was one thing, but dealing with a pregnancy was another. She sent you home to Brampton, didn't she?'

Collingstone had closed her eyes and lowered her head. She swayed slightly. Glencoyne didn't wait for an answer. She moved on as if to catch game shot out of the air:

'Who is the father of Daniel, Miss Collingstone?'

They jury were watching, heads turned. Mr Justice Oakshott was waiting, fingers poised over his laptop. Benson must have died, because he'd ceased to move. And Tess felt maybe she owed Sally an apology.

'Answer the question,' said Glencoyne.

Collingstone raised a hand and smoothed her forehead; and then, as if a battery had been taken from her back, she buckled and collapsed.

# 41

'What the hell just happened?' said Benson.

Tess followed him out of Court 1 into the concourse. 'Collingstone got convicted.'

The jury had been sent out. A medic had been called. Mr

Justice Oakshott had retired to his chambers adjourning the case until 2 p.m. Glencoyne had looked through Benson as if he hadn't been there; but there'd been the faintest intimation of a smile.

'She's finished,' echoed Benson, desperate for a cigarette.

He'd asked the question – what had happened? – but he already knew the answer. Glencoyne must have got a statement from Karen Brookland, the neighbour who'd known Collingstone's aunt. Brookland could give evidence about Collingstone knowing Bealing, but the rest was inadmissible hearsay – because she'd learned it from the aunt who was now dead. In those circumstances Glencoyne could have served a notice to introduce hearsay evidence, but instead she'd preferred to 'cross-examine in' the whole story, getting Collingstone to accept what Glencoyne was putting to her, and taking Benson by surprise at the same time. But no statement from Brookland had been included in the unused material disclosed by the prosecution prior to trial. So either Glencoyne had kept it back – a shit's trick – or Brookland had come forward over the weekend, having followed the Hopton Yard killing trial in the press. If it was a shit's trick, then Glencoyne had been running her case from a position of apparent weakness, anticipating Benson's every move, intending all along to demolish his 'success' as soon as Collingstone got into the dock. And of course, if Glencoyne had wanted to weld the jury to the Crown's case, then that would have been the way to do it. If, on the other hand, Brookland had only recently intervened, then Glencoyne had simply been very lucky; and – as Camberley often said – luck, or the capriciousness of the gods, played a great part in the running of a trial. Either way, Collingstone was finished.

'What's happened?' asked Ralph Collingstone after Benson had called him into a conference room.

'Sarah has just admitted that Andrew Bealing is Daniel's father,' said Benson.

Ralph turned to Tess as if Benson had cracked a sick joke; Tess nodded.

'But he isn't,' said Ralph, lowering himself on to a seat. 'That's impossible. Tony Greene's his father . . . he told me himself.'

Benson folded his arms, painfully aware that he had no time to be sensitive; that the court would soon be reconvened and Ralph's world was about to collapse yet again, just as it had done for Benson's father, sitting in this very room fifteen years ago. Benson had to prepare him for what was about to happen.

'I'm sorry, but Sarah has lied to you, far more than she's lied to me,' he said. 'Even if she didn't kill Andrew Bealing, there's no chance the jury will believe anything different, not now. You must try and remain calm. A long journey's about to begin.'

'I'm going nowhere, I'm staying here, with Sarah, because she's innocent. She can't have killed Bealing, it's impossible, I should know, I was with her – we were together at home, we were listening to a story and Sarah was upstairs, with the door open, so she couldn't have been at Hopton's Yard, could she? She couldn't have killed him and she'd never have . . .' – he looked faint and tugged at his shirt – 'Tony Greene is the father, I'm telling you. He told his own parents. He suggested the name.'

Benson could have cried. Ralph couldn't believe that his daughter had deceived him. And as for the rest – the horrific rest – his denial was primeval: his wonderful daughter could not have smashed a bottle and plunged the broken neck into someone's body. Benson's father had been exactly the same. Nothing the police or the lawyers said would change his mind. His son would never have killed another man. He'd been doubting himself ever since. The lobster had gone to deeper water.

'I'll give my evidence, Mr Benson. I'll tell them what really happened. I'll tell them that Sarah and I were together, at home, with Daniel.'

Benson nodded like a doctor who'd seen the size of a previously hidden tumour. The thing was a monster. Nothing could be done. Ralph wouldn't be believed; and the jury would be right to reject his evidence.

'You'll have your chance, Mr Collingstone,' said Tess, following Benson's thinking.

'But I have to see her now, I've got to talk to her about Tony Greene; there has to be some mistake, I just know, I remember Tony saying—'

'You can't speak to Sarah,' said Benson. 'I can't speak to Sarah. She's still giving evidence. She's still Miss Glencoyne's witness. Her cross-examination is only just beginning.'

'Where is she now?'

'She'll be in a holding cell. If the doctor says she's fine, the questioning will continue after lunch.'

Benson didn't say the rest: that Glencoyne was going to flail her in front of the jury. But even if he had, Ralph may not have responded. When a catastrophe strikes a family there comes a time when even a parent will think of themselves instead of their children. And Ralph had the look of a man standing in his own grave. He was just waiting for the shot to put him out of his misery.

Leaving him in that state felt like an abandonment, but there was nothing else Benson could say or do. He joined Tess for a desultory lunch and then came back to the concourse where Ralph gestured towards a conference room. Benson had to explain what had happened all over again and Ralph, rambling with the glazed concentration of the condemned, told Tess she had to tell the judge about the threat to Bealing's life, the legal highs and the missing fortune. He strained to understand Benson's repeated explanations as to why that wasn't possible, and then a court usher's voice came through an opened door:

'We're ready, Mr Benson.'

# 42

Counsel are not allowed to bully a witness. They cannot be rude or aggressive. There are guidelines for this sort of thing. But there is nothing so violent as the truth, expressed simply, if one has lived a lie, drawing in family, relatives and friends as if they were nothing more than background detail, the landscape for the deceit, giving it a fresh, convincing appearance.

So Glencoyne's flailing of Sarah Collingstone was, in fact, an extremely polite affair; more akin to putting away the Lego than a whipping. Returning to the theme of lost memory, Glencoyne dismantled eighteen years of dishonesty. Without having to build anything in its place, the real Sarah Collingstone appeared in front of the jury. She may as well have been naked under a spotlight from Hopton's Yard.

The first great lie had been given to Anthony Greene. Then a whole raft had been floated past his parents and her own father. Deceiving the midwife, gynaecologist and hospital staff had been small beer, but she'd done it nonetheless. The whole story added up, no matter who you spoke to. One could only assume that Aunt Judith was none the wiser. She wasn't speaking to Ralph, her brother-in-law, anyway, so the story was pretty tight. And then Anthony got killed and Aunt Judith fell from a ladder and broke her neck. The chances of being rumbled were nil.

Benson listened without taking notes, castigating himself for not having dug deep into the past; but he'd had no time. And Sarah's case had been so like his own.

Glencoyne lingered on these early years. Had Bealing known that his girlfriend of a month was pregnant? Yes, he had. And what had he done when she told him? He'd vanished within the week. A mutual friend at the youth club had taken her to one side. Bealing had been on about tracing his mother's family in Spain. He'd skipped the country.

'And what was your reaction, Sarah?' said Glencoyne.

Collingstone was a defeated woman. The pencil-line bones on her face looked broken. She'd been offered a seat. She clung on to a glass of water. Benson thought he might as well go home.

'I felt betrayed and angry and humiliated,' she said, crying. 'I'd thought he'd help me. I thought he'd come with me to speak to my dad.'

For a moment, she sounded like the sixteen-year-old she'd been. Frightened of her dad's reaction. Needing her boyfriend.

'Did you feel used, Sarah?'

'Yes.'

'And thrown away?'

'Yes, I did.'

Glencoyne then floated a kite: after Daniel's birth, had she met any other parents and children with special needs? Yes, she had. And had any of those children, through their parents, brought civil actions for damages alleging medical negligence? Yes, they had. One of them had suffered brain damage on a scale similar to that of Daniel. He'd won £2.5 million. A structured settlement had been approved by the court to provide the little boy with a lifetime of care and support.

'Of course, you couldn't claim anything, because no one was at fault?'

'That's right.'

'And you were a little jealous, weren't you?'

'Yes.'

'Because you've had to look after Daniel with no one to help but your father, always worrying what will happen if and when either of you die?'

'Exactly, Miss Glencoyne.'

The friendliness worried Benson. It served no purpose but to bring in a conviction. Glencoyne moved forward sixteen years, just like Benson had done in that first conference, only this time the truth came out. Collingstone had Googled Bealing's name out of curiosity.

'And you discovered he was a very wealthy man?' said Glencoyne, still friendly.

'Yes.'

'And some of that anger came back, didn't it, because you'd brought up Daniel without his assistance?'

'Yes.'

'You thought of that little boy and his claim for damages?'

'I did, to be honest.'

Collingstone had gone to see Bealing privately in early May 2014. She hadn't wanted to make a scene. But she did want help. She needed help. Daniel needed help. 'He needed a structured settlement?' interjected Glencoyne.

'Something similar, yes.' And Bealing told her he'd sort everything out. He'd been astonishingly sympathetic. He contacted the Alington Trust saying he was looking for an assistant manager; he told Collingstone to present herself in June. He then gave her a job, not expecting her to do anything. But she enjoyed it, and would have loved it, had it not been for Anna Wysocki who couldn't understand why Sarah had been appointed, given her limited experience.

'He told me he needed time to work out the finances,' said Collingstone. 'His main concern seemed to be Debbie.

205

She could never know about Daniel, he said, and I didn't want to disturb his marriage. I wasn't looking for a relationship.'

'You were looking for money?' Glencoyne's tone had subtly changed.

'Yes.'

'Did you come with figures?'

Collingstone sipped some water.

'Figures, Miss Collingstone?'

'Yes. I told him about the damages case. I said this was nothing to do with me. But the cost of nursing, day and night, is astronomical. And I had to look into the future, if I got ill, or died. You can't imagine how worrying it is.'

'So you were seeking a settlement in the region of £2.5 million?'

'Yes.'

'And he agreed to provide you with such a sum, secretly, after which you would have no dealings with each other?'

'Yes. The job was just a way of giving me some money immediately.'

'But you had sex with him on a table.'

Collingstone recoiled as if she'd been slapped.

'You put five scratches on his back.'

'That only happened once.'

'And you'd have liked it to happen again.'

'That's untrue.'

'You wanted him to leave Debbie Bealing. That's why you were pressurising him between December of 2014 and February of 2015. Anna Wysocki had nothing to do with it. You wanted to take Debbie's place because Debbie's place was there for the taking.'

'That is absolutely false,' cried Collingstone, rising to her feet. 'I did not want to have a relationship with Andrew Bealing.'

'But you did. And it happened. Kym Hamilton saw you canoodling. So did Tina Sheldon. Everybody did.'

'I wanted nothing to do with him.'

'Then why scratch his back?'

Collingstone almost shouted her reply. 'Because I made a mistake, because he'd been chasing after me, saying he wished he'd never left me.'

'But you were chasing him,' whispered Glencoyne. 'You bombarded him with phone calls, at work and to his mobile. He'd had to tell Kym Hamilton that he was out, because he couldn't get you off his back.'

'I only wanted to know when the settlement would be finalised. He'd done nothing with regard to the finances and I was worried he might be stringing me along.'

'I thought you were all hot and bothered about health and safety manuals? Or was that a lie as well?'

'I was too scared to tell the truth.'

'That's what you said the last time you tried to explain away a lie – to Mr Benson, right here in this court. Let's finally get to the truth, shall we? Andrew Bealing told you the affair was over, didn't he?'

'No, that is not true.'

'You went to Hopton's Yard to talk money and you got sex and afterwards you felt used.'

'No, no, no.'

'He told you he was staying with Debbie, and you felt the old rage. He was dropping you again, wasn't he?'

'No, no.'

'And all that humiliation and desperation you'd felt at sixteen came back, as he walked down the corridor.'

'No.'

'He was off to sunny Spain while you'd been dumped by the sewage works in Hounslow.'

'No, no, none of this is true.'

'You lost control of yourself. You smashed the bottle on the edge of the table and you went after him. And when you caught him by the door, you stabbed him.'

Collingstone's shoulders were heaving. 'It's not true.'

'And then you watched him crawl like a wounded beast to his death. You followed him, making sure he didn't reach the street.'

'No.'

'What did you say to him, Miss Collingstone?'

'I didn't say anything, I couldn't have done, I wasn't there.'

'You let him call for help and then you kicked the phone out of his hands.'

'I wasn't there, I was at home, listening to a story.'

'And then you stood over him while his blood drained on to the concrete.'

Collingstone was shaking her head and even Mr Justice Oakshott didn't compel her to answer. Glencoyne watched her patiently, as Collingstone had seemingly watched Andrew Bealing. And then, as if no one could save her now, Glencoyne said, 'You made him pay in the end, didn't you? You murdered him.'

Collingstone lifted her contorted face. 'I did not, I swear I didn't, on my son's life.'

Glencoyne paused to write down these last words. Then, eyeing them, she said, 'You really have no limits, do you? You'll even use Daniel's life. You're lying now. You can't stop yourself. It's in your DNA.'

Glencoyne sat down and Benson rose, his back and legs on fire with pain. There was nothing to clarify in re-examination. There was nothing he could do to repair the damage. He let Collingstone return to the dock. When she was seated, head in her hands, he faced the bench ready to call his next and final witness, but he felt a tug on his gown. It was Tess.

'Ralph Collingstone has just collapsed,' she whispered. 'An ambulance is on the way. Looks like a heart attack.'

# 43

After the case had been adjourned until the following morning, Tess and Benson pushed their way through the cameras and went to a pub on Cutter Street. They found a corner with an angle on to a big screen. Sky News was on with the sound off. Sarah Collingstone's collapse was already up there, on the band of text moving beneath the presenter. So was Ralph Collingstone's admission to hospital. How could a jury ever ignore the onslaught of information and comment? The Hopton Yard killing was just everywhere. On the front page. On the radio. On the telly. On Twitter. So was Benson. His face appeared on the screen. But he couldn't see it, because his back was to the room and Tess was the one with a viewing seat.

'It's over,' she said, folding her arms.

Benson agreed. Glencoyne had run a 'prince and the pauper' storyline to honour the dead and then dropped it for 'Bealing was a bastard', but only once she was sure it wouldn't harm her case: once she needed it to show why the mother of a son with special needs might lose her head and kill his father. Collingstone's denials had sounded like the death throes of a pathological liar.

'Camberley warned me,' he said, 'and I still didn't see it coming.'

'There's nothing you could have done.'

'I should have chased all my assumptions to ground and I didn't.'

Tess glanced up. A man was approaching their table. He

was stepping sideways, trying to get a look at Benson's face. She tensed and fear stopped her reacting quickly. The man was suddenly at Benson's side.

'Mr Benson, I just want to say thanks.' The man lowered himself, taking a look over his shoulder. 'I killed a man once. I didn't mean to. He'd been tracking my daughter and she was frightened and I hit him, just once, and he went down. One-punch manslaughter. I did time, fair enough. I'll never get away from what I've done. My daughter won't speak to me and I can't get a job, because, well, I killed a man. So I just want to say thanks for what you're doing. For showing we can still be decent upright people. Thank you.'

He walked off, quickly, before Benson could respond, not wanting to hear a reply. He'd delivered his message; that was all he wanted. He shouldered his way to the door and ducked into the crowd going about their business. He'd come, he'd gone.

'Well, that's answered my question,' said Benson, opening a packet of crisps.

'What question.'

'I was wondering, what's the point? Last night I got thrown into the back of a van and was beaten this side of senseless. They were ex-army, or police, or the ninjas, I don't know. But they knew what they were doing.'

'Beaten?'

'Yes. Up and down my back, my thighs, my buttocks. So I can't wear clothes or sit without pain. They left me the soles of my feet. Which shows you how stupid these people are. Because if they really wanted to stop me, they should have left my back and legs alone and beaten the soles of my feet.'

Tess was appalled. Benson's stand had literally unleashed forces that no one could control. But there was a huge issue at stake, and the stupid couldn't be allowed to win the day. It had to be decided by reasoned argument.

'You can't give up, Will,' she said. 'You represent something very important. It can't be beaten off the agenda.'

Tess felt something warm in her hand. She looked down and saw she was holding Benson's wrist. She'd gripped him. Quickly taking her hand back, she said, 'For what it's worth, in the court of public opinion, you're winning.' She nodded at the screen and he turned.

Richard Merrington was being interviewed outside Westminster. Underneath, the moving text reported the state of play in the war of petitions. 'Paul's Law' had reached 432,791 signatories; the 'Everyone Deserves a Second Chance' corner had garnered 437, 254. Benson turned back, frowning.

'I didn't set out to represent anything or anyone,' he said. 'I'm just someone who's fought tooth and nail to find a way of living with a verdict I can't overturn.'

No, you can't, thought Tess. But I can; and I will. If you're innocent.

# 44

Tess left Benson on Gray's Inn Road and went back to Coker & Dale. Seated at her desk with a second-floor view on to Ely Place, a cul-de-sac and the last privately owned street in London, she picked up the phone and rang Denis Stockwood, her contact at HM Revenue and Customs.

'I need a favour,' she said.

'Don't you always? You want it yesterday and faxed?'

'Yep.'

Tess gave him Paul Harbeton's name, date of birth, address, national insurance number and the name of his last employer, all culled from the Benson brief.

'I just want his employment history.'

'Okay. It's like you never went AWOL. Bye.'

The remark sent Tess into a reverie. She gazed out of the window at the beadle's stone gatehouse and the gold-tipped railings. It was a world away from Strasbourg, and a world away again from Benson's fishmonger conversion in Spitalfields. A world away from the sorts of client who were drawn to Benson. For all of his insistence upon elements of a vanishing legal world, he was closer to the needs of desperate people than anyone she had ever met before. Somebody out there moved . . . standing by the gatehouse was the man who'd been wearing a bomber jacket. He was in a tracksuit now.

'How are things?'

Gordon Hayward had popped his head around the door. He came in, looking desperate, in a way that even Benson couldn't assuage. Tess glanced back towards the street entrance but the man had gone.

'Are you okay?' asked Gordon.

'Yes. Fine. Grand.'

She gave him the rundown, composing herself with a flood of words, wondering why the nutter outside had shifted his attention on to her from Benson. Why was he hanging around the gatehouse? She became calmer, focusing on the bombsite of Court 1.

'It's been a disaster. We asked her if she wanted to change her plea, and she still refuses. After everything that's happened, she's still saying she didn't kill him. She's locked into a world of her own making. I suppose that's why she killed him. He offered her too much reality.'

And if it was a disaster for Collingstone, it was a disaster for Benson. Because he was tarred with the same brush. Her lying and pretence had smeared an already dirtied name. One commentator was already suggesting that he must have known about Collingstone's past and that he was implicated in her attempt to hide it. Tess hadn't said anything, but key quotations had appeared in the text band beneath the Sky presenter. Observers were within a hair of suggesting that Benson must have known that Collingstone was guilty of murder, like him, and he'd used every legal means possible to mislead the court.

'A bad day, then?' said Gordon.

'Yes.'

'I was wondering—'

'No thanks, Gordon, I've got too much to do, I'm sorry.'

'Of course. But you're missing a treat. I'd thought of seafood and Chablis.'

Tess opened the file on her desk. 'It's a prawn sandwich for me, I fear.'

Gordon didn't leave. He was still in the chair facing her. He was one of the legal profession's loud dressers. Subdued grey suit and a violent-blue striped shirt. He opened the button on his jacket, revealing wide yellow braces, which said everything. 'Tess, I've got something to tell you.'

Oh God. 'I'm really busy, Gordon, honestly.'

'This is important.'

'So is this.' She pointed at the opened file.

'No, this can't wait. I have to tell you.'

Tess closed the file, knitting her fingers together. He was a nice guy. There was someone out there for him, someone he'd find one day when he stopped trying so hard.

'This Benson business,' he said. 'It's dividing the firm.'

'And so it should, Gordon. It's an important question.'

'I don't mean about Benson. I mean about you.'

Tess gave her mind a shake. This wasn't news and it wasn't unexpected. Douglas had already told her the partners were unhappy. She raised an eyebrow.

'You've only been with us four months, Tess.'

'How could that change anything, Gordon? Would you want me to play safe until I've been here years?'

'No, of course not.' He ran a hand over his shining head. 'It's why I like you, Tess. You're not scared of upsetting the applecart.'

She felt a flush of liking for this clumsy messenger. 'Gordon, it's simple. People will have to see past me to the issues and the issues can be argued over.'

'No, Tess, you're missing the point. You've only been here four months. Your probationary period ends in two weeks. You've divided the people who can decide whether you stay here or not.'

She hadn't seen that coming; like Benson hadn't seen Glencoyne's shift in strategy. God, the legal world was a nasty, twisted place sometimes. In their own way, people tipped yoghurt on your head and beat you up in the back of a van. She no longer cared about the bearded bastard in the bomber jacket. If he came anywhere near her, she'd kick his teeth in.

'What's your advice, Gordon?' she said.

'You don't need my advice, because you know what to do. I was only warning you.' He got up and went to the door, where he turned, colouring slightly. 'The sandwich. With or without mayonnaise?'

# 45

Benson retrieved the damp Sobranies from the bin and placed them in the microwave. He gave the knob a quick turn and then paced his boat, trying to penetrate Sarah Collingstone's mind. Papillon watched from a dining room chair.

The atmosphere in the holding cells had been tense beyond

description. He had felt like one of those bomb disposal experts, wondering which wire to cut, the yellow or the green? He'd looked her in the eye, coming uncomfortably close to her face.

'Sarah, your father is in hospital, your son is with a social worker, and you are off to Holloway on remand because this judge doesn't trust you any more. All this could have been avoided. Why didn't you tell me the truth? Lie to your father for most of your existence, but why me? I represent you in a court. I'm trying to save your life.'

'Mr Benson, if they'd convict me for having sex with him on the night he was killed, what chance would I have had if I'd told them he was the father of my son, a son he abandoned even before Daniel was born? Look at my life, Mr Benson. It's a mess. It's full of disappointment and failure. Full of hopes that never got off the ground. I survived a car crash for this. And all I've got that gives me meaning is someone who most people turn away from. They can't understand how I could love him as much as I do. Do you know, once, I was standing by a bus stop in Richmond and a woman came up to me, looked me up and down, looked at Daniel, and then she said, "Why don't you put him in a home?" That's my world, Mr Benson. People look at me living by a sewage plant with my boy in a wheelchair and they think she'd kill the man who put her there. That's what Miss Glencoyne said. You heard it yourself. I was convicted the day I was arrested at Dover. I lied because even you wouldn't have been able to help me.'

'Sarah, please tell me, did you kill Andrew Bealing? If you plead now, I've got some mitigation. Hopefully, it'll shorten the number of years you go down.'

'Mr Benson, didn't you hear me? Or are you like Miss Glencoyne? I swore on Daniel's life. I left Hopton's Yard at six-thirty, feeling filthy and used and angry, and I went home to my dad and my son.'

The bright lights of the cell had blown away all the shadows from her face. Even the fine pencil lines had vanished. She'd been pale, her auburn hair disarranged, her lips cracked.

'Okay,' Benson had said. 'I'll do what I can.'

Something popped in the microwave.

After cleaning up the mess, Benson went to bed. And he thought how strange it was that the memory selects something and brings it to mind much later, without any obvious explanation as to why it selected that something in the first place. Because for no apparent reason, Benson remembered Tess de Vere's shoes. He told Papillon all about them:

'They're made of black suede on the sides with black patent leather on top. They've got a low heel and a square toe.'

Benson kept the rest to himself: he'd loved her ankle bones. They'd been like strange fruits on a vine.

Benson woke.

His mobile was ringing. The damn thing was out of reach, on a dresser. He swung his legs out of bed and growled in pain. He hobbled in the dark, banging a toe on the bedstead.

'Yep, this is Benson.' He'd got there just before voicemail kicked in.

'Do you want to know who killed Andrew Bealing?'

Benson's mouth was dry; he was still half asleep; he said he did, but—

'There's a warehouse in Shadwell.'

'Just hold on, who are you?'

'No questions, Mr Benson, just listen very carefully.' He was a Scot and spoke slowly with precision, as if making a recording. 'I repeat, there is a warehouse in Shadwell. Bewell

Street. Written on the front is 'T. W. Hesketh and Sons'. It is abandoned. You will find a door on the south-east wall facing a yard. The door is now open. I have placed a carton of milk by this door. Enter the building, turn right and go up a metal staircase. There will be night lights to guide you. On the second floor you will find another carton of milk by another door. Go through the door on to a landing. You will see a railing. Hold that railing with both hands and wait there for further instructions.'

'When do I—'

'I said no questions, Mr Benson. The night lights will burn for two hours. They have been burning for five minutes. You will find a bicycle secured to your railings. The key is in your post box. You have roughly three miles to cover. You come alone and you contact no one, not even Miss de Vere. Move silently. Wear trainers. Do not bring your phone. One final instruction, Mr Benson. I am a professional. This is how I earn my living. If you deviate from what I have told you to do, I will know. Roger Grange and his wife will end up dead, so will you, and there's a chance I might as well. Speaking for myself, I would like to live a little longer, so do only as I say. Have you understood?'

'Yes.'

'Then make your decision.'


# 46


Benson found everything as the man had said. He followed the small candles up the stairs. He opened the door and stepped on to the landing. He could make out the railing in the light thrown from the tiny flame. He gripped it with both hands. It was like the landing in HMP Beckham Heath.

'Take off your shoes and socks, Mr Benson.' The voice came from the far side, from another landing. 'Undo your trousers. Now put both hands back on the railing. Close your eyes and keep them closed.'

A bright light came on, directed at Benson's face.

'For the purposes of this conversation, you can call me Jock. I belong to an undercover police unit that does not exist. We do not even feature as a secret directory within the Serious Organised Crime Agency. For the purposes of this conversation, I will call it SOCA22. I am based in Liverpool, but we are working with a sister non-existent unit based in London. We'd been watching Andrew Bealing for five years. Tapping his phone. Tapping Grange's phone. And Wellborn's, when he was alive. Their houses are wired. So was Hopton's Yard, and the rest.'

Benson could only see orange and purple spots. Somehow, being blinded, the words seemed louder, their meaning clearer. Bealing was distributing legal highs for a Chinese gang, the Hong Hua. Gogaine. Nopaine. Burst. Banshee Dust. That lot were banned in April. After that he was moving '4-MeTMP' and 'HDEP-28'. They were banned in June. And so it went on. Goes on. The Hong Hua just find a compound that escapes the chemical definition in the law. Before he was killed, Bealing was their man. He carried on spreading the stuff like it was salt on his dinner. He made a lot of money.

'So what went wrong?' asked Benson.

'He wanted out. Went to the police – the ordinary police – and told them he'd trade information for a new identity. He'd give them names. He wanted the Chinese off his back. And he'd had enough of Debbie. The nurse could look after her.'

'So how did he end up dead?'

'We've got an agent in the Hong Hua. A prize. Someone

218

who tells us everything we want to know about rival gangs. Other importers. And distributors like Jack Felbridge who was shifting Class A round the country. Heroin. Crack. The lot. Put your hands back on the rail, Mr Benson. Keep your eyes closed.'

Benson's trousers were slipping. He widened his stance, listening to Jock's slow and precise voice. In effect SOCA22 was permitting the free flow of legal highs in order to keep one step ahead in the war against drugs. It was the lesser of two evils game, only Bealing's bid for a new identity wouldn't only end the game it would compromise a vital source in the Hong Hua, who'd probably end up dead.

'I'm just a cog in a wheel, Mr Benson. I do my part and someone else runs the machine. But it's clear what happened. Bealing went to the Drug Squad. The Drug Squad decision-makers went to SOCA22. We warned our agent. Our agent told the Hong Hua that Bealing was intending to compromise a good arrangement. My guess is that Bealing's contact in the Hong Hua was our agent. Our agent faced exposure.'

'So Bealing was sacrificed to keep a source in place?'

'It's what happens in the real world, Mr Benson. It's how we keep as many kids as possible out of a grave. It's not nice. But it works.'

'So why are you telling me this?'

'Because this isn't what I signed up for. Things have got out of hand. First Wellborn was killed, then Bealing, and now a woman faces a murder rap for a crime she didn't commit, with her father in hospital and her son in care. No, this isn't my idea of keeping the streets clean at a price.'

Benson stared into the splashes of orange and green and blue. 'You said Hopton's Yard was wired?'

'Yes.'

'Then you heard Bealing being killed. It's not a guess. You

219

listened to him being stabbed and you listened to him crawl and die.'

Jock didn't answer immediately. 'You're fast, Mr Benson.'

'You know for sure it wasn't Sarah Collingstone?'

'I do, yes.'

'But you're not prepared to step from behind that light?'

'No. I've got family who depend on me; and I want to live. That's why we're here speaking in this way. This conversation isn't even happening.'

Benson felt a flush of anger. He felt trapped. His trousers were slipping, his feet were cold and he couldn't let go of the rail. But Jock was here. Jock was talking. Jock must have a plan.

'What am I to do?'

'Roger Grange and his wife are in danger. So is Obiora. They're next, once the trial has died down. Their only chance is to speak out, and this trial is the best way. That was Bealing's mistake. He should never have gone to the police. If he'd gone to the press, he'd have been safe. No one would have touched him. Once everything's out in the open, no professional outfit would risk ordering a hit. Only the Italians do that sort of thing. They can't control themselves.'

Benson could see the logic. He liked the joke, too. 'What do I do if they won't listen? They're frightened people out of their depth. Can't you give me the recording? The recording of the killing is decisive. No one would know you'd leaked it. The operation against Bealing is over. All his assets have been liquidated. No one would be compromised. Jock? What do you think? Why not? I could play it to the judge and prosecutor and the case would be dropped. No one would know why. Jock?'

Benson waited but there was no reply. He took his hands off the rail and there was no reprimand. He opened his eyes and he fastened his trousers; he put on his socks and shoes, and he left the building. But not before he'd retrieved the torch and camera tripod from the far landing. And the milk. Benson took the milk. He'd run out.

# 47

Tess opened her eyes and sat bolt upright.

She'd heard a crack against her first-floor drawing room window. Fully awake, she listened intently. Then the window shattered. They'd come back, as she'd expected. Only this time the glass was Georgian and irreplaceable. Grabbing the Webley 455 Battlefield Service Revolver on her bedside table – at Oxford, she'd won all the target shooting competitions (organised around punch and spam fritters), so she knew what she was doing, even when drunk – she made straight for her bedroom window and quietly opened it. A man was heading off. Quite sure he couldn't prove who'd fired the shot without incriminating himself, Tess pulled the trigger, aiming for the right buttock.

The cry was a voice she knew.

'It's only an airgun. I'm so terribly sorry.'

'Well, it damn well hurt,' said Benson.

'I thought you were one of those toe-rags who'd done my other window in.'

'It was a pebble, only a pebble.'

'You should have called.'

'I don't have my phone. And what are you doing with a gun anyway?'

'I'm Irish. It's part of the lets-get-rid-of-the-Brits thing. It's in my genes. My great-grandfather was at the General Post Office in 1916. Beside Connolly.'

'It's a pity he wasn't shot as well.'

Benson went looking for the pebble but soon got distracted by the books. The mews was a sort of annex to the library back home in Ireland. The shelves were a window into her father's academic career as a historian and her mother's passions as a musician. Benson was looking at the titles, the biographies. They were all out of order: Bach, Hendrix, Walton, Elgar, Armstrong . . . he was following the shelves towards a second bookcase . . . with volumes on the Famine, the Rising, the Troubles . . . and Benson's own trial papers, laid out on a nearby table. He was standing right next to it, eyeing a framed letter from James Connolly on the wall.

Tess raised her voice, and it was almost shrill. 'You'll have some tea?'

Benson backed away. 'Absolutely fascinating. I didn't know you were so interested in history.'

'I'm not. They're my dad's.'

'History,' he mused, following her into the kitchen. 'It's always hard to know what really happened when all the main players are dead, don't you think?'

'Yes.'

'Which is why I like trials. Because a trial is an investigation into the past, too, only we get the chance to speak to the people who were there.'

'Yes, I agree.'

'We've got a better chance of getting it right. If we find someone we can trust.'

'Absolutely.

'Which is why I am here at three in the morning throwing stones at your window.'

He glanced back into the sitting room and the packed bookcases, and the table covered in trial papers.

'Sarah Collingstone is innocent,' he said. 'I thought you ought to know.'

and Kingsley Obiora. I wouldn't trust them as far as I could throw them in the air.' Glencoyne tossed the papers on to the conference room table. 'So you'll forgive me if I refuse to take this seriously. What strikes me, however, is this. It's only when your client finally shows the world who she really is that these two knights in shitty armour decide they have to save her. It's too good to be true.'

'But it is true.'

'Let's pretend, then. Grange and Obiora could have told DCI Winter what they knew ages ago. Why come forward at the last moment, in the middle of a trial?'

Benson couldn't answer the question because 'Jock' wanted to stay alive. And even if he did tell her, Glencoyne wouldn't believe him. She'd think that 'Jock' didn't exist, any more than SOCA22 did: that Benson had made up a story to twist their arms. Because when it came to throwing people in the air, she didn't trust Benson either. 'Are you behind this?'

'No.'

'Have you paid them?'

Benson refused to acknowledge the insult; but he turned white with rage.

'You're smart, I'll give you that,' said Glencoyne. 'You've got me hamstrung. I can't ask the jury to draw adverse inferences against the defendant for coming up with this nonsense overnight, first because she didn't, you did, and second because you're going to say it's all DCI Winter's fault. That he should have listened to the ravings of Debbie Bealing.'

'If he'd listened, he might have questioned Grange and Obiora,' said Benson. 'But he didn't listen. And I came up with nothing overnight. All I did was—'

'You set him up, didn't you?' Glencoyne eyed Benson with distaste. 'You asked DCI Winter about Chinese gangs on

Friday and lo and behold you have evidence about Chinese gangs on Tuesday. It stinks, Benson.'

'I'll tell you what stinks. Not bothering to tell me that Bealing was Daniel's father – that Collingstone had first met Bealing when she was sixteen.'

'You already knew.'

'I did not.'

Glencoyne began arranging her wig, making sure none of her black, sharply cut hair was showing. 'When you served that Section 101 notice on the Crown before introducing David Hamilton's bad character, I have to say I was surprised. You'd followed the rules. You'd been straight.' She paused to appraise him, as she'd appraised him in HMP Denton Fields nine years ago. 'This is what I was frightened of when you applied to join the Inner Temple. I thought there was a chance – a small chance – that you just might drag the profession into the gutter. And you have done.' She cast a sneer at the recently served paperwork. 'This sort of thing doesn't work in the long run. You'll be found out. And Camberley will have to accept that she made a mistake in joining her name to yours. You see, Benson, the Bar is an honourable calling. You can never belong.'

He followed her on to the concourse and into Court 1. He felt the choking impotence of his first night in jail. There was nothing he could do. The door had been locked. Someone else had the key. And when the door opened, another inner door would always remain closed; for he was forever a prisoner to his past. He would never get away from the stench of ordure. His own. That of Needles and Jaffa. And the security guard at Hopton's Yard. And the man who'd come into the pub on Cutter Street. They were all so much sewage.

# 50

In truth, though, Glencoyne *was* hamstrung. Benson had no difficulty explaining to Mr Justice Oakshott the reasons for a seismic shift in the defence's position and the late notice to call potentially devastating witnesses. Benson *did* say it was all DCI Winter's fault. Because it *was*. And he got a certain pleasure in stressing the point. Glencoyne couldn't object and she didn't. She was then compelled to agree with Mr Justice Oakshott that while DCI Winter had enjoyed eight months to investigate the case, Mr Benson had raised the issue on Friday and produced the evidence by Tuesday. The concession from Glencoyne's lips – in those precise terms – was music to Benson's ears. Unknown to the judge, of course, was the true state of relations between counsel. Glencoyne had never trusted Benson. Now she despised him. He could feel it; and it gave him a violent hunger to win – and not just this trial but all the others to come. In his guts he felt the defencelessness of all the Sarah Collingstones yet to appear before a court, frightened people, disbelieved and despised. And he would be their defender. The jury were summoned into court and Benson called his witness.

Roger Grange looked like a man who'd lost a lot of weight quickly. The skin on his face was pale and loose. His eyes were large in their sockets. He seemed to be wearing a suit borrowed from a broader man. A wasted neck rose from a large white shirt and tie. The slight tic – a twitching round the mouth before he spoke – created a sense of urgency and tension. He was speaking out of fear and the fear was viral.

'Andy came to see me in September. He was beside himself. He wanted to organise his finances into a trust, putting day-to-day control of money out of Debbie's reach. He was worried she wouldn't be able to cope on her own. I told him he'd have a hell of a fight, because she could contest it, but I said I'd look into it.'

'Did the matter go any further?'

'No.'

'Why not?'

'Because they got to him.'

'Meaning?'

'He was hit. Murdered.'

'Did Mr Bealing indicate why he'd decided to put his wealth into the hands of trustees?'

'Yes.'

'Please tell the jury.'

'He was worried for his life. He was convinced someone was going to kill him?'

'The mother of a child with special needs who was trying to bite £2.5 million out of his backside – to cite another witness?'

'No.'

'You're sure of that?'

'Yes.'

'Did he ever mention Sarah Collingstone to you?'

'Never.'

'Did he mention who he thought might kill him?'

'Yes. But he didn't *think*, he *knew*. He said, "I've got on to the wrong side of a Chinese gang." He said, "I know too much." He said, "They've told me. It'll look like I just went and vanished. Went missing. But I'll be dead." He said, "Roger, I don't know what to do, I'm—"'

'Just calm down, Mr Grange. Have some water. Let's take this a little more slowly.'

Grange drank a glass of water, holding it with both hands. Then Benson took him stage by stage, getting the events in the right order, starting with the death of his solicitor, Hugh

228

Wellborn. How Bealing was convinced the fatal car accident had been a professional assassination. That he'd been killed because Bealing had asked him to find a way of voiding a haulage contract. That Bealing had been unable to extricate himself from a ruthless organisation whose goods he'd been distributing. Had he named the Chinese gang? No. But then Grange volunteered something he hadn't told Tess and which was therefore not in his witness statement:

'I said I'd look at ways of putting money in a safe place for Debbie and then at the door he said there was something else. He'd been having a fling with an employee and—'

'Slow down again, Mr Grange.' Benson had to check his own surprise. He moved on cautiously, sensing sunlight, sensing the fall of shadow upon Glencoyne's mind. 'Who was the employee?'

'A Pole. Anna Wysocki.'

'By fling, you mean—'

'An affair. But it must have been pretty serious because he asked me to hold twenty grand in her name. Off the books.'

'Why?'

'Because of Debbie. He didn't want her to know. Didn't want anyone to know. Which was wishful thinking because everyone knew Andy dipped his whistle here and there—'

Mr Justice Oakshott was faster than Benson: 'Modify your language please, Mr Grange. And we are not remotely interested in what everyone knew. We only want to hear what *you* know.'

'I'm sorry. Well, I certainly knew of a couple. And Debbie must have known about Wysocki because she asked me once if Andrew was giving her one – that's her words, not mine – and I said I hadn't a clue. I didn't want to get involved.'

'And what were you to do with this twenty grand?' asked Benson.

'Andy said if anything happened to him, if he was

"disappeared", I was to give the money to this Wysocki. It was a way of putting her in his will without putting her in his will, if you see what I mean.'

'I do. And did you give the twenty grand to Miss Wysocki?'

'I did. But she wouldn't take it.'

'Where is it now?'

'I added it to Debbie's capital when we liquidated the different Hopton businesses. No one noticed given that the final figure was £11.6 million after tax.'

Benson then swiftly shut down the most obvious avenues of cross-examination open to Glencoyne. Why had he said nothing of this to the police? Because DCI Winter had only been interested in Sarah Collingstone, and he'd been terrified that he, Grange, might go the same way as Wellborn and Bealing. Why speak now? Because he was still terrified. But the defendant's solicitor, Miss de Vere, had urged him to speak out as the best way to protect himself and his family. Yes, he'd taken a risk.

Benson left matters there and he sat down, wondering how Glencoyne would handle the witness who'd obviously told the truth; who'd obviously not been paid; who'd possibly wrecked her case. She couldn't attack him for his silence without compounding DCI Winter's failure to question him. She couldn't attack what he'd actually said without rousing more fear and sharpening his credibility.

'You have been very brave, Mr Grange,' she said. 'I only have two issues to explore with you. First, in relation to Mr Bealing's financial planning. Can you confirm that he had no intention of giving any money at all to this defendant?'

'Absolutely – at least insofar as I had anything to do with it.'

'Well, in the event of his death, you alone were to handle official and unofficial disbursements, weren't you?'

'Yes, for Debbie, through a trust, and Anna Wysocki, under the table.'

'Exactly. And this defendant was to get nothing. Under the table or over the table.'

'That'll do, Miss Glencoyne,' said Mr Justice Oakshott.

'Sorry, my lord. This defendant was excluded from all arrangements, both official and unofficial?'

'So it seems.'

'And finally, let's revisit Mr Bealing's fear of being killed. You quoted him as saying, "They've told me." Did you get the impression he'd had direct contact with the person or persons who'd made the threat?'

'I did, yes.'

'And it was a very specific threat, wasn't it? He would be "disappeared"? There would be no seeming accident?'

'That's right, yes.'

'Thank you, Mr Grange.'

Benson felt the effect of this short cross-examination himself and he saw its effect on the jury. Within a matter of seconds Glencoyne had cut through Grange's evidence as if it was a baroque irrelevance. She'd underlined a Gothic motive to kill and the brutal manner of the killing: there'd been no money for Collingstone and there'd been no mysterious disappearance. The two facts seemed linked. Bealing had upset someone far more dangerous than the Chinese. A woman scorned.

No longer quite so confident, Benson called Kingsley Obiora.

And Glencoyne used the same tactic. After listening to Obiora describe his discovery of sachets containing legal highs rather than green tea and after recounting Mr Bealing's indifference, Glencoyne asked no questions at all. She hadn't even made a note of his evidence. She'd watched, she'd listened and she let him go. It simply wasn't important, she seemed to say. She looked at Benson expectantly, as if puzzled to learn what other distractions he might have procured.

'My lord, I call Ralph Collingstone.'

# 51

And – when her turn came – Glencoyne played another card from the same hand of indifference.

Ralph Collingstone had been released from hospital after a couple of hours on Monday evening. He'd been advised to rest but he'd come to court insistent on giving evidence. And now, at last, it was his turn. Benson had some difficulty controlling him because his answers were long and involved, full of affection and concern for his daughter. Full of speeches he'd make if he were Benson, which Benson had to tailor down to specific answers to specific questions. Eventually his account took form.

Sarah had left Hounslow at around 5.15 p.m. to meet Andrew Bealing. She'd gone to discuss the paperwork demanded by Anna Wysocki. She returned at about 7 p.m. and made a tuna salad, cutting herself on the tin. After supper, the family listened to a story and Sarah went to bed at roughly 10.15 p.m. The next morning, Sarah said she expected to get hell from Anna Wysocki, so she wanted to get away. He suggested France.

Again, Glencoyne wrote nothing down. But she did ask a couple of questions:

'You'd do anything to get your daughter out of this mess, wouldn't you?'

'Yes.'

'Including lie to this court as she has lied to you?'

'No, that's not fair, that's . . .'

And Ralph went into a speech that Mr Justice Oakshott cut short, if only because Glencoyne had sat down. She'd got the answer she was looking for with her first question.

And that was it. Benson proposed to call no more evidence. The anomaly of 'Alan Shaftoe' simply meant that Bealing had been shifting money abroad. Connecting that fact to his murder was tenuous. Arguing that Bealing had intended to disappear in advance of any murder attempt was pure speculation. To air it would only cloud the simplicity of Benson's argument that Bealing had been killed by the people who'd threatened to kill him. It couldn't get any simpler than that; and, as Camberley had stressed more than once, juries like a simple explanation. Benson had everything he wanted for his speech, so when Ralph Collingstone limped from Court 1, Benson said, 'My lord, that concludes the case for the defence.'

Glencoyne, however, hadn't finished. She applied to call rebuttal evidence with respect to two issues that had taken the Crown by surprise.

First – and with Benson's agreement – a statement by Luke Baker was read to the court. The accident investigator deposed what he'd said to Tess: that he'd scrutinised the circumstances surrounding the death of Hugh Wellborn at a notorious accident site shortly after the incident. In such a case he would routinely check for indications of foul play. There had been none.

Finally, Glencoyne called Cathy Turton, a pseudonym for a senior officer working in the Organised Crime Command of the National Crime Agency, which had replaced the Serious Organised Crime Agency in 2013 a group she had joined in 2006. Called at short notice, she had nonetheless studied a transcript of Roger Grange's evidence which, in effect, was a record of what Andrew Bealing had *said*. Whether or not it was *true*, however, was a different matter altogether. Because according to Turton, there were no Chinese gangs known to be operating in south London. And she ought to know, because this was her specialism; and her sources of information weren't limited to NCA operations, or previous SOCA operations, but shared intelligence from MI5, MI6, Interpol, Europol and other bodies whose remit brought them on to her patch.

'The Chinese don't work in this way,' she said. 'Haulage is too risky. For legal highs, they use the internet and the post. It's cheaper and safer and faster.'

'But we have heard evidence from the warehouse manager at Hopton's Yard and he'd come across sachets of Spice in boxes labelled as tea.'

'Sure, individual businesses might have an employee who smuggles the odd crate or two, but you were asking about organised crime and significant shipments of legal highs, and a criminal gang capable of killing a collaborator who seeks to renege on a distribution agreement . . . and this is not something I've come across in London. The internet is the preferred means of bulk trade.'

And no intelligence had ever landed on her desk regarding Andrew Bealing and Hopton's Yard. She would have expected to come across his name if he'd been hand in glove with a known gang.

'And an unknown gang?' asked Benson, before Glencoyne had even sat down.

'Well, if it was an unknown gang, I wouldn't know about it, would I?'

'Precisely, Miss Turton. Do you know everything that's going on in south London?'

'No, I don't.'

'Well, we're broadly agreed, then, aren't we?'

Benson's cross-examination had been instinctive: his mind

had been knocked elsewhere. A small and completely irrelevant detail of Turton's evidence had struck him with the
force of a headbutt. He'd been reeling, unable to work out
the full implications of the blow. In something of a daze, he
went through the motions of responding to what was now
happening in court. Mr Justice Oakshott was asking
Glencoyne if she wanted to recall Anna Wysocki and she
said, 'No, my lord' (because things could only get worse if
she did), and he then asked Benson if he wanted to cross-
examine her again, and *he* said, 'No, my lord' (because as
matters stood, things could hardly get much better). And so
Glencoyne closed her case for the second time and Mr Justice
Oakshott turned to the jury.

'Ladies and gentlemen, you have now heard all the
evidence in the case. Tomorrow you will hear speeches from
counsel. And then, after I have summed up the case, it will
be for you to decide if you are sure Sarah Collingstone killed
Andrew Bealing. For now, please bear in mind my usual
warnings . . .'

Benson's mind had cleared somewhat by the time Mr
Justice Oakshott left the bench. He was still shaken, but he
was now fairly sure he knew exactly what had happened
on the night of the 14th of February 2015. There were a
number of points to tie down, but these were mere detail.
All the evidence was tumbling in one direction, faster than
he could make sense of it.

# 52

Tess had some difficulty understanding Benson's behaviour.
He'd listened to Ralph Collingstone's complaints about
Glencoyne's upsetting cross-examination without comment,

letting the poor man blow himself out, and then he'd said, 'Well, it's over now.' Down in the holding cells with Ralph's daughter, he'd asked if Daniel was okay, only to learn what he already knew – that she wouldn't know because she'd been remanded into custody since the previous evening. As with her father, Tess had taken control, explaining exactly what would happen tomorrow, that they were to try and relax. Outside the Old Bailey, he'd been similarly distracted with Tess, not wanting her notes of evidence, finally heading off in the opposite direction to his chambers. The trial, it seemed, had taken its toll; and so had the disturbed night, and the handling of the late evidence. He looked drained.

Back at Coker & Dale, Tess found a message on her desk from Gordon: 'ECHR judgment today on covert surveillance of legal and non-legal consultations in a police station. You were right in both your predictions. If you want to discuss any of this, do give me a call.'

Tess didn't, on either score.

There was also a fax from Denis Stockwood. He'd sent on the employment history schedule of Paul Harbeton. She ran a finger down the list of employers, hoping to latch on to something but nothing obviously stood out. Then her eye caught on a place, rather than an employer. And—

The phone rang. It was Sally.

'How about the Nightjar? Just for an hour? I'd like to gloat.'

The Nightjar was a 1920s Chicago hideaway on the City Road. No flash exterior just a bird sigil on a double wooden door. Inside, lush decor. Gold light. Glinting bottles at the bar. A jazz sax-man in the corner, eyes closed. A couple of machine guns propped against the wall and it would have been perfect.

'Was I or was I not right?' asked Sally.

'About what?'

'About who, darling. Your client. I said she was hiding a great deal, and she was. I said she was hiding guilt and shame, and she was. I said you couldn't trust her and you couldn't. Which means you're paying. I'll have a Happy Buddha.'

Tess checked the menu and went for a Name of the Samurai. The waitress slinked off.

'If you want another prediction,' said Sally, 'I'd say her greatest secret guilt and shame is the only one she hasn't admitted.'

'Which is?'

'She killed him, for God's sake. You can forget about the Chinese gang. I'm right about Benson, too. You'll see. He's reinventing himself.'

'I don't think I know anyone who speaks drivel quite like you do. You sound like a quack. Hang on a minute . . . you *are* a quack. I forgot.'

'Put your money where your mouth is.'

'I'm not going to gamble on someone's innocence.'

'Bu you are doing already.'

That was true, thought Tess. 'How much, then?'

'Don't be common. I was speaking figuratively.'

'So what are the terms?'

'If I'm right about Benson, you tell me why you really went to Strasbourg. If I'm wrong, I'll pack in graphology.'

'I wouldn't want you to do that,' said Tess. 'I'd lose an *awful* lot of fun.'

'I'm sure you would. But I want to know why you up and went without a word of warning.'

As so often happened with Sally, the joke had turned serious. Between them Tess's move to Strasbourg had been passed off as a sudden whim, one of the surprise decisions to which she was prone. Something Irish. A caprice. But that was a Band-Aid. They both knew it. And out of reverence for friendship, Sally had never tried to strip it away. But it remained painful for both of them because this was the only secret to come between them. Upon Tess's return to London, Sally had taken to pulling at the edge of the plaster, hinting if there'd been a cut it should have healed by now. But she was wrong.

'Why hesitate?' asked Sally, after the cocktails arrived. 'You've already backed Benson in public. You might even lose your job at Coker and Dale. Why not risk everything?'

'Agreed,' said Tess, smiling woodenly, wishing she'd stayed at Ely Place, hoping with depth that Sally was wrong about William Benson. Her own secret was now tied to his . . . it was an intimacy she didn't want. 'May the best woman win.'

With those words the Samurai clinked into the Buddha.

When Tess got back to Ennismore Gardens she went straight upstairs to the drawing room where the Benson trial papers were laid out on a table. Still in her coat she found the pre-sentence report prepared by Geraldine Whitmore dated 21st July 1999, two days before Benson got life. There was one line in it that had come back to her when she'd skimmed over Paul Harbeton's employment history. She read the line again, as if to make sure she wasn't mistaken. She'd spotted a coincidence. Two in fact. And both of them were almost certainly insignificant but they couldn't be left unexplored.

Paul Harbeton had worked exclusively in London except for a period of eight months when he was employed by a scaffolding company based in Norwich. That was between February and October of 1992, when he was twenty-seven years old. At that time Benson's world was centred on Brancaster Staithe, where he lived with his parents and brother. However, when reviewing Benson's character and family background, Geraldine Whitmore recorded that

Benson – like Harbeton – had done a great deal of charitable work, and in 1995 (aged seventeen) he did a thirty-mile sponsored walk along the Peddars Way and Norfolk Coast Path, raising money for the Radwell Brain Trauma Clinic. Which was in Norwich.

It wasn't much, but it was something. Paul Harbeton and William Benson both had a connection to Norwich, though it was separated by a period of three years. Charitable work featured in both their histories. Histories that were joined for ever on a Saturday night in November 1998 when they both went to the Bricklayers Arms on Gresse Street.

# 53

You wouldn't know that Abasiama Agozino had lost her right leg on a land mine. You wouldn't know she'd lost her leg. You wouldn't know she'd lost anything. She was mysteriously complete. Benson marvelled at her appearance. She'd wrapped her hair in bands of coloured silk this time. Her fingers were heavy with rings, all of them cheap and possibly nasty, only they'd been transformed by her hands.

'I remembered what you said about self-hatred,' he said.

Abasiama seemed pleased. She said, 'Good, because I'd forgotten.'

'Is that why you wouldn't tell me?'

'I never repeat anything, you know that,' she said.

Benson had only recalled Abasiama's words when he found himself doing what she'd recommended.

'It was pretty trite, to be honest,' he said. His mobile phone buzzed in his pocket. 'Not something I'd have written down.'

'Perhaps you should have done.'

She'd said he'd only stop hating himself if he let someone else love him. And that meant taking risks. As long as he kept secrets, the fruit would remain in the tree. It would eventually rot. The conversation had come back to Benson as he'd watched Tess walk down Farringdon Street, trying to keep a bead on her green velvet hat as it got smaller and smaller.

'For years now I've just kept myself to myself,' he said. 'It's safer that way, for me, for everyone. But Tess is different. And not just because she comes from the time before I was convicted. She came to me. She was . . . interested in me. That's why I had that panic attack on the boat. No one's been interested in me since I was twenty-one. Except a cat. And even he's a stray.'

'Are you panicking now?'

'Yes.'

'Why?'

'Because she's pulling away already.'

'How do you know?'

'I can feel it. She doesn't look at me any more. She's frightened.' Benson's stomach turned and he broke into a sweat. 'She's got a copy of the brief from my trial. I saw it on a table. I don't know how the hell she got it but she's going over what happened.'

He rode the nausea for a while, ignoring another buzz in his pocket. Abasiama was watching him take control of his breathing, nodding as he went through the checklist. When the sweating had slowed, he said, 'She doesn't trust me. And I thought she did. I thought she was one of the few. But she isn't.'

'What have you to lose if she finds the answers?'

'Everything.'

'What have you to gain?'

Benson wasn't going to say, 'Everything', because that didn't follow at all, except as a linguistic trick.

'You've forgotten already, haven't you?' said Abasiama.

'No, I haven't,' he said, suddenly childish. 'You said I had to take risks. But I don't want to.'

'Well, that's fine, then.'

'What's that's supposed to mean?'

'Just carry on hating yourself. As you said, it's safer that way for everyone. You've always got Papillon.'

In prison Benson had learned to escape the accumulation of strong emotion by boxing up different experiences and then burying them in different places. It had taken years of practice. Contrary to the advice of the prison psychologists, it had been the only way to survive. If Needles was ahead of the philosophers and physicists on understanding the nature of time, he was ahead of Jung and the rest on questions of psychology. People who were 'in touch' with their feelings and brought them all together often killed themselves. It was a tricky one, and Abasiama was doing her best to establish connections between the different fragments of Benson's life. But keeping intense feelings in different compartments had its benefits. It meant he could be beaten up on Seymour Road and then enter the Old Bailey as if nothing had happened. It meant he could talk about the threat from Tess de Vere without thinking about the Hopton Yard killing. And it meant that he could now return to the Hopton Yard killing without thinking about the threat from Tess de Vere. He checked his phone and went to Grapeshots.

'Where the hell have you been?' asked Archie, lumbering away from the bar. 'Didn't you get my messages?'

'I did. But I've been clearing my head for tomorrow.'

'Well, I hope you've got space for this.' Archie ordered a Spitfire for Benson. 'I found out where Alan Shaftoe lives.'

## 54

The next morning Tess went to the Old Bailey earlier than usual. She went straight to Court 1. It was empty save for two court ushers. She walked into the centre of the room and looked at the exhibits table. On it lay Sarah Collingstone's hat and coat along with the broken beer bottle and various bundles of photographs. But Tess was thinking of another case. *R* v. *Benson*. Sixteen years ago this table had looked pretty much the same. Benson's jacket with Harbeton's blood on the sleeve had been laid out beside other bundles of photographs. The only difference was the absence of a murder weapon – something Camberley had stressed but to no avail. Tess turned around and looked up to the public gallery. It was empty.

But sixteen years ago it had been packed. Mainly with the Harbeton family and their supporters. The only person missing was Gary Chilton and he'd felt the exclusion ever since. Aged twelve, he'd been too young to watch the hanging. For that is what it had felt like. Some of the friends were so intimidating that Tess had been scared to be associated with the defence. God knows what Benson had felt. Or his parents, who'd been seated on the back row, utterly isolated. A fearless member of the public had taken pity on them. Tess could see her now. A woman with neat, black hair. She'd probably come to the Old Bailey as a tourist, only to find herself witnessing a tragedy. She turned up every day. She helped Benson's father when his wife collapsed on hearing the verdict; when Harbeton's family cheered as if the winning goal had just landed in the back of the net.

It had been awful. Every day had been awful. Not knowing where the evidence would lead the jury. Feeling the tension in Benson; and the tension in Camberley, who knew what

Tess had only learned much later: that a jury can swing in any direction, regardless of the evidence.

After the court had cleared, Tess had stood at this very spot. She'd been nineteen years old. Only a week earlier she'd imagined a future in shipping law because it sounded exotic. Cargo lost at sea. Proceedings in London arising from a contract signed in Cairo between parties based in Liberia and Hong Kong. She'd come to Hutton, Braithwaite and Jones of Field Court, London, intending to shadow Charles Hutton who handled this sort of thing, but then George Braithwaite had suggested she come and see a slice of real life. Standing here, Tess had asked Braithwaite if she could keep her copy of the brief. Standing here, she'd changed the direction of her life. She'd abandoned a glamorous future because of William Benson, the son of a fisherman from Brancaster Staithe. A philosophy student who loved the Proclaimers. And Tess now had a sudden burning insight. She didn't regret it for one moment. She would never regret it, even if the Buddha turned out to be right.

# 55

Tess had taken her place in the solicitor's benches. The public gallery was full. The press were squashed together. The jury were expectant. Mr Justice Oakshott was arranging his papers. Benson sat immobile. Collingstone was in the dock with the awful isolation of someone who might not be going home. Glencoyne had her eyes on the bench, waiting for a signal from the judge.

'When you're ready, Miss Glencoyne.'

'Thank you, my lord. Ladies and gentlemen of the jury, do you recall the beginning of this trial, when I first addressed you? I warned you that you'd find yourselves moved by pity. And I'm sure you have been. Who could look upon Sarah Collingstone and not feel anything but pity? But you must now examine the evidence dispassionately.'

Unlike Benson, Tess had been following the media coverage of the Hopton Yard killing. Day by day the debate about Benson's presence at the Bar had been displaced by reports of his performance in court. Commentators and columnists had expected him to falter and fall. He was conducting a murder trial without the requisite skill and experience. The tone of censure was uniformly sharp. But, come the day, Benson hadn't only skilfully exposed weaknesses in the Crown's case, he'd shown the investigation to be critically flawed. The critics, in turn, had begun to change their perception of the man who'd outraged their sensibilities. Having suggested he'd colluded with a lying defendant (after Collingstone had been stripped naked), they'd been compelled to acknowledge his unrelenting determination (after Grange had revealed the previous death threat). The trend, then, between reporters and observers was heading in the same direction. Regardless of his conviction and inexperience, Benson had the aura of a champion. All of which placed Glencoyne under intense pressure. For while the case was publicly about the murder of Andrew Bealing, in the legal world it was also about the reputation of a senior QC. She was meant to have wiped the floor with Benson. And she hadn't done.

'Mr Benson is going to talk to you at length about Andrew Bealing's secret life. The life away from Debbie with Anna Wysocki. The life away from the Alington Trust with a criminal organisation. He'll talk to you about the deadly nature of legal highs. He'll talk to you about Daniel, and how Andrew Bealing abandoned him and used his mother for a one-night stand, just to shut her up. By the time he's finished, you won't like Andrew Bealing very much. But he'll tell you that doesn't mean he deserved to die. And then he'll talk to you about sodium streetlamps and how the DNA of an innocent woman can be transferred on to a bottle. He'll ridicule DCI Winter over a tin of tuna. He'll tell you the police don't know everything, even when they work for the National Crime Agency. He'll tell you the gang that promised to kill Andrew Bealing killed Andrew Bealing. And if you have any doubts, he'll remind you about Kym Hamilton's husband, David. He'll have all the bases covered and he'll do everything he can to take your eye away from the terrible, tragic truth of this case.'

Glencoyne had spiked Benson's speech. By mapping out what he'd say, she'd robbed his words of freshness and indignation. When spoken later in the day, they'd sound slightly worn and possibly hollow. The brighter light would shine on Glencoyne's sympathetic assault upon the credibility of Sarah Collingstone. Tess listened as she went back to the summer of 1997, when a young girl who'd just lost her mother took a fateful train to Portsmouth.

The climax of Glencoyne's speech came just before the midday break. The court was left with the hideous image of Sarah Collingstone standing over her victim as he bled to death. Benson declined lunch and retired to a conference room with the brief and his notes of evidence. For a moment Tess watched him through a window: he was intensely concentrated, comparing documents. Back in court at 2 p.m., a fever of expectation joined the jury to the public gallery to the press to the ushers and to the clerks. Tess's heart was beating viciously. What was Benson going to say? Even Glencoyne looked brittle with anticipation.

'Mr Benson,' said Mr Justice Oakshott, invitingly.

'I'm grateful, my lord,' said Benson, rising. 'But I don't propose to address the jury.'

If a ceiling could fall silently, the ornate plasterwork of Court 1 seemed to have collapsed. And then the dust from the crash rose everywhere. The press were whispering, the public were talking, the usher was demanding order.

'Silence, please, or I will clear the gallery,' said Mr Justice Oakshott. And then, with great deliberation: 'I beg your pardon, Mr Benson?'

'I have nothing to say that will assist this jury.'

'Are you sure? This is a grave and unprecedented step. Counsel should never waive the right to urge a jury to have a reasonable doubt.'

'It is the step I wish to take, my lord. If I hadn't already made the decision, I'd have said that Miss Glencoyne expressed my case with commendable precision, though I would never have ridiculed DCI Winter and his colleagues. I leave matters as they are, my lord, because I am confident this jury already knows the decision they must make. I place my client in their hands. I await their verdict.'

Mr Justice Oakshott began his summing up of the evidence. But his calm, measured delivery did nothing to diffuse the atmosphere of excitement that had filled the court. Tess's heart wouldn't slow down. This had been no cheap trick. Benson hadn't outmanoeuvred Glencoyne at the last moment, spiking her strategy as she had tried to spike his speech. He'd genuinely planned to say nothing, which now made Glencoyne's long exhortation sound like she'd tried too hard. It was an incredibly daring move – a move he could never repeat in the future. Benson had told the jury he trusted them; and in return – Tess could feel it in the air – they trusted him. There was mutual respect. He hadn't tried to persuade them of anything; and in so doing he'd made his own case large in their minds. Everyone in Court 1 had been thrown by the decision, but none more so than Tess. Because she'd seen Benson hard at work in a conference room. He'd had no appetite. He'd had too much to do. But if he planned to say nothing, why had he been poring over the evidence?

# 56

Benson found the waiting excruciating. After Mr Justice Oakshott had finished summing up the evidence, the jury were sent home. Unable to bear any company, Benson shunned Archie and Tess and took to the canal. But the press were there on the banks, taking photographs, all the way to St Pancras Basin. People shouted his name. For the first time since his release, Benson couldn't work out if it was praise or abuse. He barely slept. And the next morning, he had to elbow his way through cameras and microphones fielding questions, as much about the case as about himself. The cloud he'd been living under had begun to lift. A different light was falling on him; and it was warm.

The waiting got harder as the morning dragged on. Benson was well aware that he'd taken an immense risk. Waiving his right to have the last word in a murder trial was unheard of. But Benson had felt in the marrow of his bones that it was the right thing to do, in this particular case, before this particular jury. It hadn't been a decision. It had been a kind of obedience. But the longer the jury were out, the more he began to question the certainty that had seized him when he'd opened his notebook to plan his speech, only to close it again. He began to wonder if he'd missed a golden opportunity to move hearts and minds.

It was unbearable.

The hanging around reminded him of his own ordeal. He sat with Tess as he'd sat with her all those years ago, only this time they couldn't find any words to pass across the table. She'd tied her name to his. Benson's gambit was now hers, too. If Sarah Collingstone was convicted, the decision to make no speech would mar both their careers.

But if the jury let her go . . .

They still hadn't made a decision by lunch time. Mr Justice Oakshott summoned everyone to court at 2.30 p.m. He asked the foreman if they'd reached a unanimous verdict and they hadn't. They were sent out with a direction to reach such a verdict if at all possible. An hour later, Mr Justice Oakshott convened everyone again. The same reply was given to the same question. This time, Mr Justice Oakshott said he still wanted a unanimous verdict but, failing in that, he would accept one by a majority of 11-1 or 10-2.

The jury filed out and Benson turned to leave, but Glencoyne was standing in his way.

'I regret how I spoke to you, Benson,' she said. 'I should never have accused you of manufacturing evidence or paying a witness. That was reprehensible. I am sorry.'

'Thank you.'

'Your performance in this trial has been remarkable and I congratulate you.'

'Thank you.'

'But I would be dishonest if I was to say that I will ever accept you at the Bar. I won't. For my part, your conviction for murder is a stain that cannot be erased, even by genius. I am sorry that I cannot support you.'

'Thank you.' Benson wanted to say more and he called her back after she'd moved on. 'You ought to know that I respected you for refusing my application to join the Inner Temple. I respect your honesty now. I will continue to respect your opposition in the future.'

Glencoyne offered her hand and Benson took it. Then she left court.

Fifteen minutes later he went to the toilets and threw up twenty-four hours of anxiety. By a strange quirk of circumstance, on leaving the cubicle he confronted the barrister who'd heard him vomit at the beginning of the trial. Winston Corby. And Corby looked at him very differently this time. On stepping outside, Benson heard the announcement:

'All parties to Court One, please.'

At the beginning of the trial Benson had spotted a woman juror with short curly hair. She was a redhead with strident freckles. The blouse was complimentary. White with red spots. And he had concluded that she was either a person who led others or followed them, keeping quiet. He'd gambled on the former, addressing a number of remarks in her direction. The jurors had selected her as their foreman and she was now standing, waiting for the questions from the clerk.

'Have at least ten of you agreed on your verdict?'

'Yes.'

'What is your verdict? Please only answer "guilty" or "not guilty".'

There was no pause between the question and her answer but time still seemed to crawl; and then it came:

'Not guilty.'

Benson collapsed. Not physically, but within himself. He turned towards the dock, thinking he might fall. Sarah Collingstone was weeping, her face covered by her hands. Applause was thundering from the public gallery. Members of the press were joining in. There were smiles of triumph on the faces of those who'd merely been watching. Mr Justice Oakshott was calling for order and Benson had to sit down. His vision was blurred and his throat unbearably constricted. He thought he might sob, and not just because the jury had let Sarah Collingstone go. He'd been ambushed by a memory. This is what he'd wanted for himself. Not the cheering, not the adulation. Just two words. And they'd been denied him.

# 57

Tess wouldn't dare to argue with Camberley, and Camberley had made it clear she was paying. Ever the gentleman, George Braithwaite protested for a decent interval before capitulating. Then he plumped for the Coq de Bruyère. He'd studied the menu intently, weighing up one potential rapture against another, carefully avoiding any direct conversation with Tess, for this was the first time they'd met since the day Benson was sentenced to life, when he'd urged her to keep well away from a convicted murderer. She hadn't done. Now it was too late. On shaking hands, Braithwaite's pained smile seemed to say he wished she'd taken his advice. And then he'd become indignant, insisting that Helen couldn't *possibly* meet the bill. They were seated in Le Tour de Saint Martin, a small restaurant behind the British Museum. The voice of Edith Piaf, heavy velvet curtains and an open fire transported them from London to some forgotten corner of rural France. Archie, Benson and Tess were the guests of honour, for Benson would hear of no distinction between the three of them.

Tess soon forgot Braithwaite's manner because she was watching Benson with interest. While everyone else got pleasantly drunk – Tess included – he remained sober. And she knew why. He needed to be able to protect himself. Any moments of civilised excess had to take place on *The Wooden Doll* with Papillon. But there was something else about Benson this evening. All the praise – and it was high praise

– seemed to pass him by as if he hadn't quite heard what was being said. His mind was elsewhere. But the compliments had an effect on Tess.

Combined with the country wine, the simple fare and the warbling '*Non, je ne regrette rien*', she increasingly began to think she no longer cared if Benson had killed Paul Harbeton or not. It had no bearing upon his dogged fight in Court 1. A fight that would never have been fought if she hadn't suggested that he should come to the Bar. She felt a part of his victory. She'd been there at the beginning of his journey and she'd been there for his first big case. She belonged. And what did it matter if he had orchestrated that article in the *Guardian* to bring her on board? It's what she'd wanted. And Benson needed friends in a friendless legal world. Was it any surprise that he'd resorted to subterfuge?

'*Non, je ne regrette rien* . . .'

Douglas had suggested that if Benson was guilty then he must be a pathological liar; he must be diseased; and he was probably exploiting Tess. For her own good, he'd urged her to shun him. She looked at him now, listening to Camberley: they were like mother and son, patron and protégé. If Benson had exploited Tess, he'd exploited Camberley even more . . . and that was inconceivable. Douglas, out of caution and concern, had got it wrong. Oddly enough, thought Tess, the person who'd probably come nearest to the truth was Sally. If Benson *had* killed Paul Harbeton, then he was the sort of person who'd never forgive himself. Guilty or not guilty, he still longed for his innocence. Was such a man to be shunned, if he'd paid his debt? Had Tess made a mistake by joining the small group of people who were prepared to help him?

'*Non, je ne regrette rien* . . .'

She ordered a Calva and made two decisions. First, she'd

call Sally and tell her the bet between the Samurai and Buddha was off. Second, she'd cancel the planned meeting with Angela Temple, the former manager of the Radwell Brain Trauma Clinic. Who cared if Benson and Harbeton shared a connection to Norwich? It probably meant nothing anyway.

'*Non, je ne regrette rien . . .*'

After taxis had taken Camberley and Braithwaite home, Tess, Benson and Archie lingered on the pavement of Russell Street. An evening spent discussing the acquittal of Sarah Collingstone had raised an inevitable question. Archie gave it voice:

'Who the hell killed Andrew Bealing?'

It could have been a Chinese gang. It could have been David Hamilton. It could have been anyone. Not knowing gave an unsatisfactory conclusion to the trial. It did to every murder trial where there was no conviction. The flip side of victory was unease.

'I wish I knew,' said Archie, hailing another black cab.

'So do I,' said Tess. 'But I doubt if we'll ever find—'

'I know what happened,' said Benson, opening the door for Tess, who then paused: she'd leaned to kiss him goodnight, coming so close her lips had touched the hairs on his face, but then Archie, swaying, spoke: 'What are you on about?'

Tess withdrew, fractionally, but that fraction was like a thousand miles.

'I know who killed him,' said Benson. His hand brushed against hers. 'I know how it was done and why. I'm going to bring this case to a complete close. Do you want to be involved?'

The question was addressed to both of them. Tess looked at Archie and Archie looked at Tess and Archie spoke for them both.

'Yes.'

*    *    *

The taxi dropped Tess at the cobbled entrance to Ennismore Gardens Mews. She could still feel the tingle from Benson's stubble on her lips; she could smell his skin; she could see the desire in his eyes – so different to Farsely's coarse hunger, that seeming tenderness that turned into the longing for a kebab – and it had wounded her. He was beseeching and at the same time so very far off, scared to come out of his darkness, begging her to come to him. All in a quick look by the door of a taxi. By an effort of will, she pulled herself away from the memory of his touch, settling her mind, instead, on Benson's avowal and declaration, understanding now why he'd been studying the evidence when she'd thought he was preparing his speech; understanding why he'd been distracted during Camberley's bonfire of compliments. But she was worried, because counsel aren't meant to—

'Miss de Vere, give me a moment.'

Tess spun round. The man who'd waited by the beadle's gatehouse had been waiting by her home. He stepped forward into the light of a streetlamp, drawing back the hood of his tracksuit. But she felt no fear: because, close up, this man was the frightened one. He cowered, keeping himself out of arm's reach. He glanced up and down the lane.

'Will you give a message to Mr Benson?'

'Yes.'

'Then tell him thanks. Thanks from me and thanks from all the others.'

The man's head was shaven. Old surgical scars converged on his scalp like a motorway junction.

'Thanks for what?' she asked.

'For killing Paul Harbeton, because Paul Harbeton was a bad man, and if Mr Benson hadn't done it someone else would've done, eventually. I wish I had. You can tell him that. I wish I'd had the guts to do it myself, but I'm not well, you see, even now . . .'

253

He looked over his shoulder.

'Why not tell him yourself?' asked Tess.

'I daren't be seen with him. I've tried, but I'm worried they're watching.'

'Who are they?'

'I don't know. But if they'll beat him up, they'd beat me up. You can tell him I called the police the other night. I've cleaned up the rubbish, too. It's my way of saying thanks. Tell him I put the cat in his garden. That was a present. To say thanks. And give him my message, will you?'

The man grimaced as if he'd suffered a sudden searing headache.

Tess took a step forward. 'Do you want me to call a doctor?'

'No, I just can't remember what I was going to say. I'm not too sure about what I've said, either . . . but you got it, didn't you? Tell Mr Benson, okay?'

He then backed off and ran, loping to his right side, one leg refusing to do as it was told.

Tess stayed in the street for some while wondering what to do; wondering what to make of this bizarre midnight visitation. When she turned in, she'd made some fresh decisions. She wouldn't be telling Benson; she wouldn't be calling Sally and she wouldn't be cancelling the meeting with Angela Temple.

# PART FIVE

## 'Who the hell killed Andrew Bealing?'

(Mr Archie Congreve, Clerk to Mr W. Benson Esq.)

*Benson heard a soft scraping sound and looked over. A piece of paper had been slipped beneath the cell door. On reading it, he didn't know what to feel. This is what he'd been waiting for, and now that it had finally happened, he didn't really want it.*

*'What's up, Rizla?' said Needles.*

*'I'm moving out. I've been transferred.'*

*'When?'*

*'Tomorrow.'*

*'What time?'*

*'First thing.'*

*Needles didn't seem surprised. But then again, nothing surprised Needles. He'd learned to go with the flow, to roll with whatever happened. It was another survival trick. The old man had mastered them all.*

*That night, in the dark, Benson lay on his back, hands behind his head. And he remembered his first night, when he'd curled in foetal anguish, his hands clenched, holding on to nothing but a sliver of hope. He could so easily have dropped it. But he hadn't. And that was because of Needles. He'd shown him what he had to do, which had made it possible for him to study the transcripts, the articles and the law books. And he was okay, too. Sort of. Unhappy, reserved, cautious, numbed . . . but okay. He'd make it back to the real world.*

*'Thanks, Needles.'*

*'What for?'*

*He'd just broken wind.*

*'For showing me the ropes.'*

257

'No problem, son.'

They'd spent endless hours together. They knew each other's habits as if they were family. They'd become strangely close, if only because Needles, in breaking his own rules, had told Benson every personal detail he could retrieve from his broken mind. He'd brought out these snapshots of memory over hooch as if Benson might keep them for him, put them in order, and write the names and explanations underneath.

'Thanks, Rizla.'

'What for?'

'Ah . . . I dunno.'

The next morning Benson jumped off his bunk as soon as he heard the key enter the lock. He'd warmed to the idea of moving. He could do with a change. He'd be nearer home. The door swung open, and Needles looked up and said:

'Where are you going?'

'I'm moving out. I've been transferred.'

'What? Now?'

'Yep.'

Needles gave a shrug and came over. 'Well, good luck, son.'

They shook hands and Benson's eye strayed to Needles' locker. Folded on top, neatly, was the yellow woollen scarf. Needles had finished it. The months of knitting and undoing stitches and knitting again had finally come to an end. He was about to ask for it, as a memento, when the guard pulled him by the arm.

He was taken to HMP Codrington. He was two'd up with a lad from Warsaw who didn't speak any English. Three days later Benson was lying on his bed reading the paper when he had one of those violent emotional experiences that have to be boxed up and buried, all on its own.

*Albert Seabrook, sixty-seven, a prisoner at HMP Kensal Green, had been found dead in his cell. A review was underway in relation to the effectiveness of risk assessments and the prevailing system of earned privileges at the establishment. Seabrook, serving eighteen months for non-payment of fines, contempt of court and handling stolen goods, had been granted permission to use knitting needles and wool. He'd subsequently knitted a scarf and hung himself. No one at HMP Kensal Green was available for comment.*

# 58

Papillion was purring like a Soviet tank without an exhaust system. The papers – tabloid and broadsheet – were as effusive as Camberley had been the night before. Archie had brought a selection to *The Wooden Doll* first thing in the morning. So had Tess. The two of them were reading out select passages as a preliminary to whatever Benson now planned to do. They'd been told there was no time to waste. Benson was only half listening. He was uncomfortable with the praise, somehow. But he was pleased. Pleased for Sarah. And pleased for the men and women banged up out there who might think their life is over; that they'll never make it back to normal life, and a normal job. Maybe just one of them might think they, too, could start again.

'So why won't you tell us what you know?' said Archie, throwing the *Independent* on the table.

'I know it's irritating but just indulge me, please. Call me infantile. But the resolution of this case has become personal; and I'm a private man.'

Tess folded the *Irish Times*. 'When did you find out?'

'Good question – and nice try – but you'll have to wait.

259

Fact is, the true explanation was staring us in the face from the very beginning. There's one issue I ought to have explored and I didn't – neither did Winter nor Glencoyne. Terribly basic. We were all a bit too hooked on that DNA. But no matter. In the long run, I think what we're doing now will be best for everyone.'

'So what happens now?' said Archie.

'We confront Anna Wysocki before she leaves the country.'

'How do you know she plans to leave the country?'

'Because the trial's over. She has no reason to remain in the UK. And because it's the only way to get your hands on £3.7 million.'

To make sure she was there, Archie rang her number and offered a new central heating system with free maintenance for two years. She didn't want one. She was going home to Poland.

Alan Richard Shaftoe had lived at a Clapham address registered to Hopton Residential Holdings Ltd. According to Benson's source – a well-connected member of the Tuesday Club who'd served two years for possession of false identity documents with improper intent – Shaftoe had bought a false passport on the deep web for £2000 in June 2014. It had been sent to his 'home' address, which also happened to be Anna Wysocki's – for she was housed in a HRH Ltd flat. Benson had concluded that Bealing obtained the passport as part of a plan to evade the gang he'd tried to shop to the police – the Hong Hua. That's what 'Jock' had revealed at the risk of his life. The police hadn't come up with a false identity so Bealing took matters into his own hands. Benson, while not being surprised to learn of Bealing's purchase – it confirmed what he'd already concluded – had seen another explanation. And bringing it into the open was now his prime objective, to secure a deeper kind of justice.

'The police never found that false passport,' said Tess. She was at the wheel of her Austin Cooper. Archie was squashed in the front. Benson was seated in the back.

'Which means Wysocki must have it,' said Archie.

'I'd say the killer,' said Benson, preferring a precise description.

He felt this with certainty. The finding of that document, a secret bid to escape, had sealed Bealing's fate.

# 59

Anna Wysocki no longer lived in Clapham because the property had been sold by Debbie Bealing within a month of her husband's death. She'd lost her job, too, because the supermarket in Balham had been sold to a developer a week later. Given the evidence of Roger Grange, it was clear that Debbie had relished these transactions above all the others. She'd got her own back on one of her husband's innumerable lovers. Out on her ear, Wysocki had found a couple of rooms in Streatham Vale. At trial she'd said she was now unemployed.

'Why did you do it?' asked Benson.

They hadn't forced their way in. He had given her the choice of talking to him or talking to DCI Winter who, he imagined, would want to know a lot more than the colour of her coat under sodium lighting.

'I didn't kill him.'

'The evidence says you did. You knew Bealing was at Hopton's Yard. You knew Collingstone had gone to see him. You have no alibi for that night. You saw them through the peephole in the front door. You waited until Collingstone had gone and then—'

'That's not what happened.'

'Look, Anna, I know about Alan Shaftoe. DCI Winter doesn't. I know about the £3.7 million in Zurich. DCI Winter doesn't. All it takes is one phone call and you won't see Warsaw for at least fourteen years. The tariff's gone up since my time. And believe me, Anna, you don't want to go to prison. It's very unpleasant. I knew this guy called the Gaffer and—'

'You've got it all wrong.'

Her blonde hair was dishevelled. She was sitting on the edge of a worn-out sofa picking at painted nails. Benson allowed himself a reflection: even beautiful women look awful when they're terrified.

'It's not what happened,' she repeated, placing her elbows on her knees and peering through cupped hands as if they were blinkers.

'Call Winter, please, Tess.'

Tess took out her phone.

'No, wait. Please. Just a minute. I need to think.'

'No, you don't. You've had plenty of time. This is your last chance. Tell me what you'd planned.'

Bealing said he loved her. Really loved her. He'd only married Debbie because Joe Hopton pushed him into it. His daughter was knocking thirty and he'd wanted someone to take over the haulage business. So he let himself get hitched for money, for the chance of running his own show. But Joe kept his hands on the reins and he made sure that Debbie retained a controlling interest in every new venture. As regards Debbie herself, she was fine if she took her medication, but she could use her illness to get her own way. If they had a row, and Debbie didn't like the outcome, she'd stop taking her tablets. After Joe's death, things got worse, that's why he paid for a nurse, Darren Weaver. Her dependence on Bealing had become more intense and he couldn't cope; didn't want to cope. By then, Wysocki had known Bealing for three years. The affair started like an apple falling from a tree in autumn. It was inevitable.

'I wanted him to get a divorce,' said Wysocki, her eyes wet with tears, 'but he thought it was almost impossible. Debbie would never agree. She'd harass us for ever. And she'd never agree to any financial settlement. It would be a fight in court with Debbie self-harming during the adjournments. And then Sarah Collingstone turned up.'

'Is that when he got the idea?' said Benson.

'What idea?'

'Don't be disingenuous, Miss Wysocki. The idea got Bealing killed. The idea to disappear into thin air.'

'Yes.'

'He'd already found that sachet of Spice from China with Kingsley Obiora and it gave him a flash of inspiration. Am I right?'

'Yes.'

'He linked it to the death of Hugh Wellborn – who'd simply driven too fast into a bend – and he came up with a story. A bloody good story, frankly. One that fooled everyone, ultimately. Including me, my colleagues and a jury.'

Wysocki started bending her fingers back, one after the other. 'I had nothing to do with this, I just went along with what he'd—'

'Stop washing your hands, Miss Wysocki. The blood won't come off. He started spreading a rumour that he'd been threatened by a Chinese gang, didn't he?'

'Yes. He told some other transport people and Roger Grange and Debbie. He let them all know that he was frightened and that he might just vanish one day and he was hoping the police would then start asking questions and they'd find out about the threat and that he'd tried to make sure Debbie was okay financially, with a trust, and they'd think he must have been disappeared, murdered, and after a few years he'd be declared dead anyway and we'd be free and there'd be no inquiry.'

'Seven years, in fact.'

'Yes.'

'And while that story was being put about, Mr Bealing was shifting money abroad, wasn't he?'

'Yes.' Wysocki was curling her fingers now, and making them crack, one after the other. 'And I was to join him six months after he'd gone.'

'The wait made comfortable by the twenty grand from Roger Grange?'

'Yes.'

'So Debbie would grieve and take more tablets. The nurse would come five times a week. Collingstone would crawl back under her stone. And you two would go for a walk in the Carpathians.'

Wysocki looked up. 'I never knew Andrew was the father of Collingstone's child, I swear. I only discovered that in the trial.'

'Well, you can thank Collingstone's child for the money in Zurich. Because Bealing was stealing it from him. Where is Bealing's passport in the name of Alan Shaftoe?'

'I don't know. He kept it at Hopton's Yard, away from Debbie.'

'But it wasn't there when the police found the body.'

'Then someone must have taken it.'

'I agree. You know the account number, don't you?'

She hesitated a fraction too long and Benson turned to Tess. 'Call Winter, I've had enough.'

'No, stop, please.' Wysocki pulled open a drawer and took out a brown envelope. 'Take it. I don't want it.'

Benson thought about the reply for a moment then he

said: 'You are a signatory to the account, aren't you?'

'Yes.'

'You do realise this makes you guilty of various offences – more than I care to spell out?'

'I just went along with Andrew.'

'A number of Germans said something very similar at Nuremberg. Coming from Poland, I'd have thought you were aware of that defence. It didn't work at trial. And it won't work at yours. If things go that far.'

He turned to Tess and Archie. Both of them were slightly open-mouthed. 'Do you mind waiting outside a moment? I've got one last question, and it's private.'

After they'd gone, he said, 'If you went along with Andrew, will you go along with me? This time everything will work out fine. I promise.'

# 60

Benson sat in the front passenger seat. He was dying for a cigarette. He'd spent ages that morning trying to find a packet of Marlboro that he'd hidden somewhere, but all the usual places were bare. He'd vowed to stop smoking after the trial, expecting a drop in tension, but the passing of that landmark had merely increased his desperation. Because the trial of Sarah Collingstone wasn't truly over. Neither Tess nor Archie were talking – they were staring into space, numbed – so Benson, craving a distraction, switched on the radio.

*A thirty-seven-year-old man had been arrested in relation to the killing of Diane Heybridge. The so-called 'Blood Orange Murder'. He'd been taken to—*

'I don't get it,' said Archie from the back seat. 'If there was no Chinese gang shifting legal highs through Hopton

Transport, who the hell was 'Jock', the undercover copper with an agent in the Hong Hua?'

Benson looked at Tess. Her hands were gripping the wheel as if she was shifting through Wimbledon like a bat out of hell.

'I mean this Jock was for real,' said Archie. 'He gets Benson out of bed in the middle of the night. He gives him a monumental heap of crap so that you end up putting the screws on Grange and Obiora. And they then give evidence about the Chinese . . . evidence we needed if Collingstone was going to have any chance of being acquitted. But if there's no Chinese gang, then Jock was no policeman. He must have been working with the killer. Why else go to the bother?'

*DCI Stuart Goodshaw refused to comment on the inquiry save to say—*

'I know what happened,' said Tess, her arms relaxing on the wheel.

'Well, fill me in,' said Archie.

'The explanation has been there from the very beginning. Their names keep coming up all the time. They're always on the edge of the evidence. I just didn't see it.'

'And I still haven't.'

'You have, Archie. Like Benson said, we got hooked on that DNA. Who benefited from Andrew Bealing's death? And I mean *really* benefited.'

Archie thought for a moment. 'Debbie. But she lost out, too, for God's sake.'

'Did she? Take another look. She knew Bealing had lots of affairs. She knew about Anna Wysocki. We know that Bealing was shifting money abroad and thinking of tying up the rest in a trust fund. Maybe Debbie found out. This was a business built by her father, and Bealing was planning to make her a powerless beneficiary. I reckon Debbie was pretty sick of being powerless.'

*The dead woman's family, speaking through their legal representative, had expressed relief that—*

'But she's crackers,' said Archie.

'No, she's not,' said Tess. 'She's okay if she takes her medication. She uses her illness to her advantage. She's used it to win arguments and she used it to keep herself off the suspect list.'

'God, I must be stupid, I just don't see it.'

'She had no alibi for the night Bealing was killed, Archie. The police just accepted she was at home all evening, on her own, as usual. But she wasn't at home all evening. She came to Hopton's Yard and looked through the window and saw her husband with yet another woman. Not Wysocki, but Collingstone. The husband who was planning to squeeze her out of her dad's business. She went home, all upset and then she came back later, sick of him, sick of being walked over. And Bealing, of course, let her in. She obviously went ape-shit. It was a pretty savage attack.'

*Heybridge's body had been found by—*

'You're right, Tess,' said Archie, leaning forward, a meaty hand gripping each of the back rests. 'The police never questioned her. When they came round the next morning, she got herself sectioned. Winter just accepted that she was climbing the walls. He called a doctor.'

'And a nurse,' said Tess.

'Meaning?'

'She asked for him. She only needed a doctor, but she asked for Darren Weaver, probably the person who knew her best. He'd been coming to see her three times a week for years. They were close. When Debbie couldn't make the Christmas party, it was Weaver who rang Kym Hamilton to say so. You'd have thought they were a couple, don't you think? That's what the gossip was, anyway. Remember? According to the office banter, he serviced her with his thermometer.'

Archie slowly sat back. 'They were having an affair.'

'Yes. And who'd blame her?'

*According to a distressed neighbour, Heybridge had been a quiet and—*

Benson turned off the radio and Tess turned the ignition. She pulled slowly away, flicking on the wipers. Rain had begun to fall. Benson wondered if the packet of Marlboro was in the freezer. If so, he'd have to wait until—

'Sorry,' said Archie, tetchy, 'you two might be up to speed but I'm not. Who the hell was Jock?'

'Darren Weaver,' said Tess. 'From Edinburgh. And that's in Scotland.'

'I know, but still, what was the point of getting Grange and Obiora into court?'

'Sarah Collingstone was looking a conviction in the face. She'd just been broken by Glencoyne. As for Debbie, she was in the clear – she'd got herself sectioned again, just to make sure – but she didn't want to see Collingstone go down.'

'Why not?'

'It's fairly obvious, isn't it? She'd had her revenge. Collingstone had been torn to pieces and that was enough. She didn't deserve to go to prison. And don't forget Daniel Collingstone was Andrew Bealing's son. Debbie was his stepmother. She might be an angry woman and a hurt woman, but she's not heartless. She got Weaver to trick Benson. And everyone else.'

'She's thought it all through,' said Archie. 'She's sold everything up. She's on the move. She's going to disappear.'

'Yes, with Darren Weaver, no doubt. She was released from hospital three days ago.'

Benson was fairly sure that the freezer was his best bet, and when Tess pulled up by the railings on Seymour Road, he was impatient to find out, but the planning wasn't over. Arrangements had to be made. They sat together, listening to the distinctive rumble of a sixties engine, the wipers swinging back and forth. Benson waited for the reproach.

'This is unheard of, Will,' said Tess, after a while. 'Counsel don't fight the case inside court and then go outside and resolve it. Clients will never trust you in the future. You have to stay above the fray on the ground. Your fight is elsewhere. It's not with the *truth*, with what really happened; it's with the *evidence* . . . with what might have happened. Your fight is with doubt.'

'And it's unheard of for counsel not to make a closing speech,' said Benson. 'There is no legal or moral reason why we can't resolve this case. Your reasons are practical and professional and you needn't worry. No one is going to find out. The police aren't involved. We'll never do anything like this again. But believe me, this is the best way forward. And not only for Debbie.'

The wipers cut through the spattering of rain.

'What do we do now?' said Archie.

'We confront the killer,' said Benson.

'When?' asked Tess.

'Tomorrow night.'

'Whereabouts?' said Archie.

'Where it all began and where it should end.' Benson got out of the car and leaned back inside. 'Hopton's Yard.'

# 61

Tess didn't want to see Angela Temple. She didn't want to know what she might have to say. She wanted to keep her admiration for Benson unspoiled by doubts or questions of any kind. But the recollection of the bearded man with the network of scars across his head made such avoidance impossible. This very vulnerable man had added a very different shade to the image of Paul Harbeton. He'd spoken with the anger of lost justice. He'd spoken with the ongoing grievance that a backstreet retribution can't erase. There was more to Tess's investigation now than a wager over cocktails.

Mrs Temple, now in her fifties, had been responsible for staff at the Radwell Brain Trauma Clinic in Norwich between 1991 and 1997. She'd then managed a hospice in Derry, Northern Ireland, for five years. She'd then taken a position at St Thomas's Hospital in London, overlooking the Thames, which was where she worked now. She'd agreed to meet Tess for a coffee on the Southbank. And she seemed keen to talk. Like someone who had a confession to make, or information to share that she didn't know what to do with.

'Eddie Benson had been a patient at the clinic,' she said. 'I can't give you any clinical information, obviously, so I'm only confirming what you said was in the pre-sentence report. Eddie came twice a week to see Dr Gardner.'

'For how long?'

'I can't recall. He was already a patient when I came in '91 and he was still coming when I left. So it's over six years.'

Tess did a quick calculation. Eddie's accident occurred in 1988, when he was nine. Therefore he'd been coming to the clinic, then, at least between the ages of twelve and eighteen. Mrs Temple was stirring her coffee as if making porridge, waiting for the liquid to thicken. She hadn't even added milk and sugar.

'William Benson did a sponsored walk in 1995 when he was seventeen. He raised over four thousand pounds. That's the period I knew him, if you like. Only by sight. Because he'd often come with his brother.'

Mrs Temple had then gone to Derry, so she'd missed the news regarding William Benson when he was tried for the murder of Paul Harbeton. In fact, she'd next heard of him only a couple of weeks ago when she read the article about him in the *Guardian*. She followed the uproar afterwards with a strange feeling of unease. The papers variously dissected the crime for which Benson had been convicted. And that brought back someone else she hadn't thought about since leaving the Radwell Brain Trauma Clinic – Paul Harbeton.

'You knew Paul Harbeton?' said Tess.

'Yes. I got rid of him.'

Tess reached over the table and laid a hand gently on Mrs Temple's, stopping the endless stirring of her coffee. 'Don't worry. Just tell me what's on your mind. Tell me about Paul Harbeton.'

Since the Radwell wasn't part of the NHS, the clinic relied on volunteers to help with basic admin, reception, outings, events, patient activities and, of course, fundraising. Mrs Temple had interviewed Harbeton and taken him on in 1992. But she'd asked him to leave after a few months.

'The patients at the Radwell were vulnerable. Anyone with a brain injury is vulnerable. They can have damaged memories, no short-term memory . . . they can remember things that haven't happened; they can say Gerry asked them to do something when it was Frank. And there was something suspicious about this Paul Harbeton. It looked like he'd been borrowing money off the patients, playing on the fact they wouldn't remember. We couldn't prove anything, so I just asked him to leave. And I thought that was the end of the matter.'

Only it wasn't. Because five years later, in 1997, just before she went to Derry, William Benson came to see her.

'He wanted to know where he could find Paul Harbeton.'

'Are you sure about this?'

'How could I be mistaken?'

It had been a silly question, but Tess didn't want to believe what she'd just heard. She had another hopeless go: 'You're saying he knew Paul Harbeton?'

'Well, he knew his name. He was looking for him. I told him I didn't know where he'd gone.'

Tess and Mrs Temple were now on the same page. Because Tess knew from the trial and Mrs Temple knew from the *Guardian* that William Benson's defence had been that he did not know Paul Harbeton. That he'd met him for the first time at the Bricklayers Arms in 1998. That they'd had a fight over Harbeton's rudeness at the bar. That he hadn't followed him into Soho. That Benson being found in Soho at the time of the killing was pure coincidence.

'Do I need to tell the police?' said Mrs Temple.

'No. He was convicted, remember. It doesn't matter any more.'

But it mattered to Tess.

'Thank you, Mrs Temple, you've helped me enormously.'

She left Mrs Temple quite sure that Benson's secret would remain safe. This staff manager was far too discreet to say anything to the press. She'd said nothing so far and she was unlikely to change her mind. Disclosing what she knew to Tess had been enough to salve her conscience. So, yes, Benson's secret was safe.

Tess would keep it, too. She wouldn't be blowing any whistle. But what difference did that make? Her problem wasn't to tell or not to tell . . . it was finding out in the first place. She'd hoped Mrs Temple would ease her concerns, perhaps even surprise her with evidence that supported Benson's innocence. But the opposite had happened. She was devastated. She seemed to see his eyes, dark and pleading for understanding. Her chest grew tight and she turned away.

# 62

Before going out for that celebratory meal at Le Tour de Saint Martin, the small restaurant behind the British Museum, Benson had first tried to resolve the murder of Andrew Bealing privately. To settle what really happened with an admission. But it hadn't worked. There'd been tears, shouting and accusations. The conversation had ended in minutes, so he had been compelled to force things. Tess and Archie weren't to know that what was about to happen hadn't even been Benson's idea. He'd just accepted a challenge.

At midnight Tess arrived in her Austin Cooper. Benson sat in the passenger seat, intent on deflecting any questions that she might raise as to what was about to happen, but he needn't have worried. She was evidently preoccupied. It had to be stress, he thought, because she remained just as self-enclosed after they'd picked up Archie from his flat above Congreve's. And he, too, was in no mood for idle conversation, so they went south of the river to Merton without a word passing between them. Having parked on Effra Road, they walked to Hopton's Yard where the security guard – now known to Benson as Greg – let them in. Benson had been at the premises earlier in the day, preparing the warehouse for what would hopefully now unfold. The tripod was in position, along with the torch. It was time to return them.

Four chairs had been arranged in a line. One of them was already occupied. Benson, Tess and Archie took their places. To their great credit, thought Benson, his two colleagues managed to conceal the shock they must have felt on entering the room and seeing the other spectator. They'd got it wrong; just like DCI Winter had got it wrong. Benson closed his eyes and the long wait began. He thought of Needles and he thought of Yeats: 'Our stitching and unstitching has been naught.' That was about to change.

Footsteps sounded in the darkness. A door opened. More steps echoed, closer now, slow and careful, coming down the corridor past Andrew Bealing's office. The door by which he'd been stabbed opened. Someone entered the warehouse, walking where Andrew Bealing had crawled. A man called out:

'Anna, I'm here. Where are you?'

Benson angled the torch towards the voice and switched on the light.

# 63

Tess was stunned. But she didn't have time to work out the detail because Benson got going immediately with the alarming authority he brought to the courtroom.

'Don't try and leave, Ralph,' he said. 'My friend at the door is very experienced in extra-judicial violence. Just stay right there. You're on stage.'

Ralph Collingstone was squinting, one hand towards the blinding light, a shadow falling on his face. He was hunched like a hammed-up Iago.

'Sarah came home in a state, didn't she?' said Benson. 'She was so upset she went to bed refusing to say what had happened. And you stayed with Daniel listening to yourself read out *The Longridge File*. Which is why Sarah didn't know you'd gone out, boiling with rage, wondering what he'd done this time. She'd been listening to your voice, assuming you were downstairs. The only person who knew you'd gone out was Daniel. Daniel who knows everything. Daniel who'd never tell a soul.'

Greg brought a chair.

'Sit down,' said Benson.

The light remained on Ralph Collingstone's face. He dropped his head to avoid the glare.

'Bealing let you in because you dropped your head, just like that. I don't know whether you borrowed Sarah's coat and it doesn't matter. That was always a bit of a side show. What really mattered was the hat. Because that is what Bealing saw when he looked through the peephole in the main door. He saw Sarah's hat, and he let you in. And, my oh my, he must have backed off fast. You wanted to know what he'd done. And you wanted to know when he was going to stump up, for God you were tired of waiting. Sarah might have been patient but you'd had enough. You'd had enough since the day she came home at sixteen and wrecked your career. I give it to you, Ralph. You swallowed the pill. You didn't complain. You did your best. But it's not easy, I know. People don't realise that anger doesn't go away. It just gets buried. And the deeper you bury it, the more dangerous it gets. You couldn't tell Sarah. You couldn't tell Daniel. You just had to go part-time and look at the posters on the wall and pull a few strings to get some recording work, trading on what you'd done, and not what you'd ever do. In my book, Ralph, that makes you one of the good guys. One of the people who didn't turn away, like the Greenes, who didn't care if Daniel was blood or not. But that's Sarah's story. Your story was a good story, Ralph. You ruined it here.'

Ralph's shoulders began to shake. He breathed deeply, in gasps.

'Bealing told you to calm down, didn't he? He said that

everything would be sorted out soon, that it's not easy to pull a few million from a business without your wife finding out. He said he was almost there. He was just doing the finishing touches. He just needed a couple of weeks, but you weren't having any of that rubbish. You saw straight through him, didn't you? You looked at that bottle of beer on the table and you thought, God, he's had it good.'

Ralph looked up defiantly, gasping, eyes wide open, refusing to be intimidated.

'I'm sure Bealing was pretty scared. He'd left your daughter pregnant at sixteen. And there you were, the father, staring at him like a madman. This was your first meeting. He told you to leave. Said he had a lot to do. You wouldn't go, so he left himself, so disorientated he went in the wrong direction, not towards the door, but towards the warehouse. And that's when you saw the passport, isn't it? My guess is this: earlier in the evening, after fobbing your daughter off yet again, Bealing thought of his planned disappearance. He'd taken out his new ID to remind himself that Sarah's teeth would soon be a long way from his backside. She wasn't going to get a penny. But he'd left that passport on his desk. And you had a look inside. And you saw his face. And you saw the name Alan Shaftoe. And you thought, Christ, he's going to vanish again. He's used my daughter like a doormat and he's going to leave us with nothing. The bastard.'

'You're damned right I did,' shouted Ralph, sneering at the light. 'And I thought a lot more, believe me. And I don't regret what I did. Not then, not now. He deserved it, after what he's done. After what he was planning to do. God almighty, he ruined my life, never mind Sarah's. I was going somewhere. Yeah, my wife had left me and my daughter didn't want me. But I still had the stage. I've got friends in the RSC, you know. I know people who've made it in television. And I was better than them all. I told him as he died. I told him what he'd done to me and I told him what he'd done to Sarah and I told him everything would have been different if he'd only shown a bit of decency. A bit of humanity. A bit of human kindness.'

'Is that before or after you kicked the phone out of his hand?'

'After. And it was the best speech I've ever made.'

'And then you tidied away your footprints and took the passport because you weren't thinking straight, because you thought the passport would get you to Shaftoe's millions. And, of course, you were wrong, because it won't. Because you aren't Alan Shaftoe. Which is why you came here to meet Anna Wysocki.'

'I can live without the money. I got what I wanted. He paid his debt.'

'Anger is the problem, Ralph. So much anger. All you had to do was go to a lawyer. Daniel would have got a just and fair settlement, and pretty quickly, too. The right way. And Andrew Bealing would be alive and you wouldn't be charged with his murder.'

At that moment the main lights came on. Ralph stood up, disorientated, realising suddenly that he wasn't simply with Benson and his friend at the door. That he'd been playing to an audience.

'Sarah,' said Ralph, dropping back on to his chair like a puppet, the strings cut. 'What are you doing here? What is all this?'

Tess was moved by her grace. Moved by her solemnity. Moved by her composure. This woman had endured the multiple traumas of arrest, charge and trial. She'd been stripped bare in public and humiliated. She'd been hung out to dry by the press. She'd been to hell and back, and even 'back' wasn't that far from hell, because the whole public show was about to start all over again. All because her father, the ruined actor, had refused to tell the police what he'd done. After all that, Sarah Collingstone said:

'Dad, I didn't believe Mr Benson, so I had to hear it for myself. Why didn't you tell me? You know we'd have got through this together? We've gone through everything together.'

And Ralph, at last, cracked. The rage had all gone. He looked helpless and tired and broken. He wept. 'Because I know you need me. Because Daniel needs me. Because he needs us both.'

# 64

Benson went to Hounslow on Saturday morning. Sarah wanted to see him. And he wanted to see Daniel. He'd offered to explain what his grandfather had done on the night he left him listening to a CD – if he hadn't guessed it already. Daniel, like everyone else, sat watching the news. Daniel, like everyone else, knew that his mother had been charged with murder. At least he might do. It would have been easy – unless you were Sarah or Benson – to think that the safest way out of this new crisis was to lie about Granddad's absence. But there had been enough lies. Lies can hold a family together but ultimately, if the chain snaps, they can tear it apart.

And so Benson sat alone with Daniel explaining not simply his grandfather's mistake, but his mother's story. It was a story he'd probably never been told before. How she had chosen to be with him rather than go back to school, care for him rather than place him in an institution – a host of decisions that had never registered in her mind as a sacrifice.

Because they hadn't been. She was a special person. An extraordinary person. For Benson there was a peculiar depth to the exchange. Because it had been like talking to Eddie shortly after the accident. He'd tried to tell Eddie what had happened, to explain his role in what had gone wrong, but when Eddie recovered his speech, it turned out he couldn't remember anything Benson had said; and Benson found he couldn't repeat it. He'd been imprisoned ever since. For a few flashing seconds Daniel became Eddie, and they were reconciled.

When Benson finished his mitigation on behalf of Ralph Collingstone, he joined Sarah in the room of posters and audio recordings. The room of lies and hidden resentments. And now mercy.

'How did you know it was my dad? I want to know, now. I'm sorry I wouldn't listen, before. That I shouted you down. I have to know why you saw something that I couldn't. I know how his mind works. You don't.'

Benson had got there in stages and the process began with 'Jock's' mistake.

Cathy Turton had said she worked for the National Crime Agency which had replaced the Serious Organised Crime Agency – SOCA – in 2013. But 'Jock' had talked as if the SOCA still existed. His unit didn't appear in one of its secret directories. He'd posited a fictional SOCA22 when he should have gone for NCA22. It had taken a moment or two for the penny to drop, but Benson realised soon enough that 'Jock's' revelation was based upon information reported by himself or Tess during conferences at which Ralph Collingstone had been present.

'Your defence had just collapsed in court,' said Benson. 'You were as good as convicted. And your father was now desperate. You have to understand what he was doing, Sarah.

He'd allowed you to go through a trial because if he told you on Sunday morning he'd killed Andrew the night before, he knew you'd have made him go to the police. And if he went to the police, you would lose his support. So he gambled on me winning this trial – that would keep you both free; and if you were convicted, I am sure he would have told the truth, using Shaftoe's passport to prove he went to Hopton's Yard.'

But once Glencoyne had uncovered the truth about Daniel's parentage, Sarah's case was over. So Ralph had faked a heart attack. He'd made up the best story he'd never recorded and he did some quick research on the internet. And it had to be quick because he had to act that night – and that's when he made his mistake about SOCA. But that performance in Shadwell was stunning. It was ironic because there was only one person in the audience. It was ironic because the only flaw was in the script. It was ironic because Ralph's wonderfully convincing SOCA22 was itself based on a fiction created by Andrew Bealing, and the combination of fictions then compelled Grange and Obiora to give evidence – people who'd been fooled twice: first by Bealing and now by Ralph. It was ironic because even Ralph himself had been fooled. Like Debbie. Like everyone. The fooled had led the fooled.

'Don't misunderstand me, Sarah,' said Benson. 'Yet I couldn't help but think that in a different world, a kinder and fairer world, a world without hitches, Andrew and your father would have got on very well indeed. They were both brilliant actors. Neither of them got any acclaim for it.'

She had started to quietly cry. She was nodding. Maybe so much would have been different if Andrew hadn't run off to London, leaving behind a false trail, a story about tracing his mother's relatives in Spain. If Andrew had been different; not the sort of man to abandon his own child. If

Andrew hadn't himself been abandoned. If special needs weren't seen by some as a curse.

'I understand how you realised "Jock" had to be my dad, but how did you know that Andrew's story about the Chinese had been made up too?'

'I wasn't sure, Sarah. But Cathy Turton said there were no Chinese gangs operating in that part of London. And while I could make a smart point in court, to the effect she couldn't know everything, she set me thinking. I'd been fooled once and I began to wonder if we'd all been fooled from the outset. Andrew had shifted money abroad rather than give it to you. He'd created a new identity. He'd talked about getting "disappeared". And I began to wonder if he'd been giving a repeat performance. I wondered if he'd been preparing to abandon you again.'

And if there was no 'Jock' and no Chinese gang, then who had killed Andrew Bealing? It could have been Debbie or Wysocki or one of the Hamiltons, Kym or David. They'd all had a powerful motive. As did Sarah and her father.

'And then I remembered the conference I had with your father after you fainted in court. He said you couldn't have killed Andrew because you were at home, listening to a story. You were upstairs with the door open.'

Which meant that Sarah wouldn't have known if Ralph went out. This was the one basic question that Benson had failed to explore, along with DCI Winter and Rachel Glencoyne. They hadn't dissected Sarah's alibi. If they had, they'd have seen Ralph's window of opportunity. And as he realised this error, all the evidence had come together for Benson. But he still couldn't prove it. He'd never be able to prove it. It wasn't his job to prove it. So he'd hoped that Sarah would listen, confront her father and force an admission from him, otherwise Debbie Bealing might be charged. And if they didn't charge Debbie or one of the Hamiltons or Wysocki, there was always a chance of a retrial for Sarah. But Sarah had refused to listen. She'd shouted him down, demanding proof.

'I'm sorry for lying,' she said, getting up. She was anxious. She needed to check on Daniel. She'd been out of the room too long. 'I'll be ashamed forever. But do you know something, Mr Benson. For the first time in my life I feel really free. I'm a laughing stock and the butt of dirty jokes and people pity me for the wrong reasons and I'm about to lose my dad and I can't see the end of the struggle, but I'm free. I have no more secrets. I'll never have to lie again. Can you imagine what that feels like?'

Benson couldn't answer, because he wasn't going to deceive her. But he couldn't imagine it at all. He longed for that freedom. And it would never be his.

# 65

Sarah made Benson a cup of tea. And she went back to her adolescence – the adolescence Glencoyne had only partly exposed in court. Without bitterness or recrimination she rehearsed the moment she'd arrived back home, sixteen and pregnant, obliged to face the father she'd rejected. He'd been wonderful. And it had only been years later that Sarah learned that her father had turned down roles in London. Turned down a shot at telly. Turned down all the little chances that have to be taken if an actor hopes to make it big. She'd failed to spot the loss. She'd just been proud of the fact her dad knew so many of the big names. That some of them sent him a Christmas card.

Ralph had tried to create a 'respectable' history for her. He hadn't wanted his daughter to be known as a girl who'd had a child from someone she didn't even know; and didn't even know where he was or what he was doing. So he'd tied Sarah's history to the tragic death of Anthony Greene. She'd heard it for the first time when her father gave it to the gynaecologist at the Carlisle General. The lie had been born before Daniel, and it had lived on ever since. At the time Sarah had been too traumatised to object or fight for a different narrative. If there'd been any embarrassment in a teenage pregnancy, it had been displaced by the looks of sympathy and the words of compassion. But that one lie had been a seedbed. The rest had grown like weeds around a single flower. When Benson stepped outside, he turned to her and said:

'Do you want to make a financial claim for Daniel on Andrew's estate? Miss de Vere can look after all that. But you'll need to act fairly promptly because Debbie intends to leave the country and make a new life. It will complicate things for you.'

'No, thank you. I don't want to go down that road.'

'Why, Sarah?' He asked the question but he already knew the answer.

'Right from the start, I didn't want the money, Mr Benson, I needed it. And I didn't really need it, Daniel did. But now that Daniel's father is dead, killed by Daniel's grandfather, all because I came looking for a settlement . . . well, I don't want it any more. I couldn't make the claim, even if Daniel needs it. I know he understands. We'll be fine . . . just fine.'

Benson clenched a fist, as if to hold on to a sudden rush of feeling. *Fine* was a word he'd learned from Needles. It had helped him to survive.

Benson ambled down Seymour Road rehearsing Tess's argument against Debbie Bealing. Tess seemed to have got it so right, when, in fact, she'd got it so wrong. Had it been aired in court, a jury would have believed her. Debbie may well have found herself in a cell, screaming like she'd never screamed before. All that suffering – and the injustice – had been avoided. The thought soothed his own remembered pain. He strolled on, savouring a depth of contentment he'd never known before, even as a child, for in those simpler days, it hadn't been truly deep. The hole in the heart that needed filling hadn't yet been made. And now that it had, his appreciation of the moment was almost reverential. Strangely, the contentment had little to do with himself or anything he'd done or achieved per se; it fed on what was now underway, unknown to Sarah Collingstone who knew she'd be fine.

Yes, Benson had agreed to prove that Ralph was guilty. And he'd organised Ralph's unmasking, concerned to protect Sarah or Debbie or the Hamiltons from any future proceedings. All that had been important. But Benson had also had his own secret motivation. His concern had been for Daniel, a young man who'd become Eddie, if only for a while.

And so Benson had lured Ralph back into Hopton's Yard, thinking of a boy in a wheelchair, the first step in a plan that had required the cooperation of Anna Wysocki – the one person who had access to funds that could change Daniel's life for ever. Funds that had never been available to Eddie. Of course, part of the plan involved letting Wysocki go back to Poland without being charged, but that had been a price worth paying to force Ralph into the open. Because Ralph, supported by Sarah, would now present himself at Merton police station. He'd make a complete confession, without any reference to his last great performance in the warehouse. And Sarah Collingstone would think that that was the end of the matter.

And she'd be wrong.

Because in due course, Sarah Collingstone would receive

a perfectly legal donation of £3.7 million from an anonymous benefactor who'd been moved by her very public ordeal. She would receive notification of the gift through the solicitor who'd refused to believe in her innocence: Trevor Hamsey, who was yet to discover that he'd been selected to handle the funds. For a small fee. And unknown to everyone, Wysocki would retain the loose change left over: a cool £200,000. That seemed only fair.

Benson felt like he was floating on air. Yes, he had his own problems. But he could live with them. The sun was shining. According to Archie, the phone was ringing. Hearts and minds were changing. The mob couldn't touch him. They couldn't reach the place he'd come to with the conclusion of Sarah Collingstone's trial. They couldn't deflect him from his ongoing purpose. He laughed out loud – a challenging laugh, hoping that someone out there was watching. There was rubbish heaped at his gate. More rotting fruit and leftovers, from rotting people who'd been left behind. But as he got closer, Benson stopped smiling; and he slowed, moving forward, abruptly changed, not sure that he could cope any more. His heart broke. The engine in his soul fell silent.

Reaching the pile of broken eggs, spilled milk and rotting fish, he fell on his knees. He looked up to heaven because he couldn't look down. They'd killed Papillon.

# 66

Tess was surprised not to hear anything from Benson – something which alternately pleased and troubled her. She'd expected at least a call, or a call from Archie, but there'd been nothing. Which, from one perspective, is what you would expect between counsel, his chambers and a solicitor. You're joined by a trial and then you each move on to other work, another case. And Tess hadn't called Benson. So everything was sort of normal. Only she wasn't entirely happy. She couldn't forget the man with the scarred scalp; she couldn't forget Benson's unspoken pleading. She couldn't ignore either of them. On an impulse she made a quick call. An hour later she parked outside Sally's house on Chiswick Mall in Hammersmith. It was evening and the sun was sinking behind the rooftops, blackening the old slates.

'This very damaged man told me Harbeton was a nasty piece of work,' said Tess. They were strolling by the Thames. 'He's grateful somebody killed him. And he gave me a message for that someone who, it turns, out knew Harbeton. Benson turned up at the Radwell Brain Trauma Clinic looking for Harbeton in 1997. He'd found him by 1998. He was dead the same day.'

'Won't you ever accept he's guilty?' said Sally.

Tess didn't answer, because she didn't know the answer. She leaned on a wall and watched a couple of eights fight against the wind, heading towards Barnes. She'd tried rowing at Oxford and learned that you either let it take over your life or you got out of the water. She'd got out and never regretted it for one moment.

'Sarah Collingstone was innocent,' she said. 'But her life was buried in lies, lies of other people's making and lies of her own. It took a murder to get her out of the pit. But Benson isn't a Sarah. He's not someone who got trapped by someone else. He's a Ralph. He's a Ralph who went to prison and wants to be a Sarah. He trades off the fact he went down after a fight. They got him by a majority verdict. Which means at least one and maybe two people believed he was innocent. He holds on to them like a lifeline. But I've found the first great lie.'

286

'I repeat, won't you ever accept he's guilty?'

After a long silence, Sally put her arm through Tess's, giving her a tug, not to move on, but to let her know she wasn't on her own.

'Do you want some advice?'

'No.'

'Well, here it is: stop caring. Look what Benson has done. Look what he's achieved. Andrew Bealing got justice. And so did his son. So did Sarah. And so did her father. It's monumental, because without Benson, Sarah Collingstone would be serving a life sentence. You know that.'

'I do. But I wanted to trust him. I wanted to believe in his story . . . his long walk from prison to the Old Bailey, an innocent man against the world. I don't want to stop caring. I can't pretend it doesn't matter to me when it does. I'm part of the story.' Tess watched the rowers vie against each other; one of the eights was pulling ahead. Despite her confusion, she'd come to a decision, here by the river. She had to distance herself from the eroding waves of doubt and hope. 'Care or not care, I think it's best if Benson moves on without me.'

Sally thought for a while. 'So you won't be instructing him any more?'

'I won't be proposing him to clients. It's better that way. For him and for me.'

Sally thought some more. 'We drop our investigation?'

'I'm afraid so.'

This was a resolution Tess could live with. It was honest to the moment. The only other wrinkle was a misunderstanding at Coker & Dale. Her appointment as a consultant had been confirmed but the decision had been made after she had distanced herself from Congreve Chambers. Tess had kept her job for the wrong reason. This time Sally did pull her away. 'Call me cheap and nasty and superficial, but

287

I was *so* enjoying all that brick-throwing and men in black. It was sensational.'

'It only happened once.'

'Oh, I know, but there was the promise of more.' Sally sighed. 'I suppose this means the bet is off. If we'll never know if Benson was guilty, I'll never know why you went to Strasbourg.'

'Sally, you amaze me. You've just demonstrated a grip on elementary reasoning.'

'We had a deal. You're a cheat.'

'No, it's *force majeure*.'

'In that case, can I tell you what I think?'

'I know what you think.'

'You met Peter Farsely. You fell out with Peter Farsely. He stayed in London. You went to Strasbourg. Peter Farsely goes to New York and you come back to London. Do you really think I am so stupid that I haven't made the connections?'

Tess, in a surprising abstraction, almost envied Sarah Collingstone. You could ask her anything, now, and she'd just tell you what you wanted to know and put the kettle on. That must be a fantastic way to be.

'I've never thought you were stupid, Sally,' said Tess, leaning her head towards her. 'Eccentric, annoying and irreplaceable, but never stupid.'

'Won't you talk to me? You got hurt, I know you did. I can still see you're not over it, even after all these years.'

'I will one day, I promise.'

'And between times?'

Tess didn't know what to say. She loved Sally. If she'd talk to anyone, it was Sally. But things had changed since their punch and spam fritter days; sunny days of cheap fizz and expensive cherries. Getting arrested in Vienna. The part of her that could cry with laughter had been damaged, irreparably. These days, it was cocktails with amusing names. Sophistication over simplicity. She squeezed her friend's arm and kept up the pressure, never wanting to let go.

'I'll be fine, Sally. I'll be fine.'

# 67

Benson stopped going to see Abasiama. It wasn't a formal decision as such. He just didn't want to turn up and talk about Papillon or Tess de Vere. The two sources of grief seemed to be linked. They'd gone suddenly out of his life at the same time with comparable cruelty, for there is a kind of torture watching a phone that never rings. He'd last seen Tess on the night of Ralph Collingstone's unmasking. Afterwards he'd expected – frankly – more compliments and praise, or at least the sharing of her astonishment, but the reserve shown earlier in the evening hadn't evaporated. It had been there, like a cloud, blurring her reactions. She'd said, 'Well done, Will . . .' and then she'd looked for her keys. In the cherry red Mini, on the way back north of the river, it was Archie who couldn't stop talking. No one else could get a word in. When parting, she'd shaken hands, glancing at Benson almost shyly. 'Goodbye, Will,' she'd said. And that was it. There'd been no 'I'll be in touch'. She'd looked uncertain and lost. He'd watched her drive off, remembering the first time he saw that car with its door wide open. Something had told him he wouldn't be seeing it again at Seymour Basin.

Benson was no fool. He knew this sudden withdrawal was linked to Paul Harbeton. Tess had gone over Benson's trial brief and now she doubted him. And he didn't blame her. A majority on the jury had gone in the same direction.

So it was no small wonder that a rainy day depression settled on him.

It had to be said, however, that good things began to happen. Benson's success in the Hopton Yard killing placed his name on the lips of every solicitor and potential client in London, and possibly further afield. Work started coming in. Burglaries. Criminal damage. Theft. Arson with intent. Clients were insisting on having Benson when their solicitors had expressed reservations. There was a gentle groundswell of support that couldn't be stopped. Even the Secretary of State for Justice, the Rt. Hon. Richard Merrington MP, had been obliged to fudge questions on any future legislation to prohibit his practice at the Bar. The proposal hadn't been abandoned, but nothing was going to be rushed through, and in the meantime, Benson was thriving. The two online petitions had as much as cancelled each other out. He didn't know the numbers, because it wasn't the kind of thing he followed, but the battle of public opinion was no longer news. The attacks had diminished, too. Or so it seemed so far. There'd been fewer provocations, less rubbish emptied by his door, and no beatings.

Publicity about Benson had also attracted the attention of a handbag-clutching sixty-three-year-old who simply turned up one day demanding employment. Molly Robson had been a typist at the legendary Latchford Chambers all her working life. After knocking out QC's and junior's opinions for over forty years she'd gradually become an expert in criminal pleading, evidence and practice. Inadvertently. She knew Archbold backwards and read the supplements for fun. Which would have been fine if she hadn't – when the rare occasion demanded it – dared to correct the work of her employers. Suggesting an alternative analysis. Citing cases. Changing the grammar. The young Turks hadn't liked that at all. When she was made redundant in a shake-up, she thought of Benson.

'Don't you remember me?' she asked, looking at Harold in his tank.

Benson said he didn't. She was wiry and small. Not a Congreve girl.

'Well, I remember you,' she said. 'You squatted at Latchford's for a while. No one wanted you around.'

'That's more than likely.'

'They thought you were hopeless.'

'Really?'

'Yes. Short on talent, long on influence. That's what they said. They only gave you a place because Helen Camberley leaned on Ted Ryan, the head of chambers.'

'She did a lot of leaning, Miss Camberley.'

'Your conviction didn't help.'

'No, it wouldn't.' She was a plain speaker, was Molly. 'May I ask why you'd like to work for me?'

'Well, strictly speaking, it'll be the other way around. I'd like to get my own back, you see. They'll not like me working here. So you doing the business in court while I type back at the ranch would be just wonderful. I'm hoping to use you, Mr Benson, to get at them. And that makes me a sort of boss. I won't be ordered around.'

'Of course not. Is that your only reason?'

Her large, bright eyes flashed something like excitement. 'I typed your opinions, Mr Benson. Work you devilled for Ted Ryan and the rest. I never had to change a word. You're going somewhere, Mr Benson. They don't want you to, but you are. If you could do with some free advice and typing, let me come along for the ride. They kicked us both out. We can both kick 'em back.'

And so Molly brought her own computer and took over a small room facing Archie's. She didn't only type, she dusted and cleaned. She brought Archie homemade sponges and she talked nonsense to Harold. The place came strangely alive.

But still Benson's depression refused to lift. Visits to CJ to play chess and talk about old Spitalfields had no effect, save to please the patriarch and his often-attendant daughters. Even a night out with Archie Congreve's Tuesday Club left him morose and tired, for it's exhausting to feign good spirits. The reason was simple: there'd been no word from Tess. Every day he thought of her light, lilting accent. He thought of her ankle bones. He thought of the way she screwed her eyes when she talked serious, arms folded tight, worrying about some DNA. He thought of her green velvet hat getting smaller and smaller as she walked away. He'd read every book of poetry on the shelf she'd examined, just wanting to read whatever she'd flipped through, wanting his eyes to rest on words that had held her lonely eyes. It was all ephemeral. Maddeningly, the memory of her lips grazing his cheek was fading, along with the scent from her hair. All Benson could hold on to was a handkerchief, washed free of someone else's spit. He felt ridiculous. But he wouldn't throw it away.

On a bitterly cold evening while rain and wind rattled the windows, Benson sat at his ship captain's desk reading over a letter from Ralph Collingstone. He was doing okay. There wasn't much that could disturb his peace of mind because he knew Sarah and Daniel were secure. His only anxiety was that Sarah had a boyfriend called Vincent and he wasn't sure if Vincent was more attracted to the money than his daughter, money that belonged to his grandson. It was a difficult one, that. And he was grateful, too, for Benson's advice, because Benson had told him to get a nickname asap. Needles' decision to call Benson 'Rizla' had been a far-sighted move; an old hand's ploy. Because everyone in prison wants a burn. Everyone likes someone who can give them a few cigarette papers if they're short. That name, and a stash of Rizlas, had made Benson everyone's potential friend. For very little money, he'd become a protected species. So Ralph had gone for something similar: 'Matches'. So far, it was working just fine, though he wished he'd settled on something that was less in demand. People were all over him like flies.

Benson was so absorbed in his reading that he didn't notice Archie and Molly's presence. Archie was standing in front of his desk, holding a brief by its pink string. He was smiling like the boy in shorts he'd once been, here in this room, nagging his four fish-skinning sisters. Only he was Benson's clerk, a gentleman with a silver watch chain looped across his bulging waistcoat. He tossed the brief on the desk.

'There's no stopping you, now,' said Molly, standing at the door.

The brief was from Coker & Dale of 56 Ely Place, London EC1N. Printed in the centre was the case name and indictment number. It was another murder.

Benson stood up and went over to Archie. He put his hands on those wide, pudding-filled shoulders. 'Thanks, Archie. Thanks for this place. Thanks for giving me a break. Thanks for taking the flak with me. Thanks for being my clerk.'

'It's a pleasure, Mr Benson.'

Abruptly moved, Molly scuttled out: 'I think I'll put the kettle on.'

Benson went back to his desk and pulled at the pink string. It was going to be a difficult and very public trial. The outcry against the accused had been medieval. Media speculation had been intense and hostile. Obtaining instructions hadn't been a straightforward matter. The evidence against the accused was damning. Counsel was asked to use his best endeavours.

Benson would have walked a very long way for this. A thousand miles. And more.

Tess de Vere had instructed him in *R* v. *Stainsby*, the 'Blood Orange Murder'.

# Acknowledgements

Warm thanks to the following: Ursula Mackenzie, Richard Beswick, Iain Hunt and Grace Vincent at Little, Brown, Victoria Hobbs and Jennifer Custer at A.M. Heath, Conrad Williams at Blake Friedmann, David Young, Her Honour Judge Penny Moreland, Jude Hodgson (Membership Registrar, the Inner Temple), Charles Henty (Secondary of London and Under-Sheriff, High Bailiff of Southwark), Françoise Koetschet, Sabine Guyard, Christine de Crouy Chanel, Paulinus Barnes. And, specially, Anne.

The ECHR case first discussed by Tess and Gordon in Chapter 1 is *R.E.* v. *The United Kingdom*, Application no. 62498/11. The judgment was published on 27/10/2015 (Final judgment 27/01/2016).

'Could Secondary DNA Transfer Falsely Place Someone at the Scene of a Crime' by C. Cale, M. E. Earll, K. E. Latham and G. L. Bush, appeared in the *Journal of Forensic Sciences*, 1 September 2015.

'DNA Fingerprints from Fingerprints' by R. A. H. van Oorschot and M. K. Jones, appeared in *Nature*, 387, 767 (1997).

# About the Author

John Fairfax is the pen name of William Brodrick who practised as a barrister before becoming a full-time novelist. Under his own name he is a previous winner of the Crime Writers Association Gold Dagger Award and his first novel was a Richard and Judy Book Club Selection.